This was crazy…insane… and everything she wanted

A sweet hot rush of desire swept over Paula. She'd wanted to kiss Riley for so long. She'd held back for a whole lot of good reasons.

The reasons hadn't gone away.

Reason itself had disappeared.

He began to undo her b‍____ ____ ___ ____ hands away.

"You're right. This is ina‍___

"Don't you dare apologi‍___ ___ ___ intention of stopping, ___ ___ ___ head.

Inappropriate or not, she didn't care. His touch felt like heaven. His kisses were better than chocolate. She liked him, she liked what he was doing to her. And she wanted more.

She was tired of being cautious. Tired of examining every feeling to see if she should act or clamp down on her desires. Riley was an honorable man and he was hot for her. So what if they gave each other a bit of release this once? If they were adult about this, they could have sex without it interfering with their work.

Feeling his corded muscles and broad shoulders, she'd imagined what it would be like skin to skin. Now she knew, and it was good. He claimed her mouth again and rose to his feet, pulling her up with him.

"Come with me." She took his hand and led him to her bedroom.

Dear Reader,

When my editor suggested making my hero and heroine police officers (instead of newspaper reporters) I agreed immediately. Higher stakes, more excitement—fabulous! As I began to think about the story and flesh out the characters I realized just how high the stakes could go.

What if my detective heroine Paula Drummond had a son by a drug lord she'd put in jail? What would happen when that criminal got out of jail and wanted his son? What if, by association, Paula is inadvertently responsible for hard drugs coming to her adopted town of Summerside?

That's a lot for any woman to cope with. Paula is probably the strongest and most assertive heroine I've written. She needed—and deserved—a strong partner, so I created ex-Special Forces soldier, Riley Henning. Because we writers like to make life difficult for our characters, I decided Riley had to battle his own demons—post-traumatic stress disorder from his tour of duty in Afghanistan—even as he helped Paula protect her little boy, Jamie, from his criminal father.

Protecting Her Son is the fourth book set in my fictional Australian seaside town of Summerside. In it, I introduce a new set of characters with cameo appearances from old favorites. This book stands alone but expands and enriches the picture of village life in Summerside.

I love to hear from readers. Drop me a line at joan@joankilby.com or write snail mail to, c/o Harlequin Enterprises Ltd, 225 Duncan Mill Road, Don Mills, Ontario, CANADA, M3B 3K9. Check out my website, www.joankilby.com.

Happy reading!

Joan Kilby

Protecting Her Son
Joan Kilby

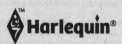

TORONTO NEW YORK LONDON
AMSTERDAM PARIS SYDNEY HAMBURG
STOCKHOLM ATHENS TOKYO MILAN MADRID
PRAGUE WARSAW BUDAPEST AUCKLAND

Recycling programs for this product may not exist in your area.

ISBN-13: 978-0-373-60696-2

PROTECTING HER SON

Copyright © 2012 by Joan Kilby

This edition published by arrangement with Harlequin Books S.A.

For questions and comments about the quality of this book please contact us at Customer_eCare@Harlequin.ca.

® and TM are trademarks of the publisher. Trademarks indicated with ® are registered in the United States Patent and Trademark Office, the Canadian Trade Marks Office and in other countries.

www.Harlequin.com

Printed in U.S.A.

ABOUT THE AUTHOR

Joan Kilby is a great believer in law and order, but like many people, gets nervous for no reason when she sees a police car following her on the highway. So it was with some trepidation that she wrote a story about a couple of cops. She felt better once she was done. Somehow the police seemed more human now that she knew them better. (Yes, she knows she's writing fiction and these people aren't real. They just seem that way.) Joan lives in Melbourne, Australia, with her husband and three children. She's the law-abiding and award-winning author of more than twenty Harlequin Superromance books.

Books by Joan Kilby

HARLEQUIN SUPERROMANCE

*Summerside Stories

Other titles by this author available in ebook format.

To police officers everywhere
who put their lives on the line to serve and protect
the community.

CHAPTER ONE

Seven years earlier

DETECTIVE PAULA DRUMMOND'S long-legged stride through the bull pen was more of a wiggle than a walk in her tight skirt and teetering high heels. Her clinging silk blouse with plunging neckline displayed a generous cleavage.

Catcalls and wolf whistles erupted in her wake. Paula grinned, flipped up her middle finger and exaggerated her hips' sway as she carried on to the detective sergeant's office.

Tim Hudson's shiny bald head was bent over his computer keyboard as he typed furiously with two fingers. Knocking once, Paula entered and lowered herself onto a guest chair. She crossed her legs, one rhinestone-studded shoe bobbing briskly. "What's up, boss? Why did you call me in?"

Hudson hit save, leaned back and squinted at her. "Drummond, is that you? I barely recognize you."

"That's the idea." Paula pushed back the blond hair streaked with mink hanging over her heavily made-up eyes. "Nick's ready for his daily massage. He doesn't like it when I'm late."

She inspected her nails, kept short and blunt. Her prep for this operation had included six weeks intensive training in therapeutic massage. Once they'd learned Moresco had a chronic shoulder injury, her cover ID was a cinch.

"I wanted to know if that slimeball is pressuring you," Hudson said. "Sexually, I mean."

Nick Moresco was a drug lord but he liked to think of himself as a businessman. He was rich, handsome, charming, sophisticated and intelligent. He liked women. Of course he was pressuring her.

Paula shrugged. "Nothing I can't handle."

The detective sergeant leaned forward, his brown eyes glittering. "I hear he's hot stuff. An Italian stallion."

Paula met Hudson's leer with a steady gaze. "Nick's a criminal. Like you say, a slimeball."

"You're sure you're not losing your objectivity? Horowitz is transcribing the tapes. He reckons you're flirting with Moresco. And liking it."

"I'm doing my job. And Horowitz wouldn't know whether a woman was *liking it* if she held up an Olympic score card." Paula picked a fleck of lint off her mini skirt. But yeah, flirting with Nick was disturbingly easy. The man had charisma.

Hudson leaned back, flicking a pencil between

his fingers. "I think we should pull you off the case."

Paula's hand tightened on her purse strap. "This op has been going for nearly a year now. Nick's close to making a major deal on meth production. If I suddenly quit his therapy, it'll look suspicious. He's always asking me questions as it is, testing me."

"As long as you remember you're a cop. There are lines you don't cross."

"Jeez, boss. What do you think I am? Nothing is going to stop me from the satisfaction of hearing those handcuffs click into place when we arrest the bastard."

Hudson was silent for a long ten seconds, studying her. "All right. Just don't say I didn't warn you."

Present day

"JAMIE, ARE YOU DRESSED for school? You don't want to be late on your first day." Paula paused the hair dryer to listen for a reply. Across the hall in his bedroom her six-year-old son was playing with his cars.

"Vrooom! Smash! Ka-blam!"

Paula put down the dryer and went to look. Jamie was sprawled on his stomach in the middle of the carpeted floor, creating a fifteen Matchbox car pileup. He had on the school navy polo shirt, superhero underpants and one navy sock. His school shorts and the other sock were still on the bed where Paula had laid them out half an hour ago. Young for his age and easily distracted, Jamie could be a challenge.

"Look, Mum." Jamie's curly dark hair bounced as he made a giant plastic T. rex stomp over the wreckage.

"Right you go, mate." She hauled him up by his armpits with him clinging to the T. rex, grabbed the shorts and helped his knobby-kneed legs into them. "You're a great big boy in grade one. You shouldn't need your mum to dress you."

Jamie clamped the T. rex's jaws around his own forearm. Through the gap where his right front tooth had been, spit sprayed as he made sound effects. "Chomp, chomp, chomp."

"Get your other sock on," Paula said. "And come eat breakfast."

In the kitchen, the phone rang.

Great, another distraction. Jamie wasn't the only one who couldn't be late this morning. Today was her first day on the job at Summerside Police Station. She hurried down the hall, tucking her blue uniform shirt into pressed navy pants. Her hair, still only half dried, swung around her shoulders.

Paula leaned across the counter and grabbed the receiver on the fifth ring. "Hello?"

The phone went dead.

Odd. She slotted the receiver into the wall mount. Then set out a bowl of cereal and glass of milk for Jamie and dropped a couple of pieces of bread in the toaster for herself.

Back she went to the bathroom, passing Jamie in the hall carrying a plastic brontosaurus. She ruffled his hair. "Your cereal bowl is not a prehistoric swamp."

She tied her hair back tightly and turned her head to check in the mirror for stray wisps. First impressions were important and hers had to be stellar. Busted back to uniform, she'd been transferred twice since Nick's arrest and both times she'd copped flack from the other cops. She was tough—she could have dealt with the animosity. But the commanding officer at each station eventually moved her on, like a vagrant they wanted off their clean streets.

Well, screw them all. She was fed up with being jacked around, tired of dragging her son from town to town. It was bad enough that she was raising him on her own without a father. Now that Jamie was starting school she couldn't be moving every couple of years.

This time things would work out. She would survive long enough at Summerside to make detective again. She jammed in a last hairpin and looked herself hard in the eye. Third time lucky.

"Mummy, your toast popped," Jamie called, his speech garbled by a mouth full of Weetabix.

The phone rang again as she entered the kitchen. If this was one of those automated marketing programs dialing her number repeatedly...

Tucking the receiver between her ear and shoulder, she put the hot toast onto a plate, grabbed a knife and started buttering. "Hello?"

Silence.

The fine blonde hairs on Paula's arms stood up, her fair skin pimpled. Like most cops, her number was unlisted.

"Hello," she repeated sharply. "Who's there?"

"Mio amore," a silky male voice said in her ear.

Nick Moresco. The butter knife clattered from her hand onto the counter. "What do you want?" she whispered, her throat suddenly dry.

"Just to know that you are there."

The phone went dead.

Paula fumbled the receiver onto the hook. Her gaze shot to the wall calendar. February 1. Which meant Nick had been out of jail for a month. In all the confusion of moving house, Jamie starting school and her starting a new job she'd completely forgotten.

Her stomach churning, Paula tossed her uneaten toast into the garbage. "Are you finished, Jamie? We have to go. Quickly brush your teeth."

Jamie took one more mouthful, grabbed his

brontosaurus and ran down the hall. Paula swiftly put the breakfast dishes in the dishwasher, dismayed to see her hands trembling.

Get a grip! Think. How had Nick gotten her phone number? Only a handful of people knew it—her mother, a couple of friends, Senior Sergeant John Forster at the Summerside Police Department and Jamie's school. None of them would have given her number to a stranger.

She ran her hands over her chilled arms. Nick had ways and means that were beyond those available to ordinary folk. He had a vast network of employees, spies and bodyguards. Plus an enormous extended Italian family who were loyal to every member.

Paula spent the next ten minutes going around the small one-story house making sure every window and door was locked. She'd meant to have a deadbolt installed on the exterior door in the laundry room door but she'd had so many other things to take care of she'd put it off. Wincing, she pressed the flimsy button lock in. First chance she had…

"Ready, Mum." Jamie stood before her, baring his gap-toothed grin to show her he'd cleaned his teeth.

Her heart melted. His freckled face was scrubbed shiny. His small shoulders were squared to bear the weight of his backpack. His *Toy Story* lunch box, which she'd packed the night before, was clutched tightly in his hand. He was still in his sock feet, one navy, one black, but there was no time for him to change.

"Bring me your shoes. I'll help you with the laces."

"I can do them myself." Off he ran again, his lunch box banging against his side.

If Nick had found out her phone number, he could find out her address.

Paula pulled back the drapes and glanced around the quiet court. Across the street her neighbor was backing his car out of the driveway. Farther up the road some teens in the sage green and brown high school uniform were walking to school.

Jamie returned and plumped himself down on the foyer tiles. He yanked his black leather shoes over his wrinkled socks. The tip of his tongue tucked in the corner of his mouth, he concentrated on laboriously tying his laces in a bow.

"You're doing great," Paula said, her voice too tight to really be encouraging. "You've nearly got one. Do you want me to do the other?"

"Nope." He moved on to the other shoe, his small fingers clumsily manipulating the black laces.

The phone rang *again*.

Paula walked slowly to the doorway to the

kitchen. What did he want from her? A chill flowed over her. Jamie?

"Aren't you going to answer it?" Jamie demanded, still struggling with his shoelaces.

Her crepe-soled shoes squeaked slightly on the tiled floor. Her heart thudded in her chest. Her hand shook as she answered the phone for the third time that morning.

"H-hello?"

"Hello, darling," her mother said in the cheery voice she used when she wanted to settle down for a good long chat.

Paula's knees gave way and she leaned her elbows on the counter for support. "Mum, I can't talk now. Jamie's school starts in ten minutes and I'm late for work. I'll call you tonight."

POLICE CONSTABLE RILEY HENNING opened his locker and took down his protective vest and checked over his equipment—baton, pepper spray, ammunition, handcuffs, police radio and a semi-automatic .38 Smith and Wesson—making sure every component was clean and operational.

The order and discipline, the camaraderie of the guys at the station, reminded him of the army. He liked that. He also liked that pleasant leafy Summerside, his hometown, was light years away from bleak, dusty Afghanistan.

His cell phone rang. Shift hadn't started yet so he answered it. "Hello?"

"Dude, did you get my email about the reunion in Canberra for the ANZAC Day parade?" Gazza, his old army buddy from the Special Air Service, said. "It's less than two months away. If you want to get a cheap airline ticket, you should book now."

Riley sat on the bench in front of the row of lockers. He and Gazza had trained together and fought together. They were bonded as only soldiers in combat could be—like brothers. And yet he'd avoided answering that email.

"Sorry, I meant to reply but it's been hectic. I'm in the middle of moving houses. You know how it is."

The truth was he didn't relish attending the annual ceremony to honor Australian soldiers. He'd been out of the SAS for nearly a year. His injuries from the suicide bomb explosion that sent him home had healed. A reunion would mean an inevitable swapping of stories, reminiscing about the dangerous and difficult tour of duty in Kabul. Maybe one day he'd be open to that, but right now he wanted to forget, to enjoy his new life.

"So are you coming?" Gazza said. "The guys are all going to be there." He paused briefly and his voice went quiet. "We're worried about you, dude. After the bomb explosion you disappeared—didn't answer anyone's emails or phone calls."

"I'm fine." Riley didn't need to force the note of contentment. "Don't worry about me. I'm healthy, happy. Glad to be back here among friends and family. Got a great job. I'm living the dream."

"Cool." Gazza sounded doubtful. "But if you ever want to talk about stuff, I'm here. Kabul, the explosion, it's a lot to process by yourself."

"To be honest, I don't remember much about that so it doesn't worry me—"

The door to the locker room opened. Delinsky, Crucek, and Riley's partner, Jackson arrived. Lockers clanged. Laughter and boisterous talk rang out.

"Gaz, I'm going to have to call you back sometime. Shift is starting."

"Okay. But you think about ANZAC Day."

"Sure." Riley said goodbye and hung up. He turned his phone off and put it away. Then he strapped on his vest, adjusting it so the weight settled evenly over his torso.

"You're always here first, Henning. Did you even go home last night?" Jackson, his partner, said good-naturedly. "What do you do with your time?"

Jackson was forty-three-years old and comfortably married with the beginnings of a paunch and a receding hairline. No doubt he spent his evenings happily watching TV with his family.

"I did some target practice at the shooting range

last night, if you really want to know." Riley closed his locker and spun the combination lock. "This morning I got up at six and went for a run. Early bird gets the perp. Anything else?"

"Guys, I'm starting a football pool." Crucek straddled the bench with a clipboard in hand. With his large nose, carroty hair and mottled complexion, he was no male model. "Who's in?"

"Put me down," Riley said.

"Me, too." Delinsky, who had blond good looks and a buff body Jackson and Crucek could only envy, was stripped down to his boxers. "The new cop starts today. I saw her in John's office as I came in."

"I wonder which of us lucky stiffs will get her as partner." Jackson pulled on a starched navy short-sleeve police shirt.

"Better not be me," Riley said. "I hear she's trouble."

Rumors had been flying about this woman for weeks that she was bent. Until her fall from grace seven years ago she'd been a hotshot detective at the Melbourne Police Department. Her infraction, related to her final investigation, a covert drug bust, was apparently so serious it was never made public. No one knew exactly what she'd done but they all agreed it had to be bad.

"I'll take her." Delinsky combed his hair in front

of the mirror. "She's a babe. You should see her ass."

The door opened and Senior Sergeant John Forster entered. "Delinsky, I hope you weren't referring to our new recruit in such crass manner. These walls aren't soundproof."

John Forster was tall, with a swimmer's shoulders and sun-streaked blond air. He might look like a surfer dude but he commanded the men's respect.

Delinsky wiped the leer off his face. "No, boss."

"Listen up, men." John looked to each in turn.

Jackson hastily tucked in his shirt. Crucek rose from the bench and put his clipboard with the footy pool in his locker. Even Riley, who'd been best mates with John since high school, came to attention.

"I want to go over the new roster," John said. "Jackson, from today you're partnered with Crucek. Delinsky, Stan Grant is switching from night shift to partner you. You boys okay with that?"

The men exchanged glances then nodded. But Riley knew no one liked a shake-up, least of all him. He was a little pissed, to tell the truth. Over the past six months he'd gotten to know Jackson, liked and respected him. He'd expected they'd be partners for a good long time. Now the stability and continuity he craved since getting out of the army had been ripped away.

John turned to Riley. "Come with me. I'll introduce you to your new partner, Paula Drummond."

A chorus of whoops and jeers from all but Riley met this news. John cleared his throat pointedly and the noise died down. "Dismissed."

The men went about the business of getting ready to go on duty. Riley followed John out to the bull pen, an open area of desks, computers, photocopiers and filing cabinets. Over in Dispatch, red-haired Patty answered the telephone with her distinctive Irish lilt. A couple of admin staff were talking by the copier.

"Why me?" Riley asked as he and John wove through the desks to John's office on the far side of the bull pen. "I'm the new guy on the block."

"Our new recruit has had a rough road over the past seven years," John said. "She's had trouble fitting in. I picked you because you get along well with people. I want you to turn on the charm. Make her feel welcome."

Riley was tempted to play the friendship card and ask to stay with Jackson. But he'd been trained to follow orders, to put on his soldier face and say *yes, boss.* Still, he couldn't resist a dig. "So this is my reward for being Mr. Nice Guy? Thanks, mate."

John glanced around to make sure they weren't being overheard. No one was paying attention. "I also want you to keep an eye on her. This is strictly off the record. I know I can trust you to be discreet."

Riley considered that. John trusted him with extra responsibility—good. But having to watch another cop for wrong-doing? Bad. Who wanted a partner who wasn't straight up? "Are you afraid that whatever she did, she'll do again?"

"I'm not going to prejudge her. But I have the integrity of this station to consider. My attitude is welcoming but cautious."

"What's the deal with her anyway? What kind of wrong turn did she take?" Riley didn't have a lot of time for people who screwed up professionally. In the army, if you screwed up, people could die.

"I wasn't given the details. She doesn't talk about her past. She's a single mum with a young son who wants to start fresh. We're going to give her a fair go. You probably won't be with her for long. She applied for detective and sat the exams at her last station. Most likely she'll get the promotion and be out of your hair in a few weeks. Okay?"

"Who's in charge, her or me?" Going from leading a platoon to being a beat cop meant Riley had taken a step down, career-wise. For the moment he was okay with that but he liked to know where he stood.

"She's got years more experience. But you've

been with the department longer." John mulled it
over. "Let's just say you're equal partners."

"Suits me."

Riley passed young rookie Simon Peterson
seated at a computer laboriously typing out a report, and gave him a commiserating grin. The
endless paperwork of police work was annoying.
But the Summerside force was a good place—too
small for corruption to flourish the way it did in
some of the big city stations. Riley felt at home
here. And he liked working with a small team of
dedicated people who believed in what they were
doing.

Which begged the question, how was he going
to believe in what he was doing partnered with a
cop who might not be trustworthy? He and this
woman were supposed to be equal and yet he was
being asked to keep an eye on her. How did he do
that and still develop the bond of trust he needed
to do his job?

The more he thought about it, the more distaste-
ful he found his situation. He didn't blame John,
who was only trying to do what was best for the
station. No, it was Paula Drummond who had gotten herself in trouble. There was no smoke without a fire, as the saying went. And now he had to
compromise his integrity for her.

Inside John's office, a woman in uniform stood
with her back to them, gazing through the partially

open blinds at the main street of the village. She was tall and athletic-looking with her blonde hair pinned tightly back. Her stance appeared casual but for the rigid set of her shoulders and her white-knuckled grip on the window ledge.

Outside, the morning rush hour was in full swing. Riley guessed there must be, oh, four or five cars backed up at the town's only set of traffic lights. It was a typical morning in late summer—shoppers going about their business, newly-liberated mums having coffee in the sidewalk cafés, seniors gossiping on the wrought-iron benches beneath shady trees. Nothing Riley could see that would cause the new recruit to be so tense.

Hearing their footsteps she turned. She had blue eyes with enough crinkle at the corners to suggest she'd seen everything yet still found humor in life, an assertive nose and full lips lightly glossed. Riley schooled himself not to react. Delinsky was right. She was hot. Put a dress on her, let her hair down, and she'd be right…kissable. Not that he'd ever get busy with a coworker. He happened to agree with the unspoken rule that cops didn't screw their partners—in any sense of the word.

John made the introductions. A phone call interrupted and he excused himself to take it. His murmured conversation faded into the background.

Riley nodded to Paula, extending his hand. "G'day."

Her gaze took in the rank on his uniform. "A rookie. Excellent." *Not*, her blue eyes added silently. Her firm grasp brought a jolt of awareness, a primal zing of flesh on flesh he wasn't expecting.

"An *ex*-detective," he replied with subtle emphasis. He squeezed hard, feeling the softness of the skin on the backs of her fingers. "I'm sure you can teach me a lot."

Riley had never gotten into a pissing contest with a woman before, especially not a woman this attractive. It kind of threw him. Those eyes that had his stomach in free fall contrasted oddly with a bone-crushing handshake. They were still eyeing each other warily when John finished his call.

"All acquainted?" John walked around his desk and headed for the door. "Let's introduce Paula to the gang."

"After you." Riley gestured to Paula. Despite his good intentions his gaze dropped to the trim round butt encased in snug navy trousers. Again, Delinsky was right. She had a great ass.

Eyes front, solider. Paula Drummond would probably pull out her gun and shoot him if he made a pass.

John summoned Delinsky, Jackson, Crucek and Grant who were hanging around the coffee machine, waiting to go out on patrol. The guys checked her out covertly while they said all the nice things, like *welcome* and *glad to have you aboard*.

"Delinsky and Grant, follow up the liquor-store break-in," John said, moving on to the morning debrief. "Jackson and Crucek, you're liaising with Frankston P.D. on the new drug task force. Detectives Leonard and Cadley will meet with you at ten o'clock. Drummond and Henning, you're on traffic patrol."

The crew began to disperse.

"Excuse me, boss," Paula said. "I've had extensive experience in large-scale covert drug investigations."

"I'm aware of that, Constable," John said evenly. "The bend on the highway after you exit the village is a good spot to set up the radar."

Paula's wide mouth tightened. "I only meant, if the team wanted to make use of my expertise—"

"Thanks, we'll keep that in mind." John nodded a dismissal and went to his office.

At the counter in Dispatch, Riley signed out a patrol car. Patty picked the keys off the Peg-Board and tossed them in Riley and Paula's general direction. Riley raised his hand to catch them. Paula snatched them out of the air.

"So, it's going to be like that, is it?" Riley said, teasing.

"Like what?" She gave him a blank stare.

Hadn't even been aware she was taking control. Okay, he could be magnanimous. "You can drive."

PAULA PROPPED AN ELBOW on the car window ledge and stared at the highway. They were parked behind a large ti tree, radar gun mounted on the dash. Nearly two hours had passed without them collaring a single speeder. During that time her partner had chatted endlessly, trying to draw her out. Normally she wouldn't be quite so uncommunicative. After all she had to work with this guy and she couldn't afford to put anyone off—but she couldn't stop thinking about Nick Moresco's phone call.

Just to know you are there. What had he meant by that? Was he planning something? Did he know about Jamie? She hadn't been showing when she'd given evidence at the hearing and by the time the case had gone to trial she'd given birth. But Nick had spies everywhere. It gave her shivers to think he might know where she lived, where Jamie went to school…

"How long have you lived in Summerside?" Riley passed her the thermos of coffee they'd filled at a local café.

"Sorry? Oh, less than a month." She dug out her cup wedged next to her on the seat and filled it.

"You're going to love it here. John said you had a kid. Boy or girl?"

"Boy."

Riley crossed his arms behind his head and leaned back. "Summerside is a terrific place to raise children. Parks, the beach, trails through the bush...loads of places for your son to explore."

Isolated areas where a small boy on his own could be snatched. "You don't have children, do you?"

"Me? Nah. I'd like to someday," Riley said. "I've been too busy till now but I'm ready to settle down. I'm moving into my childhood home this weekend now that my father and stepmother bought a unit close to the village. They haven't done much to the old place over the years so I'm planning to renovate..."

Paula tuned out. He was probably trying to put her at ease but the constant stream of words was making her more uptight. What was she going to do about Nick? There was nothing she *could* do until he made another move.

If he made another move.

Riley had stopped talking. He seemed to be waiting for a response from her.

"Sorry, I missed that last bit."

"You're not one for chitchat, are you?"

"I'm worried about my son," she admitted guardedly. "It's his first day of school."

"How old is he? My sister Katie teaches at the primary school."

"He's in grade one." She'd met Jamie's teacher briefly. Now that she knew Katie Henning and Riley were related she swiveled to study him more closely, noting his dark hair, dark eyes and rugged features. Her gaze lingered a moment on his sensual mouth. Something tugged deep inside, desires half-forgotten, wishes unfulfilled. Nope, not going there. "I can see a family resemblance. Your sister, huh?"

"There, you see? I knew we could find something in common." Riley leaned against his door, as if settling in for a long chat. "What's your son's name?"

"Jamie." She lifted the cup to her mouth, conscious a second later she was exposing her bare ring finger. Sure enough, Riley had noticed—and quickly looked away. For crying out loud, it was the twenty-first century. If there was one thing in her life she wasn't ashamed of, it was giving birth to her son. "I've never been married." She hoped her cool tone would deter further questions.

Riley's hand shot up. "Hey, it's none of my business. Live and let live."

"You're older than most rookies," Paula said, turning the conversation away from herself. "What did you do before you joined the police force?"

"I was a bouncer at a nightclub in Frankston."

"A bouncer," she repeated dubiously. Riley was tall and strongly built, in his mid- to late-thirties.

His skin had the deeply tanned look of someone who'd spent a lot of time outdoors. Bouncers usually looked pasty, as though they'd crawled out from a cave. She doubted he'd worked nights long term. "Before that?"

He faced forward again, turning his gaze away from her. "Special Air Services Regiment."

Her eyebrows rose. Impressive. "Were you deployed overseas?"

"I was in Kabul." It might have been a trick of the dappled light flickering through the ti tree, but a shadow seemed to cross over Riley's face.

Before she could ask another question, he smiled easily. "So, what sports do you like?"

Maybe they did have something in common. He didn't like to talk about his past, either.

"I used to play basketball—"

A school bell chimed in the distance. She glanced at her watch. Lunch hour was over. She imagined the kids filing into class. Had Jamie made any friends? Had he eaten the sandwich she'd packed for him?

What if Nick showed up at the school?

Paula shifted restlessly. "I don't know how much more of this thrilling police work I can handle." She fiddled with the radar gun settings. "Is this thing even working?"

Riley let a beat go by. "Why are you so tense?

I noticed that back at the station. Is something wrong?"

"Nothing's wrong. I'm not tense." Tapping the steering wheel, Paula watched the curve in the road.

What if Nick was driving down this highway? He always obeyed the speed limit so he didn't get pulled over. That could be him coming toward her right now, in that black sedan, and she wouldn't know. She felt for her gun, snug and reassuring in its holster.

"We're partners," Riley said. "Partners are supposed to bond. That means opening up to each other, getting to know and trust each other. Be friendly."

"All we need to know is that when the going gets tough, we have each other's back." Turning to face him, she leaned forward a little, gripping the steering wheel. "Can I? Can I count on you?"

Riley drew back, shaking his head. "Lady, you *are* tense."

A bright red Ferrari screamed past so fast the draft shook the patrol car and rattled the branches of the ti tree.

"Finally, some action." Paula locked in the clocked speed on the radar gun and started the car engine. "Let's get this jerk."

CHAPTER TWO

RILEY STACKED HIS guitar case on top of a box of kitchen stuff and carried it from his car up the gravel driveway to the single story weatherboard home. Purple bougainvillea trailed over the veranda, annuals bloomed in loamy beds next to the house.

He set the box on the wood floor in the entry hall and went exploring. It felt weird, walking through the empty rooms. So many years had gone by since he'd lived here, so many changes in both himself and his family. Mum had passed, his father remarried...

The living room was smaller than he remembered, the dining room, tiny. He would need to knock a few walls out. He wandered in and out of his old room, Katie's room, the master bedroom, peeked into the bathroom, then went down the hall to the kitchen, the center of their family life. At least it had been while his mother was alive.

On the doorframe of the laundry room were the incremental marks where Dad had measured his and Katie's growth. God, had he ever been that short? He twisted his head sideways to look at the dates.

One stood out from the rest.

The year Mum died he'd been twelve years old, and five foot six inches tall.

There was a big gap after that, as if normal activities had ceased for a time. Riley dragged his gaze away.

The old-fashioned kitchen looked exactly as he remembered. White-painted cupboards, worn linoleum, green-tiled walls up to shoulder height, then yellow paint above that. It was cramped, not enough counter space.

You'd never know a professional cook had worked there. His mother's weekdays had been spent testing recipes and typing up notes for her next cookbook, her electric typewriter all but lost among the clutter on the counter while two or three pots bubbled on the stove. Her brown hair would be tied back, her brow lightly creased in concentration as she tasted, adding a bit of this or that, then tasted again.

Riley especially loved the dessert section of Mary Henning's healthy-lifestyle cookbooks. The red ceramic cookie jar was always full when he came home from school. He'd grab a handful of oatmeal and raisin cookies then run outside to play cricket or footy with his mates.

He glanced at the mark on the doorframe and

ran his thumb across it, feeling the indentation of the pen in the soft wood. The beginnings of a headache stabbed his right temple.

Why hadn't he hung around and talked to her more often, just for a few minutes? She'd always stop what she was doing when he or Katie came into the room, ready to chat or give tastings. It pained him to think how he'd brushed her off. He'd give anything now to be able to ask how her day was, if her work was going well. To hear the sound of her voice.

A lump formed in his throat, making swallowing difficult. Kids didn't think like that, though. At twelve he'd thought his mum would be around forever.

"Riley?" Katie called through the open front door. She'd followed him from his rental unit in her car.

"In the kitchen." Riley blinked rapidly. Jeez, any minute now he'd break down and cry like a girl.

Katie carried in a box of dishes. To help him move she'd worn old jeans and a shirt with the sleeves rolled up, her dark hair swinging in a ponytail.

"Dad and Sandra just pulled up. The moving truck isn't far behind—" She set the box on the floor. "Hey, what's wrong?"

"Nothing." But he and his little sister were close. She always knew what he was thinking.

Katie's gaze swept over the kitchen. Her arm stole around his waist. Softly she said, "It almost feels as if Mum's still here."

Riley cleared his throat. "This room is too poky. I think I'll knock this wall down between the kitchen and dining room." He swept a hand across as if waving a magic wand. "New appliances, new flooring, the works. What do you think?"

"It's your place now." Katie gave him a one-armed hug. "Do what you want."

"Are you sure? By rights, you should get half the house."

"I'm happy with my little cottage. I—I couldn't live here."

The catch in her voice wasn't only about their mother. Katie had gotten breast cancer in her early twenties and come home to live while undergoing treatment—and to nurse her broken heart after John had abandoned her.

"But I'm glad you're here," Katie said. "I think Mum would have liked knowing one of us, at least, was still living in the family home. She was so much a part of this place, especially the kitchen."

"Yeah. Moving in is a bit more emotional than I expected." Riley sucked in a breath. "Let's get the rest of the load." He led the way back through the dining room. "How was the first day of school?"

"The children are so gorgeous. I know, I say

that every year but it's true. Grade one is such a cute age."

"My new partner has a kid in your class. Small world, huh? Her name is Paula Drummond."

"Drummond…" Katie frowned, thinking. "I haven't got all the names memorized yet. Boy or girl?"

"Boy."

"Ah, Jamie. He's sweet."

Riley hauled a box out of the trunk of his car and placed it in Katie's arms then picked up his army boot locker.

"I'm planning our annual bike safety lesson," Katie said as they went inside. "Do you know who at the station will be doing it this year?"

"Not a clue."

"Well, since your partner's son is in my class and you're my brother, what if you two did it? What do you think?"

Riley didn't particularly want to spend any more time than necessary with uptight Paula and since events like the bike safety lesson were usually conducted on their own time, this was a particularly unwelcome idea. But he didn't like letting his little sister down. "Sure, that sounds like fun."

Katie beamed at him. From this angle with her oval face framed by long black hair, and her green eyes, she reminded him of someone…. A stab of pain made him wince. He pressed his fingers to his temple.

"Are you all right?" Katie asked, pausing in the foyer. "You went pale all of a sudden."

"A bit of a headache. I'm fine." Outside, a car door shut. "I think the others have arrived."

His dad's white Ford sedan was parked at the curb. Then a truck rumbled to a halt, its air brakes hissing. Barry Henning's voice carried as he issued instructions to the driver backing up the narrow curving driveway.

"How did you accumulate enough stuff to fill a moving van in less than a year?" Katie said.

Riley leaned against the veranda post. "Imagine a man living out of a footlocker for ten years. Then imagine him moving into his own home, even if it's just a two-bedroom rental unit. A trip to the home furniture store is like taking a kid to a candy shop."

"Hey, you two." Sandra, their stepmother, came across the lawn, avoiding the truck. Her gray-blonde hair was softly waving, her smile big and bright. She presented Riley a casserole dish. "Your mother's famous chicken cacciatore. You won't have time to cook today."

"Thanks." He gave her a peck on the cheek. "You shouldn't have."

He exchanged a furtive grimace with Katie. Since she married their father Sandra had taken up cooking out of their mother's cookbooks. It was nice of her, but in her hands the recipes didn't always turn out—to put it mildly.

"Save that for another time," Barry ordered, striding up onto the porch. His gray hair and moustache were regulation army length, his carriage erect. "We'll order pizza after we get him moved in."

"Yes, sir, Major Dad." Katie saluted. She gave Sandra a wink.

"We've eaten out twice already this week." Sandra was briefly crestfallen. Then she put on a brilliant smile. "Never mind, I'll tuck this in the fridge." She carried the casserole into the house.

One of the moving men trundled the first dollyload—a walnut dresser—to the steps. "Where do you want this?"

"Right this way." Riley led them into his house, rubbing his aching temple. What was up with the headache? He rarely got them and then only when he occasionally drank too much. There weren't even any painkillers in his belongings. But the pain was nothing compared to what he'd experienced in Afghanistan. He would soldier on.

"MORNING, PATTY," Paula called out as she passed Dispatch on Monday morning. The young Irish woman waved.

After the phone calls last week, Nick had gone

quiet. When Paula had arrived home that night with Jamie, her house had been exactly as she'd left it, every door and window locked and untampered with. It should have reassured her. Instead, all weekend she'd been jumpy, obsessively checking over her shoulder, looking for Nick's face in the crowd, keeping Jamie in sight as they wandered through the monthly outdoor market in the village.

She wasn't naive enough to think Nick had gone away. He seemed to be biding his time, trying to make her nervous. What did he want from her? Did he hate her for betraying him? Did he want revenge?

Or did he want Jamie?

This morning she'd called Sally, Jamie's afterschool caregiver, and asked her to be at the school at 3:00 p.m. on the dot. Then Sally's toddler started crying and the other woman had to go. This afternoon, when Paula picked up Jamie, she needed to have a proper talk with Sally.

She found a desk and a spare computer and got caught up on paperwork, working steadily for an hour before her shift started. She and Riley were supposed to be equal partners but from things the guys said she'd deduced he was the boss's best bud. And even though she was senior in years on the force, her past tainted her. She didn't know if it was her imagination or her insecurities showing but she had the uncomfortable feeling that Riley was watching her every move, waiting for her to slip up. Well, she would show him. She would show everyone. She would work twice as hard as any one of them.

John came through the door heading for his office. He carried an athletic bag with a beach towel stuffed inside and his hair was damp. His early morning ocean swims were legend around the station.

"Excuse me, boss. Can I have a quick word?"

"Sure." He glanced at her computer and at the clock. "You know we don't have the budget for overtime, don't you?"

"I know." She saved her report and rose to follow him. "I hate getting behind on the report writing."

"The trouble with policing today isn't the crime, it's the paperwork." He opened his office door and flung his bag in the corner. "What can I do for you?"

"I wondered if you've heard anything from District Headquarters about my application to detective."

It was too early to be asking about a promotion but chances were Moresco would revert to his old ways. She didn't know if she'd be allowed to work on any case that involved him but if she was, she wanted to be ready. This time she would take him down for good. She couldn't do that sitting on the side of the road working a radar gun.

"I reviewed your application when you joined Summerside," John said. "Your qualifications are excellent."

She studied his face, trying to decide if he genuinely supported her career ambitions or if he was like her previous commanding officers, letting her put in time till she could be sent on her way. "But?"

"All promotions are on hold due to budget cutbacks." His expression was open and frank. "Funding cuts have been looming for some time but the memo came yesterday afternoon. The economy dips and the government tightens up on new spending. I'm sorry. There's nothing I can do."

Paula struggled to hide her disappointment. She believed him about the budget cuts but she'd been burned before and she wanted to know where she stood with him. "This knockback doesn't have anything to do with my past, does it?"

"I know very little about your past." John's gaze was steady, inviting her to open up to him.

The silence stretched. Sounds of the outside office filtered through the door. Her fists balled on her thighs. What did he expect her to say? Did her future at Summerside depend on whether she told him her history right this minute? It sucked that her career still hung on one stupid choice she'd made years ago.

She could see his point of view. John didn't know those days were over, but she'd be a fool to expose herself in case he had some discretionary spending or the economy turned around. He sure as hell wouldn't be in a hurry to promote her if he knew what she'd done. But she wouldn't whine that she'd learned her lesson. She would have to bust her hump and prove to him she deserved her detective stripes. If that meant taking Nick down on her own time, so be it.

Speaking of Nick, should she tell John that Moresco had contacted her? Not yet. Not till she knew what Nick wanted. She was in no hurry to associate herself with that loser. No, the past was still a closed subject.

"I should go finish my report before shift." She rose. "Boss."

Paula walked over to the coffee machine, nodding at bleary-eyed officers from night duty on their way home. Third-time lucky? Ha. She'd been dreaming. She stirred cream into her cup and took a sip, taking a moment to collect herself.

She checked the big wall clock over the copy machine. Almost time to hit the locker room—a daily ordeal she hoped would pass if and when she became accepted. The station was so small she was the only female cop. That in itself showed how far she'd dropped since she'd been part of a big bustling city station, in charge of her own vice unit and leading a major undercover drug investigation. Add in the fact that she had to share locker space with the guys and Summerside P.D. started to look more like a boys' outdoor camp than a fully fledged police department. Mind you, she would never say such a thing to John who was proud of his little band of brothers.

But she was a big girl; she could handle the arrangement. It was the guys who seemed to have a problem with it. Whether they resented her for disrupting their routine or they simply didn't like her, she had no idea.

Take the issue of changing into their uniform at work. Jackson was on the pudgy side and self-conscious. He waited until she left the room to get dressed. Crucek grumbled and turned his back as he quickly shucked his civvies. Delinsky obviously worked out and thought he was hot stuff. He liked to parade around bare-chested, flaunting his sculpted body at her. *In your dreams, mate.* She didn't go for that over-developed look. Or the leering attitude.

Riley was the odd one out. Every morning he was there when she arrived, already fully kitted out. She might have thought he slept in his uniform except that it was always immaculately cleaned and pressed.

Sighing, she set her dirty cup by the sink. Time to man up.

"Morning, gentlemen," she proclaimed loudly as she pushed open the door and stepped inside.

"Morning." Riley was seated at the table, shining his already spit-polished shoes.

Despite the fact they hadn't exactly hit it off the first week, he was a prime example of a good cop. Always professional, always smartly decked out, every detail of his uniform top notch. He was good looking, too, since she was noticing. His shoulders filled out his shirt nicely and the fabric of his pants stretched over long thigh muscles. *Smarten up, Drummond. Mind on your job.* The last time she'd given in to an inappropriate attraction it had cost her her career.

Instead of greeting her, Delinsky, Jackson and Crucek retreated to the far side of the room and began whispering like teenage girls. Normally she ignored their behavior—she had bigger things to worry about than guys acting goofy—but since Nick's phone calls her control was stretched thin.

She twirled the combination lock. "So much for my high hopes of working with men instead of boys."

More giggles.

It sucked being the new person. But she was damned if she would let the guys think their treatment bothered her or that she was going to kiss their collective asses.

Paula swung her locker door open. A plastic bag containing white crystals fell onto the floor. She jumped. In the background excited whispers rose in volume. Slowly she bent to pick up the ziplock bag. Her stomach turned over.

"Hey, watcha got there?" Crucek swaggered forward and took the bag from her hand. "Lookie here, guys. Our new constable is into drugs."

"Don't be an idiot!" She made a swipe for the bag but Crucek whipped it out of her reach, holding it high so she would have had to jump to get it.

Delinsky and Jackson crowded around. "Does Sergeant Forster know about this?" Jackson said, eyes wide. "Maybe we ought to get him in here. Let him know what his new constable has been up to."

"Screw you." What the hell was this about? Were they teasing? Was this a lame joke because she was a woman or because she was new? She should laugh it off but she couldn't find her sense of humor.

"We know about you," Delinsky crowed.

How could they know about her past? That was supposed to be a secret. Was she imagining the menace in Delinsky's voice? Were they trying to get rid of her? Whatever they knew, or thought they knew, would they tell John? If so, there went any hope of her promotion, if not her job.

"Nothing to know." Her voice was too loud, bouncing off the pale green walls. "Piss off, jerks, and let me get ready for work. Shift is about to start."

"We think there's plenty to know, don't we guys?" Crucek glanced around for support and received grunts of assent and nodding heads.

Had Nick gotten to them? No, that was plain paranoid. She swallowed. *Wasn't it?*

They had her surrounded, Crucek and Jackson in front, Delinsky's hot breath on the back of her neck. These men were supposed to be her coworkers, her support system. Yet at this moment she felt that if she showed any weakness they would tear her apart like a pack of wolves.

"Back. Off." She spoke more forcefully, spinning to snap at Delinsky. "You, too, hotshot."

Jackson took a step closer. As if by agreement, the others did, too. "We don't like bent cops."

"Do you know what happens to bent cops?" Crucek sneered.

Paula scowled, adrenaline rushing through her body, making her feel sick. Her heart was beating so loudly she could barely hear them. She had a crazy urge to pull out her gun and start firing. Maybe that's what they wanted, for her to lose control.

Riley rose and walked over. Although he was junior to the others he had a battle-hardened air that gave him an innate authority. "Give me that." He reached between Jackson and Crucek and yanked away the plastic bag. He held it up to the light, turned it this way and that.

Paula clenched her fists. If her partner was in on the plot to break her, she would never forgive him. If she was found in possession of drugs, all her credibility was gone. Whatever the guys' motivation was, this had the potential to hurt her. Badly.

Riley opened the bag and shook a large irregular crystal into his palm. He brought his hand to his mouth and took a lick. Ran the taste around in his mouth. "Rock sugar. The kind some people put in their coffee."

Sugar. Relief flooded her, weakening her knees. She hadn't been set up with real drugs. They didn't know anything. No one was out to get her. Nick hadn't infiltrated the station. John wouldn't find out about her past.

The men erupted in roars of laughter.

Jackson slapped her on the back. "We got you good, Drummond!"

"Welcome to Summerside P.D." Crucek had tears in his eyes from laughing so hard.

"You're a good sport." Delinsky grinned and squeezed her arm.

The men drifted away, still crowing. "She took

it so seriously." "Did you see her expression?" "I could hardly keep a straight face."

Paula stood where she was, trembling and trying not to show it. Bloody bastards thought they were so clever. She'd love to give them a dose of their own medicine. But she didn't dare, not with even a faint possibility of her detective stripes dangling in front of her. She had to keep on the straight and narrow, regardless of how much she'd like to grind these backwoods amateur cops into the dirt.

Riley took her arm and led her to the bench, gently pushed her onto it. He sat beside her and put a hand on her shoulder. "It was just a joke."

She shook off his hand, turning her pent-up fury on him. "Stay out of it. I can fight my own battles."

"They hid my gun the first week I was here," Riley went on as though she hadn't bitten his head off. "I thought I'd lost it. I was shitting myself. Idiot that I was, I didn't even get that they were hazing me. They waited until I wrote up a missing-equipment report and was about to give it to John before they brought out my revolver from wherever they'd hidden it."

"What did you do?" Paula asked. Was there a way to get even without cost to her? Doubtful. She knew how hazing worked. If you got mad, you were a poor sport. If you tried to get even, the jokes escalated.

"Nothing. There's nothing you can do. But it's not so bad here in Summerside. I've seen army squadrons where newcomers are hazed for months. But these guys will do it only once. They called you a good sport—after today you won't have to worry about them." Riley paused. "You did take it awfully seriously." He waited, as if for an explanation.

"I was never treated like that in my other units." She didn't mention the moving of files, the swapping of her hat for one three sizes too big. But those pranks happened years ago, when she was a rookie. This seemed malicious. Or was she being overly sensitive? "Were you in on it?"

"No. I'm not a fan of practical jokes." Riley drew a thumbnail along the grain of the bench, making a shallow crease in the wood. "I don't think they meant to upset you. Maybe they inadvertently hit close to the bone." He searched her face. "Did they?"

Really? He wanted her to cozy up and confide in him? *Think again, mate.* He might be handsome and sexy and professional and a whole lot of things she admired, but they had a job to do and that's where their connection ended. Besides, she'd rather do a month of solid paperwork than trust someone she'd just met with her past.

Paula got to her feet. She unclenched her fingers

and felt the blood flow into them. "Shouldn't we be out on traffic patrol, nailing speeders?"

Riley continued to regard her with that measured gaze. She shifted edgily, twisting her cap. Finally he rose and tipped a sardonic finger to his brow. "Okay. Partner."

PAULA KNOCKED ON THE open classroom door, arriving for her parent-teacher interview. The walls were lined with brightly colored student artwork. Tables, not desks, were used for seating. At the back of the room beanbags formed a reading circle next to the bookshelf. Her new job might be less than she'd hoped for but at least for Jamie the atmosphere was warm and welcoming.

Katie Henning, seated at her desk, glanced at her schedule. "You must be Paula, Jamie's mum. Please come in."

"It's nice to have a parent-teacher meeting early in the year," Paula said, taking a seat. Katie had her brother's dark hair, high cheekbones and sculpted mouth. But instead of dark brown eyes, Katie's were pale green.

"We like to get parents involved in their child's education right from the start." Katie leafed through the stack of folders on her desk. "I've got some of Jamie's work to show you."

"We have someone else in common besides Jamie," Paula said. "Your brother, Riley."

"I know, he told me." Katie pulled a folder with Jamie Drummond written across the top. "I asked Riley if you two would give my class a lesson in bike safety. Would you be up for that? I'll bet your son would be thrilled to show off his mum, the cop."

Paula wasn't sure she wanted to draw attention to Jamie being her son. But she guessed if Nick were going to find out about the boy, he would do so regardless of a bike safety talk. "That sounds fine."

"We'll schedule it in a few weeks, when the kids have settled in." Katie smiled. "Jamie's a lovely boy."

Katie probably said that to all the parents but Paula couldn't help feel a rush of maternal pride. "He's enjoying school. Is it too early to ask how he's doing in class?"

"He's adjusting well, playing with the other children. Judging from his drawings he has excellent fine motor skills."

"So you have no concerns at this point?"

"There is one thing. The other day I asked the children to draw pictures of their parents' occupations. He depicted you in a police uniform. All good there." Katie removed a drawing from Jamie's folder and passed it across the desk. "But is his father really an astronaut?"

Paula pressed her fingers to her mouth at the

cartoon-like figure of a man in a space suit. Poor Jamie. School activities and interacting with other students would inevitably highlight his lack of a father. She'd tried to prepare him but she couldn't foresee every contingency.

"I'm sorry. I should have spoken to you about Jamie's father before."

"You can tell me now," Katie said. "This meeting is for parents and teachers to talk about any issues or special problems."

"Jamie's never met his father. N-Nicholas and I separated before Jamie was born. He isn't an astronaut. He's…a businessman," she lied, choosing her words carefully. "He's not in our lives. Never has been and never will be. I have full custody. I've provided a copy of the court order to the school office. If Jamie's father were ever to come to Summerside, he's not to have any contact with Jamie. That's *extremely* important. No contact. At all."

"We have a couple of students where custody is an issue," Katie said. "Jamie's not alone there."

Paula doubted her son's situation was remotely similar to the other pupils'. She didn't want to be one of those overprotective helicopter mothers hovering over her child, but Nick's re-emergence had spiked her sense of vulnerability. She gripped her purse as Katie once again leafed through Jamie's folder.

"Ah, yes. I see you've noted on his information sheet that you, Karen Drummond and Sally Leeds are the only people authorized to pick him up from school."

"Karen is my mother. Sally is Jamie's after-school caregiver," Paula explained. "I've spoken to her about the situation. Sally's very reliable. But in the event that she's late, what safeguards are in place to prevent someone else taking Jamie before she gets here?"

"A teacher is always on duty outside at the front of the school at home time," Katie said. "With so many students it's difficult to ensure each child goes with the correct adult. It's up to the authorized person picking up to get there on time."

"As I said, Sally's dependable. However, I'd like this information to be circulated to every teacher." Paula pressed her hand on the sheet. "I can't stress how important this is."

"I'll make a note of that." Katie wrote a brief memo on the info sheet. "Cops. You're so security-conscious. Riley is always installing some new alarm in my house. I'm not complaining. It's good to know someone's looking out for you."

Paula nodded politely, unable to relate. She looked out for herself.

"I don't blame you," Katie added. "Children are precious and so vulnerable."

"Do you have kids?"

Katie shook her head wistfully. "Someday. If I meet the right guy."

"It's not easy, is it?" Paula gave her a wry smile, one single woman in her thirties to another.

Katie's dry lift of her eyebrows acknowledged the truth of that. "However, I'm too busy right now with work to be looking for anyone permanent."

"Same." Although it was more complicated than that. She would love to find a wonderful man and have another child or two. But a proper home and a family felt out of reach with Nick lurking in her background. *Oh, by the way, Jamie's dad is a drug lord but don't worry, I'm over him.* Understandably, any worthwhile man would run a mile once he knew that about her. What was wrong with her that she could have fallen for a criminal?

"Anything else I can tell you?" Katie asked.

Paula would have welcomed knowing why Riley shunned questions about his past. What bad-ass thing had he done? But that probably wasn't what Katie meant. "No, I think that's it. I know you have a lot of parents to see tonight. It was nice to meet you."

Katie got to her feet and shook hands. "I'll be in touch to organize for the bike safety class in a few weeks. Thanks for agreeing."

"I'm happy to do it." Paula said good-night and walked through the corridors, thinking ahead to picking up Jamie from Sally's house, then going home. After she got Jamie into bed, she might treat herself to a nice hot bath. Riley was right. She *had* been tense lately—for good reason—and the incident with the rock sugar hadn't helped.

Thirty minutes later she turned into her driveway, half listening to Jamie's chatter about the game of hide and seek he'd played at Sally's house. Nearly eight o'clock, it was still light. Her glance automatically went to the front door—

Her hands tightened on the wheel. Sitting on the mat was a bright red remote-controlled racing car. She couldn't afford toys that expensive. Her mother would never splurge unless it was a birthday or Christmas present. Nor would she leave it sitting on the front porch. It definitely wasn't Christmas and Jamie's birthday was in July.

Only one person would have given such a gift. *Nick.*

CHAPTER THREE

PAULA DROVE INTO the carport, hoping Jamie hadn't seen the toy. Somehow she had to get him into the house through the back door.

"What's that on the porch?" Jamie unbuckled his seat belt even before the car had stopped.

"Nothing. Jamie—"

Too late. He was out of the car and running across the lawn and through the flower bed. "It's a car."

"Jamie, honey, don't get excited." She hurried after him, dropping her purse in her haste. She grabbed it from among the petunias, wasting precious seconds. "It's probably a mistaken delivery."

"It's for me," Jamie said. He kneeled on the mat, a gift card in his hand. "My name's on it, see?"

Jamie might not be able to read yet but she'd taught him to recognize his name and phone number and to print both. He also knew the alphabet.

"It's from..." His small brow furrowed as he laboriously spelled out, "D...A...D." He looked up at her. "What does that spell?"

Paula gazed into her son's small trusting face and felt her heart break. She never lied to him. Ever.

"Mum?" His eyes searched hers.

Taking a deep breath, she swallowed. Her hands felt clammy. "D-dad. It spells, *Dad*."

Jamie went still, his eyes wide and unblinking. "But I thought— You said he was overseas."

Okay, maybe that one lie.

"Um, he was." Her fingers curled into her palms. How dare Nick disturb their peace? How dare he think he could buy his child? "He must be back."

"Yay!" Jamie stood and ran down the steps as if expecting to see his father out on the sidewalk. "Where is he?" Looking up the street he took a step forward and called tentatively, "Dad?" Another step. "Dad! I'm home."

Though it was a fine evening, it was past dinnertime and no one was outside. There were no strange cars parked nearby that she didn't recognize. Through the curtains in the houses across from hers came the blue flicker of TV screens. Chances were no one had seen who'd placed the toy car on her step.

"Jamie." Paula ran to take his hand and tugged him toward the porch. "He must have gone."

Jamie dragged his feet, looking over his shoulder. "He'll come back, right?"

"No." Her free hand curled into a fist she would dearly love to smash into Nick's face for raising a little boy's expectations.

Jamie stopped dead, crestfallen. "But he'll want to see me if he's back from his trip. Won't he?"

Oh, God. "I don't know. He's not—" She thought desperately, agonized at seeing her son hurt. "His job doesn't allow him to be a family man."

"But he came here. We weren't home. He'll come back," Jamie said logically.

"Let's go inside," she said, leading him up the steps. "You'll have your bath and get ready for bed. Then we'll talk about your father."

"I want to play." Jamie crouched beside his new toy. Gripping the slick red hood of the racing car with small fingers he tried to pull off the wires holding it on to the cardboard packaging.

"No!" Paula snatched up the toy. "I'm sorry. You can't have it."

"It's mine!" He scrambled to his feet, his arms reaching upward. Tears rolled down his cheeks. "My dad gave it to me."

Paula fumbled with the key, stabbing it into the lock as she held the car high, feeling like the world's meanest mother. She got the door open and dragged Jamie, kicking and screaming, into the house. She put the car on top of the bookshelf in the living room.

"Why won't you give it to me? I hate you!" Jamie yelled, his face red.

Paula crouched and took him by the shoulders. "Listen to me. I know you're angry and upset. But your father is not part of our lives. We can't accept presents from him."

"Why not?" Jamie wailed, rubbing his eyes. "Why can't I see him? He wants to see me."

"Just because."

Because he's a bad man. I'm afraid he'll hurt you.

"I want my car. My daddy brought it to me!" He was working himself into a full-blown tantrum such as he hadn't had since he was three years old.

Paula tried to fold him in a hug to rock him but he tore away from her and flung himself face down on the carpet, his ribcage heaving.

"You have to trust me, sweetheart," she pleaded. *Only me.*

A knock sounded at the door. Great. All she needed was some nosy neighbor thinking she was beating her kid.

She left Jamie pounding his fists on the floor while she answered the door. "This isn't a good t—" Riley stood there wearing a pair of faded jeans and a black polo shirt. "What are you doing here?"

Riley began to speak but Jamie's howls were too loud to ignore. He peered past her, into the house. "Is something wrong?"

"Did you come by for a reason? Because I'm pretty busy. As you can hear."

Suddenly Jamie stopped howling. His footsteps

thudded behind her. "Is that Dad?" Seeing Riley he stopped short, suddenly going shy. His anxious gaze tore at Paula's heart. "Is he...?"

"No, sweetheart." Her cheeks burning, she said to Riley, "You should go."

Instead, Riley crouched, eye level with Jamie. "I'm Riley, your mum's partner at the police station. What's your name?"

Jamie pressed back into Paula's legs. Her arms went around his shoulders. His small chest jerked as he hiccupped.

"My sister Katie is your teacher at school." Riley spoke with the studied casualness of a cop talking down an out-of-control offender. Any other time Paula would have admired his technique.

Jamie sniffled. "Ms. Henning?"

"That's right. What's your name?"

"Jamie," he mumbled.

"Nice to meet you." Riley held his hand.

Jamie hesitated then placed his small hand in Riley's to be given a hearty man-shake. Wiping his eyes with his sleeve, he stood a little taller. "Do you have a gun? Mum won't let me hold hers."

Oh, no, not the gun conversation. Jamie asked at least once a week to see her gun despite her constantly telling him it wasn't a toy. At least he seemed to have forgotten the car—for the moment. "Not now, Jamie."

"When I'm not on duty my gun is locked up,"

Riley said. "Your mum's right. No one but a police officer is allowed to touch our weapons. One day I might show you my gun."

"Cool," Jamie said shyly.

"It's time for Jamie to get ready for bed." Paula rubbed his arms. "Go on, mate. Into your pajamas."

"Aw, do I have to?"

"I'll read you the dinosaur story tonight."

Jamie went, dragging his heels and glancing over his shoulder at Riley. Paula watched him with a tiny frown. With her father dead and her only brother living in Sydney, Jamie didn't have many male role models in his life.

"So," she said, turning back to Riley. "To what do I owe the pleasure?"

"I was passing on my way home from the shooting range and thought I'd see how you were doing after the hazing." He shoved his hands in his back pockets, making his shirt stretch across his chest, hinting at some serious pecs. "You seemed to take it hard."

"I didn't take it hard." Paula lifted her gaze— and her chin—a fraction. "I simply wasn't expecting it."

"Okay." He studied her, relaxed but assessing, then seemed to decide to take her words at face value. "Nice kid, Jamie. Something upset him before I came?"

"It's really none of your business." Riley's earlier words sank in. If he was at the shooting range he would have his gun in his car. When it counted he'd backed her up. A small thing, but she liked him for it.

"I appreciate you not bringing out your gun. Jamie can make a pistol out of a slice of bread but I don't want him anywhere near a real weapon." She sighed. "Plus, you made him forget what he was crying about."

"I guess he was disappointed at not seeing his father." Riley tilted his head, his eyes narrowing. "Doesn't he know what his dad looks like?"

"His father is not in our lives." She crossed her arms over her chest. "That's all I'm going to say. I don't mix work and home."

"No worries." Riley held up his hands, palms out. "Just curious."

"'Curiosity killed the cat.'" The phrase she threw at Jamie when he got into stuff she didn't want him exploring popped out.

"Satisfaction brought it back." Riley's sudden, sexy grin made her think of a tomcat, whiskers dipped in cream, sensual, sleek and satisfied.

Sensual? Yessiree. With the porch light gleaming on his dark hair, his broad shoulders and long-limbed athletic stance, there was no getting around the fact that Riley was hot. And tonight he'd shown he was sensitive to her wishes regarding her son. But he was her partner, out of bounds on every level. She was trying to get her career on track, not become sidelined by another inappropriate attraction.

"I need to go to Jamie. He's waiting for me to read a story."

Riley nodded, and backed through the door. "See you tomorrow."

Paula resisted watching his butt move in snug jeans as he walked to his black sports car. Instead she closed the door firmly.

Before she went to Jamie she removed the toy from the high shelf and carried it out to the carport. She started to lift the lid on the rubbish bin then changed her mind and put it in the trunk of her car to take to the thrift shop tomorrow. No reason some other little boy couldn't benefit from Nick's largesse.

After she read Jamie a bedtime story she stayed in his room until long after he fell asleep, watching over him. A glimmer of moonlight through the curtains shone on his mussed hair and bunched pajama top. She might not be enough for him anymore but he was everything to her.

Please, don't let anything happen to my boy. Don't let anyone hurt him or try to take him away from me.

FROM THE SQUAD CAR'S passenger's seat Riley watched Paula covertly through his dark glasses.

They were parked on the side of the highway again, in the shade of the ti tree. Without the air-conditioning the heat of the day was almost unbearable, even with the windows rolled all the way down.

Paula was preoccupied, staring intently out the window in silence, a slight frown marring her near-flawless complexion. Was she thinking about her ex, Jamie's father? What was the story there— love of her life or rat bastard?

Last night in her foyer, for a moment, a spark had jumped between him and Paula. It must have been seeing her in a clinging blouse and short skirt instead of her uniform that had him noticing her breasts, her legs and pretty much everything in between. Their little verbal exchange toward the end had been out of character. Not professional, almost flirting.

She'd realized it, too, and backed off so quickly she'd practically left skid marks. And if she hadn't, he would have. He liked how she was strong as a cop and as a mother, but they worked together— a no-go zone as far as he was concerned. And it didn't take a genius to work out that she had issues with her ex. He didn't want to get in the middle of that.

The radio crackled.

"Code twelve on Nepean Highway at Wooralla Drive." Patty's Irish accent became more pronounced the more urgent the situation. "Repeat, code twelve, Nepean at Wooralla. Fire and ambulance dispatched to the scene. Car sixteen, do you read me?"

Paula started the engine and hit the switch for the flashing red and blue lights. Siren blaring she forced her way into the stream of traffic.

"Copy that, Dispatch," Riley said into the radio. "Estimated time to scene, five minutes." He glanced at Paula. "Correction. Officer Drummond at the wheel. Make that two minutes."

"Right outside the primary school," Paula muttered through gritted teeth, as she slowed behind a vehicle whose driver was oblivious. "Idiot."

"That intersection is notorious." Riley braced a hand on the dash as she swerved to pass on the wrong side. "It's worse now Summerside has gotten so big."

"Big?" Paula spared him a brief glance sideways. "I'd hate to have seen it when it was small." She fixed her gaze on the road again. "School lets out now. You'd think people would drive more carefully."

"Must be hard having a young kid," Riley said. "Every time there's an accident near the school, wondering if your child has been injured."

"Let's not go there, okay?" Paula crested a slight hill and slowed as she approached the intersection. Heat shimmered off the pavement, making wavy lines in front of the crashed vehicles—a black SUV and an electric blue Holden sedan. The fire engine was there, the crew swarming over the road, directing traffic, putting out cones to block off one lane.

Children, teachers and parents congregated on the corner nearest the school. Some stood and watched while others hurried away.

Riley's vision blurred suddenly in a haze of red and black. A convulsive shudder ran through his body. Dizzy, he dropped his head forward. *Dozens of school children. Innocent, defenceless.*

Paula screeched to a halt diagonally across the intersection. She frowned at him. "What's wrong?"

"Nothing." He raised his head, tried to shake off a lingering chill. Good thing he hadn't been behind the wheel or there might have been another accident.

Paula gave him a hard look. "Take over from the firefighter directing traffic."

Still dazed, Riley didn't quibble with Paula taking command. He waved cars through the intersection, watching events unfold as if watching a movie. An ambulance siren wailed, approaching rapidly. In the Holden a man in his early twenties was slumped behind the wheel, unconscious. A blonde woman was climbing out of the SUV, her arm bleeding. She was crying. Her two kids were in the backseat, also crying. The fire crew brought out the Jaws of Life to pry open the Holden's smashed-in door.

Riley was beset by a feeling of unreality, of being disconnected to events going on around him. What was going on? Had he come down with some sort of flu bug? He didn't feel sick so much as disoriented. And that damned headache was back. He'd left his cap in the squad car and the hot afternoon sun beat on his unprotected head.

Another squad car pulled up. Crucek and Jackson climbed out.

"Take a break." Crucek jerked a thumb over his shoulder. "You're white as paste. Thought you would have seen worse in Afghanistan."

Riley started to protest then gave up and walked to the Holden where Paula and the paramedics had congregated. The medics were loading the unconscious driver onto a gurney. His hair was stringy and lank, his emaciated arms covered from shoulder to wrist in tattoos. He had the sallow, unhealthy look of an addict.

"Alive?" Riley asked one of the paramedics.

"Barely."

"Are you taking blood samples? Testing for alcohol and drugs."

"I can tell you right now he's using." The paramedic nodded to the track marks on the driver's arms.

Paula held up a used syringe between gloved

fingers. "This goes to the lab for analysis. Somehow I don't think the guy's injecting insulin. And I want this car back at the station so we can search it properly." She unclipped the radiophone on her vest and pressed buttons. "Patty, get a tow truck out here."

She turned to Riley. "Hey, rookie, are you okay? You seem like you're about to faint."

He tried to pull himself together. He and Paula were supposed to be equal partners but he'd just behaved like the greenest recruit who'd ever thrown up at an accident scene while she had effortlessly taken control and directed operations. He had no problem with women being in the police force or in command. He did have a problem with himself looking like a pansy ass.

Protecting people was what he did. If he couldn't do that, who was he?

"I'm fine," he growled. "Just a touch of sun."

IN THE PARKING LOT behind the police station Paula popped the trunk on the blue Holden. From the interior of the car came the sound of cloth ripping as Riley tore apart the backseat. Simon Peterson was on a dolly underneath, shining a flashlight into crevices.

The direct afternoon sun turned the pavement and brick building into a recipe for heatstroke. Paula barely noticed she was perspiring. Finding that syringe had given her a rush of adrenaline. Mentally she ran through the illicit injectable drugs—speed, heroin, crack cocaine...

Finally she was involved in a task she'd been trained for, a potential drug investigation. This could be her break-out opportunity, a chance to shine, to earn her detective stripes, budget constraints or no.

She stuck her head inside the trunk, letting her eyes adjust to the shaded cavity. It was loaded with junk—oily rags, empty black garbage bags, a pair of worn leather boots and a stack of tattered men's magazines. Her hands protected by gloves, she threw these items onto a large tarp spread on the pavement.

An ancient first-aid kit was tucked at the rear of the trunk. She opened that and pulled out rolled bandages and dressings encased in yellowing paper. She threw them on the tarp, too.

Paula wiped the sweat dripping down her neck with the back of her hand and called to Riley. "Find anything?"

"Not yet," came his muffled reply.

With everything out of the trunk the stained mat lining looked lumpy. Paula tried to lift it. The clips holding it down were rusted shut on one side. The other side of the mat was stuck beneath the spare tire. She pulled on the tire. It was wedged in tightly. Bracing her foot against the bumper, she hauled on it harder.

Riley backed out of the car, his hair mussed, a smear of dirt across one cheek. "Need a hand?"

"Nope." With a grunt she gave a final tug. "Got it." She staggered backward. The tire flew out of her hands, bounced across the tarmac. Something fell out—a plastic bag half full of white crystals. "Jackpot."

Riley walked over and picked up the bag. He opened it, tasted a bit and grimaced. "This ain't no coffee sugar. It's crystal meth."

Crystal methamphetamine. Her skin prickled. Nick Moresco had built an empire around this drug.

Paula tore the trunk liner away. Approximately two dozen plastic bags of crystal meth were lined up in neat rows, flattened to avoid detection.

Riley whistled. "We've got ourselves a dealer."

Peterson, a skinny twenty-two-year-old with pimply skin, asked more eagerly than was seemly, "Do you think he's local?"

"We've never seen this junk in Summerside before." Riley gestured to a peeling bumper sticker. "But Bayside Holden is in Frankston."

Paula felt the heat now. She wiped her forehead again. It was clammy. Moresco was fresh out of jail. Hard drugs had come to town. *Her town.* Where she lived and worked, where Jamie went to school.

Coincidence, or something more sinister? Suddenly light-headed, she bent over, her hands on her knees.

"Hey, what is it?" Riley gripped her shoulder. "You okay?"

"It's frickin' déjà vu," she mumbled.

"Sorry, I didn't quite catch that."

"It's the heat." She tried to suck in a breath. Spots danced before her eyes. If those bags of crystal meth were Nick's doing...

She dug deep and found the resolve to straighten her spine. If the drugs were his doing, he would be caught and punished. "Let's get these bags logged and put in the evidence room."

More paperwork. At least it took her mind off Moresco. It was after five o'clock before she and Riley had filed the last report. She pushed away from the computer. "I'm beat."

"Let's take a walk," Riley suggested. "Have you tried the ice cream on the corner yet?"

"Not yet." Ice cream. Cold, sweet, tempting. The man doing the offering was sexy, smart and strong.

Wouldn't it be nice to do something simple like go for ice cream with a man she was not only attracted to but beginning to like and respect? But her life wasn't simple. And Riley had never given the slightest indication he'd like to hang with her after work. He had to have an agenda. And she suspected she knew what it was.

"I have to pick up Jamie." She made a show of checking her watch.

"Fifteen minutes." He gave her a disarming smile. "My treat."

Might as well get this over with. She put in a quick call to Sally to let her know she'd be there by six at the latest. No problem according to Sally. Jamie was happily playing with another little boy in her care.

Outside the station Riley turned into the arcade that led through to the main street. In the narrow shadowed lane she was more aware than usual of his sheer physicality. His height and the breadth of his shoulders were accentuated. His stride seemed longer, his demeanor relaxed but alert.

"What's your favorite flavor?" Riley asked. "Chocolate, vanilla, rocky road...?"

"Pistachio."

"You can tell a lot about a person by the ice cream they choose," he confided, his head tilted toward her.

"Bull." He was softening her up. Even knowing that, she grinned, fascinated.

"You have a taste for the exotic. You're not afraid to be different. You don't care what people think of you as long as you do what you believe is right."

"You're making this up."

His dark eyes danced. "Am I wrong?"

Not entirely, but she wasn't going to give him that. "What's your favorite flavor?"

"I have no favorite. I love them all."

"Ah, you're a commitment-phobe. You flit from ice cream to ice cream."

"No, I'm a man who keeps his options open."

"Same thing." She gave him a nudge, her bare elbow making contact with the damp cotton of his shirt, and below the cloth, his rib cage.

Teasing felt surprisingly good. The moment would be fleeting so she allowed herself to relax and enjoy for a change. The scorching heat of the day had died, leaving the air pleasantly warm as the shadows lengthened. They strolled down the sidewalk, Riley nodding and greeting people as they passed.

A bell over the door tinkled as they entered the air-conditioned ice-cream parlor.

A blonde fiftysomething woman behind the counter had a ready smile for Riley. "How did you enjoy the casserole?"

"Um, yeah, it was great," Riley said, scratching the back of his neck. "Paula, this is Sandra, my stepmother. Paula's my partner," he said to Sandra. "She has a craving for pistachio."

"I don't—" Paula started to protest then got distracted by the twinkle in his eye. Hmm, maybe she did have a craving. But she would have to be satisfied with a frozen treat. Her awareness of him was growing, no doubt due to spending hours sitting in the squad car together. She would have to be careful not to encourage him.

Sandra handed Paula a waffle cone piled with three fat scoops of pistachio ice cream. "Complimentary to Summerside police officers."

"Thank you." Paula took a lick and her eyes closed briefly. "Heavenly."

Sandra began to construct a second cone for Riley at his instruction—raspberry, butterscotch and licorice. "Are you all settled in at the house?"

"That's a way off. Tonight I'm going to start tearing apart the kitchen." He was nodding at the display of fresh cakes and pastries under glass covers on the counter. "You're selling desserts now."

"The new owner wants to expand the fresh-food line," Sandra said.

"New owner?" Riley's eyebrows rose. "Shane Kennedy has owned this place since I was in high school. Never thought he would give up such a prime location."

"Apparently he was offered a price he couldn't refuse," Sandra said. "It was all very sudden. I didn't even know the shop was up for sale."

The bell above the shop tinkled. A teenage boy with blond curly hair and a pretty dark-haired girl in school uniform entered holding hands.

"I'll let you go," Riley said to his stepmother. "Catch you later."

"Thanks again for the cone," Paula called.

Outside Paula lapped at the cone to stop the rapidly melting ice cream from dripping onto her hands. "It's a bit undignified, don't you think, for cops to be eating ice cream on the street corner?" She couldn't conceive of doing this in her city precinct.

"The locals are used to it. But let's go sit." He started walking toward the grassy square and a wrought-iron bench beneath a shady gum tree.

Paula sank onto the slatted seat. For a few minutes she concentrated on her cone, enjoying the cool sweetness of the pistachio confection.

"You have a bit of ice cream..." Riley touched her nose.

She batted his hand away and fished in her pocket for a tissue. "Have I got it all?"

He pretended to scrutinize her, his eyes amused.

"Never mind." She threw the remains of her cone in a nearby bin and wiped her fingers.

"Feeling better?" Riley was sober now.

"Yes," she said warily.

"Good." He looked away, at the row of shops and cafés, post office and supermarket, then at her. "Suppose you tell me what you meant by *déjà vu*."

Paula stilled. Pedestrians walked through the little park but she couldn't have said whether they were male or female, young or old. She knew Riley had picked up on her muttered comment. He came across as laid-back but he was always on alert.

"I didn't want to say anything until I was sure…"

"Maybe I can help."

She studied his intelligent eyes, his determined jaw, his sensitive mouth. "Maybe you can. I think I know who's behind the crystal meth we found in the Holden."

"Who?" Riley prompted.

"Nick Moresco, the drug lord I put in jail seven years ago."

CHAPTER FOUR

RILEY KNEW IT, knew she'd been hiding something earlier. Her doubling over hadn't been due to the heat but to the drug cache itself. And maybe to its discovery in Summerside. She'd gone quiet while they'd documented the haul, her mouth pulled down in a grim expression. Did she still have connections to Moresco? Was this why John was worried about her?

She was innocent until proven guilty, Riley reminded himself. "What makes you think Moresco is involved?"

Paula gripped the iron slats on either side of her knees. "He got out of prison last month."

Riley thought about that. "Didn't he operate out of the inner city? Why would he come all the way to the peninsula to set up shop?"

She shrugged, eyes down. "I don't know."

Riley was no detective but he'd been trained in interrogation techniques. He could tell when someone was lying. The rumors about Paula came to mind. She'd done something so bad that it couldn't be talked about.

"A woman and her two children were almost wiped out today by a sleazebag shooting a light. If Moresco has something to do with the drugs in that car, and if you know something, you'd better tell me about it."

"I can't be positive the crystal meth came from him. I'm only speculating. But—" She glanced up. "He called me the day I started at Summerside P.D. He has my phone number. He knows where I live."

No wonder she'd been tense. Riley lifted his cap and dragged a hand through his hair. "What did he want?"

Again she hesitated. Riley got the feeling she was choosing her words carefully.

"He…didn't say. Maybe just to scare me. Maybe he wants revenge." She straightened and scowled at Riley as though he were the villain. "He'd better look out before he tangles with me again."

Riley studied her, frowning. One minute she was hesitant and uncertain, the next minute she was full of bravado. Was she hiding her own wrongdoing, laying the groundwork for a cover-up by admitting Moresco had called her? Or was she simply justifiably anxious because a drug lord was contacting her?

"Have you told John? If you're in trouble, the police force will back you up."

She gave him a look that was part scorn, part pity for his naivety. "Yeah, right."

"What happened seven years ago to get you busted back to uniform?" Riley asked. "You reacted strongly to the hazing. Did you get caught pilfering drugs from the evidence room? Are you an addict?"

"No! Are you nuts? I would never do drugs." She was really angry now. "My father was killed by a junkie while he was trying to resuscitate the man's girlfriend."

"Oh." Riley sat back. "I'm sorry. Was he a doctor?"

"Paramedic." Her shoulders squared. "I went into policing so I could bring creeps like the one who killed my dad to justice."

"Then what did you do?" He returned to his initial question. "Why has your past followed you here?"

"I don't talk about it. I made that clear to John. What's done is done."

"But it's not, is it? Not if crystal meth is showing up in our sleepy little town because you're living here."

She shrank away, her face pale and drawn.

"You need me to watch your back?" Riley said. "I need to know what I'm watching out for. A soldier doesn't go into a dangerous situation without intel. His mates wouldn't let him." He hardened his voice. "So what's the story?"

"I'm not required to divulge that information to you, or anyone." She got to her feet. "I've got to go. My son is waiting for me."

Riley watched her stride off. Was she really bent, as rumor had it? Why else would she have moved from station to station? In a long, deep-cover investigation sometimes the line between good guys and bad guys blurred. Boundaries shifted, cops began to see the law from the dark side. Maybe she had money problems. A cop's salary wasn't that great. Undercover vice cops were vulnerable to all sorts of illegal temptations besides drug use. Taking bribes, selling drugs or protection, tampering with the evidence. She had definitely overreacted to the bag of sugar in her locker.

Was Moresco threatening her with violence if she spoke up? Paula didn't seem like she scared easily. Or maybe it was the other way around. Maybe she'd gotten too close to Moresco.

Riley had known from the beginning that Paula wouldn't be an easy partner. She could be abrupt, she had a giant chip on her shoulder and at times, talking to her was like chatting to the sphinx. Then there was her attitude to traffic duty. Clearly she felt it was beneath her and what a joy that was to work with.

On the other hand, she was gutsy and he liked a bit of attitude. Being a single parent couldn't be easy, dealing with the guys at the station was a pain sometimes and she had to be disappointed that her career was at a low ebb. But she worked hard and didn't complain—unless it was that there was too little to do.

He'd expected she'd be difficult, but he hadn't thought she'd bring her problems to Summerside. She was his partner, yes, but if her actions violated his moral code, if he found any evidence of illegal activity on her part, either now or in the past, he was going to John, he was taking her down.

Riley pushed off the bench. She'd dodged his questions but the interrogation wasn't over.

Hours later Riley was still mulling over the drug haul and what exactly Paula's deal was. After she'd left he'd made a trip to the Frankston hospital hoping to question the driver of the Holden. Timothy Andrews had severe internal injuries and kept slipping in and out of consciousness. The nurse told Riley to call in the morning.

Paula thought there was a connection between Moresco and the crystal meth. What was the connection between her and Moresco? Her behavior didn't add up. Was it merely a coincidence that Jamie must have been conceived around the time she was working on the Moresco case? Surely she was too smart, and too classy to get mixed up with a lowlife like Nick Moresco.

Hell. Why was he wasting his free time trying to figure out his partner when she so obviously intended to keep her secrets?

Instead he took out his frustrations by dismantling his kitchen. He disconnected the plumbing to the sink. The stove he'd removed to the corner of the room. There was a gaping hole where the fridge had been.

Riley levered a crowbar deep into a gap between the wall and the cabinet. Bracing his foot on the wall, he hauled on the crowbar. With an ear-piercing screech, the screws holding the unit pulled out of the wood and the cabinet shifted, buckling the ancient linoleum.

Riley staggered backward, panting, to survey his efforts. His mother's kitchen was well and truly on its way to being destroyed. In a way it felt wrong, as if he were being disloyal to her memory. But she'd be the last person to want him to make worn cabinetry and old-fashioned appliances a shrine to her.

Damn, the pain in his right temple had started up again. His heart raced with an irregular, thready pulse. He must be breathing in too much dust. The paint was so old it might even have lead in it. He hadn't thought of that. He could be getting brain damage.

He opened the back door and sank onto the steps. The air, cooler now it was evening, was heavy with the scent of the red roses climbing the trellis on the wall next to him. Mum had planted the rose bush the first year she and his dad had moved into the house. Riley picked up a petal and held it to his nose.

His dad and Sandra hadn't changed much about the house and grounds over the past ten years. The huge fig tree that shaded a corner of the backyard still held remnants of the cubby house he and John had built in its branches when they were ten years old. His mum used to bring out cookies and lemonade and they'd winched them up in a bucket.

In the other corner of the yard was her gardening shed where she grew seedlings for the vegetable patch on the sunny side of the property. Smack in the middle of the grass was the rotary clothesline where she'd hung out the laundry. Summers had been cricket on the lawn, barbecues, the sound of his parents' conversation continuing into the warm night as he lay in bed lulled to sleep by his father's deep rumble and his mother's soft musical laughter.

Heat pricked the back of his eyes. Part of him was grown up and practical. He recognized the value of the property and wanted to improve it, making a nice home for himself in the process. Another part of him wanted to preserve the small shabby dwelling as a time capsule, a tribute to the golden days of his youth and, yes, as a shrine to his mother.

His head throbbed harder. He let the petal in his fingers fall to the overgrown grass and pushed to his feet. He couldn't stay a kid forever. And he didn't have time to sit around being sentimental.

He would take a couple of painkillers and get back to work. The kitchen wasn't going to renovate itself.

PAULA STOOD BEFORE the bathroom mirror, pinning up her hair while Jamie brushed his teeth at the sink. Nick and his crystal meth had followed her to Summerside. She couldn't be *positive* he was the source but the timing was too close to be a coincidence. Was he taunting her? Trying to get her blamed for his presence in the community?

Freshly washed, her hair was slippery and unmanageable. She jammed a hairpin in only for it to pop out immediately. Already on edge, she swept the box of pins off the counter. She'd been aiming for the garbage but most of them scattered over the tile floor.

Jamie's eyes went round at her uncharacteristic loss of control. Toothpaste foam dripping from his mouth, he crowed, "You've got to pick those all up."

"Yes, sir." She pulled her hair into an ugly ponytail, ignoring the flyaway wisps. Then crouched to retrieve the pins.

The house needed a good tidying. She picked up the book she'd been reading in the bath last night, *Get Out Of Your Mind and Into Your Life*. She was a sucker for self-help books, not that they ever seemed to fix her. If she could figure out what exactly her problem was, that would be half the battle. She knew where she'd gone wrong—getting involved with Nick—but not why. Until she understood that she was in danger of falling into the same trap in the future.

She put the pins in the cabinet and carried the book to the spare bedroom. There she kept her private bookshelf crammed with titles like, *The Courage to Be Yourself*, *Women Who Worry Too Much*, *Get Out Of Your Own Way*. But pride of place went to her sewing table and quilting materials.

A half-finished crazy quilt was spread over the table. She touched the patchwork wistfully, itching to piece a few scraps and forget about everything for a while. Ironically, quilting did for her what the books couldn't do. Fully absorbed in sewing, she didn't have time to dwell on herself.

She dropped Jamie off at school and went in to work early to have a chat with Patty. As well as operating Dispatch she was in charge of requisitions.

Paula handed Patty a list of items she thought she and Riley would need for the investigation.

Patty looked at the list and laughed. "You're pulling my leg."

"No. It's not an ambitious list. A camera, a high-powered flashlight, a dedicated laptop—"

"Half the time we don't even have spare batteries. Most officers use their own cameras." Patty shrugged. "The station doesn't have the resources toward the end of the financial year."

"I see. I'll file this, then." She crumpled the list and dropped it into the rubbish bin.

She started to leave then noticed her reflection in the window onto the bull pen behind Patty's desk. Her hair was already springing out of the elastic band. Using the glass as a mirror she rearranged some hairpins. She was so focused on what she was doing she didn't notice Riley on the other side of the glass until he rapped on it.

"Inside," he mouthed, and jerked his head as if to tell her to get her butt in there.

What happened to Mr. Affable this morning? If she hadn't been on unofficial probation, if Riley wasn't the senior sergeant's best mate, she would slap him down and put him in his place. "Gotta go. The rookie commands my presence."

"Riley?" Patty swiveled in her seat, discreetly craning her neck. "He's hot."

"Is he? I hadn't noticed," Paula lied. She finished with her hair and jammed on her cap. Oh, yes, Riley was hot. In another world, another life, she would have been the first girl in line at his kissing booth. But since Nick, she'd learned her lesson. Compartmentalize. Trouble was, between the box surrounding her job, and the one containing her as a mother, there wasn't any room left in her life for a romance box.

She grabbed her purse, quickly smoothed down her shirt and went to join Riley at the desk he shared with his counterpart on night shift. "What's up?"

"Before I forget, Katie called. She asked if we could do the bike safety talk tomorrow," he said, ignoring her question. "It's our day off so I said yes. Is that okay?"

"I've got nothing better to do. Jamie's hoping you'll bring your gun." She shot Riley a glance. "I'm counting on you not to take it out of your holster."

"That's a given." Riley picked up the phone. "I'm about to call the hospital to see if Meth Head is awake so we can grill him. Thought you'd want to be in on it. If you're finished primping, that is."

"Can't a woman look at her reflection for two seconds without being accused of fussing over her appearance?" She didn't wear makeup on duty and she didn't paint her nails. She didn't even really have what you could call a hairdo. "I don't primp."

"Looked like primping to me." Riley pulled his notebook from his breast pocket. "Looking forward to seeing your old pal Moresco again?"

Paula stiffened. She wished she'd never said anything about Nick to Riley. She hadn't pegged him to be someone who poked at a person's sore spots. "Why do you say that? Has he been sighted?"

"Not that I'm aware of. It's just that I wouldn't have thought the first person a crim would call when he got out of jail would be the cop who put him away." Riley narrowed his gaze at her. "Are you sure he didn't threaten you?"

"No." She in turn, studied him closely. There were shadows beneath his eyes and his shirt was wrinkled, unusual for Riley. He looked tired and crabby.

"But you won't tell me why he called. Are you protecting him?"

"All he said was that he wanted to know if I was there." *Mio amore*. A delicate shudder ran across her shoulders. To cover, she tried to diminish Riley's suspicions by making fun of them. "If I didn't know better I'd say you sounded jealous."

"Don't be ridiculous. Maybe Moresco's trying to scare you, as you say." Riley threw her a hard look and picked up the phone, consulting his notebook before dialing. "Or maybe there's another reason he's calling you."

"I don't like what you're implying." Had he heard rumors? Or was he fishing? Riley was her partner. She owed it to him to come clean. She was torn between wanting to sweep her association with Moresco under the rug and needing an ally to help take him down. But could she trust Riley to be on her side? "Why are you being such a T. rex?"

Phone to his ear, Riley said impatiently, "Sorry?"

"It's what I call Jamie when he's in a bad mood."

"ICU," he barked into the receiver before turning to Paula. "I didn't sleep last night. And I have the mother of all headaches."

"I didn't sleep too well myself." She perched on a neighboring desk and crossed her arms.

"This is Police Constable Riley Henning inquiring about a patient who was brought in yesterday afternoon." Riley consulted his notebook again. "Timothy Andrews. Is he well enough to answer a few questions?"

"Tell them it's a narcotics investigation," Paula suggested.

Riley held up a hand to shush her. He listened, his expression blank. "I see. All right. Thank you." Then he put down the phone and scrubbed a hand over his face, looking more tired than ever. "Andrews passed away at four o'clock this morning, poor bastard."

"Dead. That son of a bitch."

"Your compassion for the deceased does you credit."

"He was our only lead to whoever's manufacturing and distributing the drugs."

Riley folded his notebook and slid it into his breast pocket. "Let's have a look at the stuff found in his car, see if we can find something to connect him to Moresco."

Paula went to Dispatch for the key to the Evidence Room, a locked cupboard in the office supplies closet. Riley was waiting for her. She opened the cupboard and did a double take. The bags of crystal methamphetamine were missing.

"What's that about?" Paula tried not to jump to any paranoid conclusions. "Don't they trust us?"

"The drugs would have been taken to Frankston P.D." Riley hefted the trash bag containing the miscellaneous junk cleared out of the Holden. "They have a special safe for illegal substances."

"Right, of course." She wasn't used to working in a small station that didn't have its own narcotics squad.

Riley dropped the bag and sucked in a breath, pressing his fingers to his forehead.

"Jeez, Henning. Should you be at work today? You look like hell."

"It's nothing."

"For crying out loud, will you stop being such a guy. You're sick."

"I think I've got a migraine. I've tried three different painkillers and nothing touches it."

"How long have you had it?"

"It came on yesterday afternoon. It was so bad I could hardly sleep. When I did, I had nightmares."

"I've never heard of nightmares with a migraine," she said doubtfully. "But I'm not a doctor. Did you have flashing colors in your peripheral vision, nausea?"

"Bit of nausea. No flashing colors. I'm renovating my kitchen. I think it's all the dust I've been breathing in. I've started wearing a mask."

"All sorts of things can trigger it. I get them occasionally. I've got something that might help."

"At this point I'm ready to lop off my own head if it would take away the pain." He reached for the bag.

Paula signed the book hanging on a string and relocked the cupboard. She went to the locker room, got the medication from her purse then met him in the Incident Room. Handing him the packet of tablets and a glass of water, she said, "Take two."

"Meds for menstrual pain? Are you kidding?"

"Read the fine print. They work on migraines, too." When he hesitated, she added in a tone she used with Jamie, "Be a big brave boy and take your medicine."

Giving her a dark look, he swallowed a couple of tablets. "Don't mention this to the guys."

"Your secret's safe with me. I don't want anyone to know my partner is a girl."

Riley made a low inarticulate growl in his throat. She repressed a grin, deciding not to torment him with any more barbs. Instead she spread the contents of the bag over a long table. They donned gloves and got down to the grubby business of sifting through the rubbish from Andrews's car.

"I don't think this guy ever cleaned out his car." Paula opened a crumpled fast-food bag. She tossed it into the bin with a shudder. "Yuck. I think something's crawling in there."

"Look at this." Riley held up a teddy bear with a torn pink ribbon around the neck. "Andrews might have been a father."

Paula imagined a little girl clutching the teddy, hearing the news that her daddy had died. "Don't. I don't want to feel sorry for him."

"I feel sorry for his kid." Riley pressed his fingers over the bear's belly. "Do you suppose there could be more drugs in there?" He took a knife and slit the side seam, pushing his fingers into the stuffing, probing. After a moment he gave up. "Nothing."

He started to toss the teddy bear into the bin, then instead he pushed the stuffing back in and set the toy aside. Paula pretended not to notice. Did he plan to take the bear to Andrews's family? It surprised her that a tough character like Riley could be sentimental. He'd done a nice thing.

A half an hour later, they'd gone through nearly the entire pile without finding one useful item. Paula took a porn magazine off the stack and riffled the pages upside down in the off chance that something would fall out, like a slip of paper with a list of drug contacts. Yeah, right.

Something did fall out—a business card. She reached for it and her fingers stilled. The card bore the logo of an Italian restaurant in the city. She glanced at Riley, oddly reluctant to bring it to his attention. The cop in her wanted to put Nick back in jail. As a mother…suddenly she wasn't so sure.

Was she protecting him? The thought brought her up short. What changes had Nick undergone while in prison? She hadn't kept contact. Was it possible he'd rehabilitated? Did part of her not want to cut off all possibility that someday Jamie might meet his father?

Her silence made Riley glance up. "What have you found?"

She thrust aside her hesitation. The business card was evidence. Regardless of her private issues she couldn't suppress it. "This is from a restaurant that Moresco owns. It doesn't prove anything, of course. Andrews could have simply eaten a meal there. Or someone else could have dropped it in his car."

Riley held the card by the corner with gloved fingers. "The restaurant is in Carlton, an hour away from Summerside."

"I know, I went there with him," Paula said.

That earned her a sharp glance from Riley. "Sounds like you were pretty tight with Moresco."

"I was investigating him. Undercover. I was his massage therapist." She'd assumed Riley would know that. Her photo had been in all the newspapers at the time of Nick's trial. Then she remembered he'd been in Afghanistan.

Riley's eyebrows rose.

What was that skepticism for? What assumptions was he making about her and Nick? She wished she could tell him the truth and that he would be different, that he would believe in her and not judge her.

Who cares what he thinks? He's nothing to you—a partner. Do your job.

She took a few paces away but couldn't let it go. She spun around, years of pent-up frustration at being judged—by herself as much as by her fellow officers—spilling out.

"Do you have any idea what it's like working deep undercover? You live, eat, sleep and breathe your persona. You become that person, that qualified but slightly sleazy masseuse who walks a fine line between legitimate therapist and someone who consorts with criminals. So, yeah, I had dinner with Moresco. Many times. Any other questions?"

"I wasn't aware I'd asked a question," Riley said quietly. He stripped off his gloves. "Timothy Andrews may have gone to Moresco's restaurant for linguini and clam sauce but I'm betting he didn't. The business card is a link between our local dealer and Nick Moresco. Time to go to John with what we've found."

"You've got nothing that would stand up in court. No fingerprints, no phone conversations, no paper trail." John ticked the deficiencies of the evidence off on his fingers. "Write up your report and send it to the Frankston Drug Investigation Unit. They'll take it from here."

Riley glanced at Paula who was being conspicuously quiet. John had told him she wanted to make detective again. She'd offered her services to the Drug Unit once before and been turned down. Things were different now.

"Under the circumstances don't you think we should have a role in the investigation?" Riley said.

John twiddled a pen between his fingers, clearly impatient to wrap this up. "What circumstances?"

"Paula's past dealings with Nick Moresco."

Paula frowned at him as if she was worried

about where he was going with this. As if she didn't quite trust him. Well, the feeling was mutual. "Do you want to tell him about the phone call or should I?"

Her frown deepened and she shook her head. "It's irrelevant."

"I disagree." Riley turned to John. "She received a phone call from Moresco ten days ago." He filled the Senior Sergeant in on the few details he knew.

"Is this true?" John asked Paula.

"He wanted to know if I was there." She shifted on her hard chair as if she couldn't get comfortable. "He was confirming my location. For what reason, I have no idea."

"Did he threaten you?"

"Riley already asked me that. The answer is no. Nick was never violent to me."

She was hiding something, Riley was more certain of it than ever. She said she wasn't worried about Moresco being violent toward her but she was scared. Scared of being caught out in some wrongdoing? Should he talk to John about his suspicions? No, too soon. He didn't have enough to go on. And besides, they needed her cooperation in going after Moresco.

"Riley's right, this does make a difference," John said. "Frankston will want to set up surveillance on your house. A phone tap—"

"No." Paula got to her feet, brushing her hands down her pants. Agitated.

"I beg your pardon, Constable?"

"I'm a cop. I can take care of myself." She paced the small office between the window looking onto the street and the glass wall showing the bull pen. "I don't need, or want, surveillance."

"This isn't about your competence as a police officer," John said. "As a former detective, I'm surprised you object. Surveillance is standard practice."

"A phone tap, in case Moresco calls you again, makes sense," Riley added. "Why are you being uncooperative?"

"Think about it." She rolled her eyes. "I don't want Delinsky, for example, listening in on my private calls. A phone tap is intrusive. Give me a bit of time."

"To do what, exactly?" John asked.

Paula dropped into her chair. "Talk to Nick, find out what he wants without alerting him to the fact that he's under investigation."

Riley hadn't missed that she referred to the drug lord by his first name. She'd had a personal relationship with Moresco. "Do you have his phone number?"

Paula looked him in the eye. "No," she said firmly. "And I don't know where he is. If he calls me back, I'll find out what I can. He's recently released from prison. He's going to be wary. We need to proceed with caution or we'll scare him off."

That made some sense, Riley acknowledged grudgingly. "What about your safety? And the safety of your son?"

"Trust me," Paula said. "No one is more concerned about Jamie than I am."

"How do you know Moresco will contact you again?" John asked.

She shook her head, shrugged. "A hunch."

"All right." John laid down his pen. "We'll hold off on surveillance. But I want to know if and when he contacts you. I don't need Frankston Drug Unit giving us grief because we've withheld information crucial to an investigation."

"Will do." Paula got to her feet. "Now if you don't mind, I'm late for picking up Jamie."

Riley was about to rise and follow her out when John gestured to him to stay. When Paula was well away from the door, John asked, "What do you think of her attitude toward this development? Do you trust her to cooperate?"

Riley's first loyalty was to the law, and to John—his boss and his best mate from high school. Fair or not, Paula was tainted by her past association with Moresco. On the other hand she was his partner and the partner bond was sacrosanct. Beneath her tough exterior Riley sensed vulnerabilities and that aroused his protective instincts.

That was the crux of it. He might not trust her completely but he would do his damnedest to protect her. Even from John and the police force? He was on shaky ground now, getting himself into something he didn't fully understand. In the process he was making himself vulnerable.

Yes, even then. And what the hell that was all about, he didn't want to think.

Riley drew his line in the sand. "She's a good cop. I believe she'll do what's right."

PAULA KNOCKED ON SALLY'S open front door after work and stepped inside the foyer cluttered with shoes, school bags and toys. "Hey, Sally. It's me."

"Come on in," Sally called. "We're in the kitchen." She was at the stove preparing dinner, her brown hair in a messy knot on top of her head. Fourteen-month-old Chloe played on the floor with a wooden spoon and saucepan.

Jamie and another little boy, Trevor, were in the adjoining family room, driving small cars around a foldout road map spread over the carpet. Appropriate sound effects competed with the TV tuned to a children's show.

"How was school today?" Paula crouched to hug Jamie. His hair and clothes smelled of school hallways and crayons and lunchboxes. As usual, he had one sock on and one off.

"I got a gold star for my drawing." Jamie squirmed free of Paula's embrace and went back to his cars.

"Well done." Paula retrieved his sock from beneath the coffee table. "Pack up your things. We need to get home, have our dinner."

Jamie drove a fire truck around a bend and smashed into a parked car. "Are we going to McDonald's again?"

"Maybe." Paula threw a guilty glance at Sally who was cooking something from scratch. Pots and pans bubbled on the stove. The counter was cluttered with a chopping board and the remains of fresh vegetables. "I don't normally give him fast food every day but with the move…" She trailed off lamely.

"Forget it, you don't have to explain," Sally said. "You're welcome to stay and eat with us. Rick is working late tonight."

"Thanks—it smells delicious—but I need to get home." And see that her house and everything in it was exactly as she'd left it. She still hadn't gotten around to putting a new lock on the laundry room door. Procrastination wasn't like her, especially with something as serious as security. Did she *want* Nick to get to her and Jamie? Was she that desperate for him to have a father? The thought made her feel sick.

"All right. But listen, we've been invited to a barbecue, an engagement party for our friends, Lexie and Rafe, next Saturday. Why don't you come? I know they wouldn't mind and it would be a chance for you to meet some people."

It wasn't the first time Sally had made friendly overtures. Paula was tempted. She'd left friends behind in her old suburb when she'd moved but an hour and a half drive was too far for casual visits.

"An engagement party is special," Paula protested. "I'd be intruding."

"No, it's fine, really." Sally waved that off. "Lexie isn't organized enough to actually send out invitations. It's a word of mouth party."

"Thanks. I'll think about it, see how I go."

Sally turned down the burner, hoisted Chloe onto her hip and walked them out. "See you tomorrow, Jamie." She ruffled his dark hair as he ran between the two women and out to the car. "He must take after his dad, you being so blonde."

"With those detecting skills, you should be on the force," Paula said lightly, sidestepping her question.

"I've got enough to keep me busy with this little miss." Sally tugged on one of Chloe's brown curls and the little girl dimpled.

"Mum! Come on." Jamie stood by the car, swinging his backpack.

Paula held up a hand to let him know she'd heard. Then she turned to Sally. "I should have mentioned this before but well, there's been so much to do I've been distracted. Jamie's father doesn't have any visitation rights. If he were ever to come around, I don't want him seeing Jamie or talking to him. In fact, if he came to your house, even if Jamie wasn't here, don't let him in. Call me immediately."

"Sounds serious." Sally's expression turned troubled. "But how will I know it's him?"

"You'll know." The dread Paula had been carrying around in her stomach ever since she'd gotten the first phone call felt heavier than ever. "Jamie looks just like his dad."

CHAPTER FIVE

RILEY'S EYES WERE gritty from staring at the shaft of moonlight inching across his bedroom ceiling for the past two hours. He never used to have so much trouble sleeping. Was it about Paula? About fighting his attraction, worrying whether she was trustworthy, torn loyalties? Wondering what happened between her and Moresco?

Again Riley pondered the apparent coincidental timing of her covert investigation and the age of her son. His mind couldn't compute a cop who would sleep with a suspect. But what else could account for her strange behavior whenever he asked her about Moresco? Had he pressured her into having sex, or even raped her? While that would account for Jamie, it didn't explain her getting busted back to uniform.

The digital bedside clock read 3.25 a.m. He gave up trying to sleep and got out of bed picking his way between the unpacked boxes cluttering his bedroom. He'd been spending all his time on the kitchen and it seemed counterproductive to bring out his valued possessions only for them to get covered in drywall dust during the renovations.

Picking up his guitar, he went to the living room and sat on the couch to strum a few chords. Lately he'd been trying to teach himself classical but in the wee hours when the world was blackest old ballads were more comforting. Tonight he was having trouble recalling the chords. His fingers felt clumsy and he was out of sorts. He ought to go to bed so he'd be fresh for the bike safety talk tomorrow. But he was too wired.

Riley set the guitar aside and went to his room to find some sheet music. He rooted through one box without success then lifted it aside to look in the one below. What he uncovered wasn't a cardboard box but his battered army footlocker.

Which reminded him, he still hadn't called Gazza back. Why was he avoiding his friend? All it took was a quick call to say he wasn't going to make it to the ANZAC Day parade.

Riley stared at the footlocker. He hadn't opened it since Afghanistan. Well, why would he? He'd left the hospital with his arm in a sling and his head and ribs bandaged, packing in a hurry so he could catch the air-force jet leaving Kabul for Sydney.

He pushed the locker aside and went through another box where he found the sheet music. Turning to go, his gaze lit again on the footlocker. An odd feeling of dread came over him, surprising him. Was he *afraid* to open it? Lumps in his throat, taking menstrual meds…he *was* becoming a girl. To hell with that.

He found the key in the drawer of his bedside table and inserted it in the brass padlock. The metal lid creaked open.

One by one he pulled out mementos of his army life—his black beret, neatly folded; an envelope containing his discharge papers; a leather case holding his Victoria Cross for Australia. He opened the case and glanced at the bronze medal and crimson ribbon with the motto that read, For Valour. He felt…nothing. He'd "earned" it for his role in the suicide bomber blast that had sent him home. Earned it? Didn't think so. Although he didn't recall details and hadn't asked about the incident, he did know that everyone involved died but him.

He tossed it aside and moved on to the next item.

A photograph of a young Afghani woman.

She wore a blue burka with the veil flung back, showing an expectant smile and light green eyes filled with laughter. On the back of the photo was written in pencil, Nabili.

Riley sat back on his heels, baffled. Who was she? Did he know her? She probably wasn't a random figure in the street. She must have trusted him to show him her face. Why had he taken a photo of this woman—assuming he had taken it?

He peered closer at the photo. Something about her face both drew him in and haunted him. His memory of the final few months of his tour was spotty. He couldn't, for instance, recall who he'd been on patrol with the day of the explosion that had injured him and sent him home. He couldn't even recall where in the city it had taken place. He supposed he could find the answers to those questions if he wanted to. Gazza would probably know, or one of his other SAS mates.

Riley shifted closer to the lamp, squinting to see more clearly. That smile, those eyes... The migraine, which Paula's tablets had banished, returned suddenly with a vengeance. His eyesight blurred, distorted by bright lights in his peripheral vision. His stomach roiled with nausea.

Riley dropped the photograph and staggered to his feet, scraping a shin on a box. He stumbled blindly to the bed, sank onto it and flung an arm across his pounding head.

He knew what upset him...Nabili reminded him of his sister, Katie.

THE ALARM CLOCK JOLTED Riley out of a troubled sleep. His face was taut with dried sweat from a nightmare—a hellish vision of explosions and flying body parts.

He'd been looking forward to meeting Katie's class and doing the safety talk. Now he wondered if he would make it through the day.

He dragged himself out of bed and into the shower, tuning the waterproof radio to loud trance music. He stood under the pounding water and let the pulse of the showerhead and the staccato computer-generated music obliterate his thoughts.

Breakfast was cold cereal eaten standing up amid the rubble of the half-demolished kitchen that now consisted of a lone section of counter supporting the huddled microwave, toaster and electric kettle.

Riley's migraine worsened as he drove across town. The closer he got to the school, the slower he drove. By the time he turned into the street the black Audi was crawling like a beetle.

He hated that Paula was going to see him like this. Hated showing any weakness, especially when he needed to be on his toes around her. He was attracted to her and yet suspicious of her. She would probably take one look at him and make some snarky comment about him resembling road kill.

He glanced in the rearview mirror at his red-eyed reflection and ran a hand over his bristly jaw. A chill curled down his spine. How could he have forgotten to shave? He swiped his tongue across his teeth. They weren't brushed. Hell, was he sleepwalking?

A glance at the dashboard clock told him it was far too late to go home and clean up.

Children's laughter and high-pitched voices came to him through the open window as he cruised the curb looking for a parking spot. A gym class was on the field to the left of the school buildings, engaged in some rowdy game involving hoops and balls.

Sweat broke out along his hairline. His foot trembled on the accelerator as he fought the urge to stamp down and speed off. Instead he pulled into a parking spot half a block away.

Only his sense of duty—to Katie, to Paula, to the kids, to his job—made him drag his ass out of the car. He looked toward the school. The vague feeling of dread that had dogged him all morning, intensified.

PAULA STOOD JUST INSIDE the classroom door, near the front of the room. The grade one students were restless. Katie had given them a coloring assignment while they waited for Constable Henning but having been primed for an hour of outdoor activity they weren't taking well to staying between the lines. Or keeping quiet. Or staying in their seats. A group of boys, including

Jamie, had lined up at the window to watch the older children in P.E. class.

"Quiet, please, class," Katie said. "Sit down, boys. We'll be going outside very soon."

Paula paced out the door into the empty corridor. She checked her watch for the umpteenth time. "I'm surprised he's late," she said in a low voice to Katie. "Something must have happened to him."

"I'll give him a call." Katie reached into her desk drawer for her phone and punched in the number. It rang and rang. Her worried glance met Paula's. "You should go ahead and start without him."

"Let's give him another minute." He'd roped her into this on her day off and while she thought it was a worthwhile event, she didn't want to do it on her own. Then because *she* couldn't stay still, she added, "I'll check out front. Maybe he's lost."

RILEY CROUCHED BY THE school gate, unable to take another step. A moment ago he'd heard children laughing. Now their laughter had turned to screams. The billowing clouds above the school were smoke from the explosion.

Oh, God. No. No. No….

Sweat soaked his uniform shirt. His heart tripped over itself, beating scary-fast. Was he having a heart attack? He was holding his gun. His hand was shaking. Had he fired? No, he couldn't fire. He was a coward.

A blonde woman in a uniform came out of the school and stood on the steps. She seemed familiar.

"Riley, what are you doing?" she called. "Come inside. The children are waiting."

There *were* no more children. Only pieces.

A stab from the migraine distorted his vision. His eyes squeezed shut. *It was just a nightmare, just a nightmare, just a nightmare, just a nightmare…*

A hand was shaking his shoulder. "Are you okay? Riley, are you all right? Can you speak? Answer me."

He opened his eyes. Blinked against the bright sunshine. The pebbled concrete path dug into his knees. *Paula,* that was her name. "What happened?"

"You tell me." Her piercing blue eyes searched his face. "You look like hell. Are you sick?"

"I'm fine." The safety catch was off on his gun. Breath held, he cracked open the chamber. And breathed out his relief. He hadn't fired. "I heard a gunshot."

"I didn't hear any gunshot." Paula pressed the back of her hand against his forehead. "You feel feverish."

"I'm fine." He ducked away from her hand.

Great, now she was treating him like a child. He holstered his gun and staggered to his feet. Did a check of his heart rate. Not quite normal but getting there. The palpitations had died down. The clouds were white fluffy balls of water vapor, not smoke. The children's laughter was...joyful.

"It looked as if you were having a panic attack," Paula said.

Special Forces soldiers didn't have panic attacks. Riley brushed the dust off his pants and re-tucked his shirt. Refocused his thoughts, refusing to dwell on the mortifying incident that had taken place. "We should go inside."

He started up the path to the entrance. Sick dread was lodged in the pit of his stomach. He ignored it.

"Are you seeing a doctor or therapist?"

"There's nothing wrong with me. I had a bad turn."

She held open the door for him. "Where did you say you lived, on De Nial Avenue?"

"Very funny."

"It *isn't* funny," she said with no trace of a smile. "You need to get your act together."

He threw her a look. She dared tell him to get his act together? She who most likely had crossed the line with a suspect?

Their boot heels echoed as they walked side-by-side, two feet apart, down the empty school corridor.

Of all people who had to witness him having a flashback… He didn't need her nagging at him. She didn't know him. Who was she to say anything?

Katie's classroom was coming up. Children's voices spilled through the open door. Riley's steps slowed. His palms grew damp and his heart began to race. Oh, crap, not again.

"You're not well," Paula said bluntly. "Go home."

"I'm fine." He marched on. "Katie is expecting me. I can't let her down."

"She'll understand."

"I don't want understanding," he shouted. "I just want to do my damn job!"

Down the hall, a door opened. Katie stuck her head out. "Riley?"

Damn. He was overreacting, not in control of himself.

"Go home, Henning." Paula planted her fists on her hips and blocked the corridor, her knuckles brushing her gun butt. "That's an order."

He scowled, ready to refuse. But below the bravado, lurked the fear that he would disgrace himself again. He'd had his gun drawn, the safety off, a bullet in the chamber…all without even being aware of what he was doing.

"This isn't real police work anyway." He turned on his heel and marched down the corridor and outside.

On the steps he paused to grip the railing and suck in fresh air. A magpie warbled from a pine tree on the edge of the schoolyard. Bright sunshine and sparkling blue sky contrasted with the seething blackness inside his head.

What the hell was wrong with him?

"RILEY WENT HOME. He's not feeling well," Paula told Katie. "I'll take the class if you can assist."

"No worries." Despite her words, Katie frowned. "He had a headache the other day. Riley never has headaches. I hope he's not coming down with something."

Riley was already quite ill, unless Paula missed her guess—post-traumatic stress syndrome. She'd seen it before in police officers. But she didn't say anything to Katie. The room full of six-year-olds was like a box of puppies, spilling over with high spirits and restless energy.

"I'll leave the blackboard portion of my talk until afterward. These kids need activity, stat."

Katie clapped her hands. "Children, line up in twos at the door. When we get outside, go to the racks and get your bikes. Walk, don't ride, to the basketball court."

Chattering and laughing, the children followed

instructions. Paula was pleased to see that Jamie had made a friend, partnering with a towheaded boy with a cheeky grin. They squirmed, play-punched and giggled in the line until Katie admonished them. The kids maintained ranks until the door to outside opened. They spilled onto the schoolyard to get their bikes.

Paula set up traffic cones on the basketball court and had the kids ride through, one at a time, giving arm signals as they turned corners and getting off and walking when they came to the "street."

"Has Riley had any problems since he came back from Afghanistan?" Paula asked Katie while they watched from the sidelines.

"What sort of problems?"

"Post-traumatic stress disorder, or PTSD." She stepped forward to call out to her son. "Jamie, wait your turn." Then she turned to find the young teacher staring. "Soldiers are exposed to things we can't even imagine. My cousin was in counseling for months after he was discharged."

"Riley's the same as he always was," Katie said, bewildered. "Outgoing, confident, cheerful. He didn't enjoy being a bouncer, but once he joined the police force he's been as happy as I've ever seen him. I can't believe he has PTSD. Why do you think that?"

"He was in the middle of some sort of episode when I found him earlier, outside the school."

Paula blew her whistle and waved the next child through the course. "It looked like a panic attack."

"Panic attack." Katie shook her head. "That doesn't sound like Riley."

"I hope you're right. He could be simply under the weather." No point mentioning the gun. Any teacher would freak out at the thought of a man standing outside a primary school with a loaded revolver. She herself had been shaken. Riley was normally so controlled and professional. It had been a shock to see him disheveled and wild-eyed, waving a gun.

"Riley and I are close," Katie said. "I'd like to think he would say something to me if he was having problems."

"Not if he's in denial."

"He's never liked admitting to weakness," Katie conceded. "I've had some health issues in the past. He had to leave for Afghanistan in the middle of that. But his letters were all upbeat, no death or destruction though I know he must have witnessed a lot of bad stuff. He hasn't even talked about the explosion that injured him and sent him home."

"He hasn't mentioned it to me, either."

"That's because he tries to protect all the women in his life. Not have them look after him."

Paula shook her head with a dry smile. "I'm his partner. As far as he's concerned, I'm not a woman."

Katie laughed. "Do you really believe that?"

"I have to believe it to do my job properly." Paula watched the children go around the course, concentrating on making the turns between the cones.

As a rule she didn't need looking after but with Nick on the loose… Well, Riley was her partner—he was supposed to have her back so she could make an exception and accept help. It had nothing to do with her gender, or any unacknowledged feelings that might have sprung up between them. "I'll go see him after I leave here. Make sure he's okay."

An hour later Paula drove to the address Katie had given her, a neat weatherboard bungalow at the end of a narrow curving driveway on a quiet street. Well, it would have been quiet but for the sounds of demolition coming from inside. She winced as a huge crash sent puffs of dust shooting out of the open window on the right side of the house. For a second she wondered if he'd gone totally insane and started destroying everything around him. Then she recalled him mentioning renovations.

She pressed the doorbell. And waited.

He wouldn't hear the bell over all the banging. She tried the handle. The door opened. "Riley?"

She followed the sounds of destruction, skirt-

ing the mountain bike in the foyer to go through
the arched doorway on her right, into the living
room. The furniture was new, chain store but comfortable and mostly covered with drop cloths. A
stack of cardboard boxes sat next to the fireplace.

She moved into the adjoining dining room. The
oval oak table was covered in a plastic sheet. The
wall that presumably backed onto the kitchen vibrated. Plaster crumbled away from a jagged di-
agonal crack running floor to ceiling. Chips of
off-white paint fell to the pale green carpet.

Paula approached cautiously. She fished in
her pocket for a tissue and held it over her nose.
"Riley?"

A sledgehammer crashed through the plaster.
A chunk of plaster fell into the dining room, creating a hole the size of a basketball.

"Riley." She could see part of his T-shirt.

The sledgehammer withdrew only to reappear,
making the hole double in size. Wearing headphones and safety glasses, he swung the sledgehammer for another strike. His white T-shirt was
wet under the arms and across his chest. His bi-
ceps and forearms gleamed, the muscles flexing.
Hot? *Whoo boy.* This was Riley as she'd never
seen him before—pure male beefcake.

She dragged her gaze away from his body and

trained them on his face. Sucking in a deep breath, she fought to control her response. He wasn't a man to her any more than she was a woman to him.

That was her story and she was sticking to it.

Paula stepped in front of the hole in the wall and waved her arms. "Yo, Riley."

He let the sledgehammer fall and lifted his goggles. "What are you doing here?"

"We need to talk."

"Later. I'm busy." He replaced his goggles and raised the sledgehammer, ready to strike again.

Before he could swing the hammer, Paula reached through the broken wall and grabbed the front of his shirt. "We talk now."

Pushing back his safety glasses he stuck his face close to hers. His nostrils flared. His eyes sparked. Something flashed between them that had nothing to do with his panic attack or the fact that they were partners. It was the chemical reaction that had been on a slow burn, waiting to combust since they'd first shaken hands in John's office two weeks ago.

Hell. The last thing she needed was this kind of complication.

Riley lowered the sledgehammer.

Paula loosened her fingers, releasing his shirt.

He backed away from the wall. She took a moment to regain her breath and slow her heart rate.

When she walked into the kitchen Riley was pulling a beer from the fridge in the middle of the room.

He held one out to her. She shook her head. Flipping off the cap he pulled over a kitchen chair and offered it to her. Again she shook her head, too wound up to sit.

He perched his denim butt on a sawhorse. "I apologize for my behavior at the school today. It won't happen again."

"Really?" She paced the dusty linoleum floor, hands on hips. "Can you be sure of that?"

Riley examined the top of his beer bottle.

"Listen, Henning." She jabbed a finger at him. "I've been in uniform for seven freaking years. I was once a detective, a damn good one. I'm going to be a detective again once the departmental budget promises are kept—*if* all goes well here in Summerside. I don't need anyone wrecking my chances."

Riley took a swig of beer and backhanded his mouth. "What does that have to do with me?"

"You've been cracking onto me about my personal life while acting as if butter wouldn't melt in your mouth. Today at the school you lost it. If you've got a mental health issue I need to know."

"I doubt my missing a bike safety talk is going to wreck your application."

"Okay, forget about my plans. Let's talk about your ability to do your job, to provide me with backup. I need to know what's wrong with you."

His face was stony blank. "There's nothing wrong with me. I've got your back, don't worry."

"If you won't talk about it I'll have no choice but to go to John." Paula let her words sink in. "Is that what you want? Oh, yeah, and thanks for outing me the other day, by the way. I really appreciated that."

"I did it for your own good." Riley dragged both hands down his face then looked at her with bleary eyes. "Okay. We'll talk. I have no ongoing mental health issues. Lately I haven't been sleeping well. I have nightmares. I get headaches. Today was the first time I've had a panic attack or whatever that was."

"What's the cause?"

"I don't know." Riley glanced away.

"Could it have something to do with Afghanistan?"

Silence.

"I knew it," she said, flatly. Wonderful. She was saddled with a partner who had serious issues. Not only that, he was deluded about them. And in typical male fashion, he shut down in response to her show of concern. "What happened over there? What was the big bad that's got you freaking out a year later?"

Riley shrugged helplessly. "That's just it. I don't know. Before I was discharged I was injured in an explosion. That's all I can remember."

"You never asked your colleagues or your superior officer for details?"

"I wanted to get the hell out of there. What's the point of dwelling on it? Shit happens all the time—suicide bombers, improvised explosive devices, unexploded ordinance that blows up in your face—"

"But not to find out what happened? That's not a normal reaction."

"What makes you the arbiter of normal?" he demanded angrily. He got to his feet, kicking aside shards of plaster and offcuts, to pace away. Then he turned to her, his eyes desperate, his voice pleading. "Don't go to John. I can't go back to cracking heads outside a nightclub at 3:00 a.m."

"Don't you get it? I'm trying to help you. And yeah, I'll admit it, I'm also worried about myself. I can't do my job effectively if I have to watch you and make sure you don't go over the edge." She paused, then drove her point home. "Make sure you don't draw your gun on a bunch of kids."

He winced.

"You're in trouble, mister. Headaches, nightmares, panic attacks—classic PTSD. Did the army give you any counseling?"

"I didn't tell you my symptoms so you could psychoanalyze me," he growled. "Now that you know, we can forget it."

"No, we're not going to forget it. PTSD can be treated. Promise me you'll talk to John yourself. Get some therapy."

Riley took a swig of beer. "I'll think about it."

That was it? That was the best she would get from him? A wave of anger and frustration swept through her. Here she was, stuck in this pissant little town where no major crime happened and when it did, they passed the case to Frankston. Not to mention she had a partner with big problems who wouldn't admit to them or do anything to fix himself. Her promotion to detective looked further out of reach than ever.

As she stared at the wreck Riley had become, she realized it wasn't the title and the stripes on her epaulet she wanted. It was the redemption for her sins, validation that she was indeed worthy of wearing the badge. It was about her life-long commitment to avenging her father's death.

And what about Riley? He was a good man—strong, compassionate, intelligent. A man with a commitment to duty, who acted with honor and integrity. He wasn't taking care of himself. And he wasn't letting anyone in, least of all her.

She stomped through the house and out to her car, furious and upset and confused. One thing she knew, whether Riley liked it or not, she had his back.

CHAPTER SIX

PAULA KNEELED ON the floor and peered beneath her bed, looking for her other sandal. Why had she let Sally talk her into going to an engagement barbecue for a couple she didn't even know?

The doorbell rang.

She got to her feet to hurry down the hall. Probably Jamie had left behind one of his favorite toys and begged her mother to come back for it. That kid couldn't spend a night away from home without fifty Matchbox cars and half a dozen dinosaurs.

Paula spoke as she swung open the front door. "What did you forget?"

Nick Moresco stood on her doorstep.

She went very still. His olive skin was paler and his toned frame thinner than she remembered. But his gray suit fit him perfectly—as a custom-made suit should. His dark hair had turned silver at the temples, not surprising since he must be fifty years old by now.

She started to shut the door.

Nick gripped the edge and pushed back, easily

creating an opening wide enough to step inside. "To answer your question, *cara,* I have forgotten nothing."

Paula stepped backward, her mind whirling. Her gun was in her bedroom, her phone in her purse on the kitchen counter. "Go away. Now."

Nick closed the door. "Not until I see my son."

"Who?" She forced her voice to stay steady. "I don't know what you're talking about."

"Don't play games." He produced a grainy black-and-white photograph of her and Jamie at the zoo. Jamie looked about three years old. "Don't pretend he's not mine. He's got the Moresco eyes and jaw. Not to mention my coloring."

Paula felt bile rise in her throat. For three years Nick had been looking at that photo and plotting... revenge? Abduction?

He strode into the living room, his gaze sweeping over the red L-shaped couch, glass coffee table and gas fireplace. Jamie's brontosaurus lay on its side on the hearth. Nick picked it up and stroked the plastic tail. "Where is he?"

"Staying overnight at a friend's house." Paula had had a lot of practice lying to Nick and the words came smoothly. "And no, I'm not going to tell you where."

"You won't mind if I look around." Without waiting for an answer he walked to the hall, heading toward the bedrooms.

Paula followed him, pressing her clammy palms to her dress. He strolled into her room and glanced around, his gaze lingering on a lacy bra lying on her bed. Her stomach dipped sickeningly. How could she ever have found him attractive? Yet she had.

Over her twelve months of undercover work she'd been drawn in by his charisma. She'd become part of his world. She'd ignored the gun he carried in a shoulder holster. And the long thin knife in a special holder inside those fine Italian leather boots.

"My shoulder bothered me a lot in prison," he said, smiling. "I could do with one of your massages."

He was playing her. He had to be angry that she'd sold him out. Nick Moresco *didn't* forget. And he never, *ever* forgave.

She could try to throw him out. But if he refused to go she would be left looking weak. She could send Riley a text message. But what if he was having one of his episodes? Not good. Plus she didn't want him to see her with Nick who might give away that their relationship had been intimate. No, she would handle this on her own. Knowing Nick and how volatile he could be, she would have to find herself a position of strength then get him off guard.

"I was on my way out when you arrived." Casually she glanced at her watch. "People are expecting me. They'll wonder if I'm late."

He walked to her bedroom door but instantly dashed any hope that he planned to simply leave. "Jamie's room?"

"Across the hall." She waited until he'd left then crossed to her bedside table, her heart racing. The time was now.

A moment later, she stood in Jamie's doorway watching Nick pick up a soccer trophy. She raised a straight strong arm and leveled her Smith and Wesson, aiming at Nick's head. "Put. That. Down."

His eyebrows rose in an expression of mild surprise. "Such melodrama. Is it so strange that a man would like to know his son?"

Her finger stroked the trigger, itching to pull. "Leave my house before I do something you'll regret."

He set the trophy on top of the dresser. "You won't shoot me, Paula. I'm the father of your son. How would you explain that to Jamie?"

Her hand wavered. Was a criminal father who loved him better than an absent father he pined for? She was still the center of her son's life but she had to face facts—she wasn't enough for him anymore. But Nick, a convicted drug dealer? No, surely no.

"If I shot you, Jamie wouldn't have to know who

you are. You'd just be an intruder I shot in self-defense, a criminal who attacked me out of revenge."

"My family wouldn't let that pass, you know that. My mother knows about Jamie. The whole family does. If anything happened to me at your hand, they would raise a stink. You and me—it would all come out."

She knew it was true. And hated that he was using Jamie as leverage over her.

She set her jaw, making her molars grind together, and readjusted her aim, firming her grip on the revolver. "I'd live with it," she growled.

She hoped like hell he wouldn't call her bluff. Hoped she looked tougher than she felt right now.

Nick raised his hands as if in surrender. "Paula, I swear on *my* father's grave, I mean my son no harm. He is family. Family is everything. I have no other children."

"That you know of," she said flatly, not lowering the gun.

Nick lifted his shoulders in an elegant shrug. "All the more reason to meet Jamie." He glanced around the room. "I don't see the car I left for him. Did he like it?"

"I got rid of it." Her arms were getting tired but she wasn't about to let Nick out of her sights.

"I mean him no harm," he repeated. "I only want to get to know him. I will go through Child

Services if necessary. Social workers are all about
father's rights these days."

"You're a convicted drug dealer. You would
never get access to a child."

"I want to meet him. Just once." A note of pleading crept into Nick's voice. "Would that be so terrible?"

Ah, he'd shown a sign of weakness. Her resolve firmed. Now she had leverage. "Not going
to happen."

"I wouldn't be so sure. I've reformed, found
God. In prison I was a model of good behavior."

"I'll fight you in court."

"A court order won't keep me away from my
boy."

"Is that a threat?"

"No." Nick chuckled softly. "In spite of how you
betrayed me, I don't mean you any harm, either,
cara mia. You are the mother of my son."

Paula held her gun steady, refusing to let his soft
low voice sway her. "If you truly care about Jamie,
think about his welfare. Think what it would do
to him to have a convict for a father."

"I've paid my dues. Now I'm a businessman. I
still own the restaurant in Carlton. I intend to continue running it."

"What do you know about a recent influx of
crystal meth in Summerside?"

"Nothing." His baffled shrug would have been

convincing had Paula not known what an accomplished liar he was.

"What's your association with Timothy Andrews?"

"Never heard of him. I tell you, I'm not in the business of drug manufacture anymore."

"I don't believe it."

"Believe what you like. But don't deny me my son. Don't deny your son his father." Nick strolled around the room, looking at the posters on the walls, the red plastic box full of toys, the comforter printed with racing cars. Turning to Paula he tilted his head, his gaze wistful. "Does he ask about me? What do you tell him about his father?"

Trust Nick to zero in on his opponent's weakness. She needed to stay strong, not let him see he could get to her. "I told him you were a bad man and he couldn't have anything to do with you."

"Paula." Nick shook his head. "You shouldn't have done that."

He skimmed the back of his knuckles down her cheek. A shiver rippled over her belly. She didn't know if her reaction was desire or fear or a combination of both. She told herself his touch was a threat.

But it felt like a caress.

She forced herself to stay ramrod-straight, not wanting him to misinterpret her body language. "I'm leaving for my date. I'll see you out."

"A date?" he said skeptically. "For seven years there's been no man in your life. Now suddenly you're seeing someone? Who?"

How did he know all these things about her?

"I'm going out with another cop. My partner," she blurted before she could think.

Immediately she knew it was a mistake. She didn't even know if Riley would be at the barbecue tonight. If Nick had her followed, he would know she wasn't with anyone.

"We haven't gone public yet," she added. "Not a good idea when we work together."

"You've been at your new job only a few weeks," Nick mused. "That's fast work."

"As you say, it's been a long time for me. But when you meet the right man, you know." Referring to Riley as Mr. Right, it was hard not to let out a bitter laugh. She wanted a man with fewer problems than she had, not more.

From her purse in the kitchen came the muffled ringing of her cell phone. "That's probably him now."

"Go on, answer it."

"First I want you out of my son's room." She stood back and made Nick precede her down the hall. He'd said he wouldn't harm the mother of his son but just in case, she was keeping her eyes on him. She reached into her purse and flipped open her phone. "Hey, Riley, I'm on my way."

"Paula?" her mother said. "Is everything okay?"

"Fine. Half way out the door."

"Jamie won't eat his dinner. Did you promise him McDonalds tonight?"

"I can't wait to see you, too."

"What's going on? Should I call emergency services?"

"No. Everything's under control." Paula clicked the phone off. She flicked the gun at Nick, gesturing in the direction of the door. "Get out."

Nick complied. But before he closed the door behind him, he added, "I'll be back."

Paula kept her gun raised, trained at where his head would be for another ten long seconds. Slowly she lowered her aching arms. "Over my dead body."

RILEY CRUISED SLOWLY past the school on his way to Lexie's house and stopped out front, letting the car idle. With the school windows dark and the playground empty, the building posed no psychological threat. He felt a little tense but that was undoubtedly from recalling his humiliating breakdown.

Nothing like that had ever happened to him before. He'd been trained to be in control. Not knowing what he was doing or being able to stop the craziness and the panic was scary.

Maybe Paula was right and he was suffering

from post-traumatic stress disorder. He'd gone onto the internet and researched PTSD. Symptoms could come on months, years, even decades after the original trauma. It might not even be the explosion that caused his problem. He'd spent five years in and out of Afghanistan. The trauma could have happened earlier—seeing a buddy killed by Taliban snipers, a local family wiped out by a misdirected drone hit, witnessing a Coalition tank blow up after hitting a land mine.

These were facts of war. Every soldier had similar experiences. What made *him* so weak that he couldn't deal with them? Well, damn it, he wasn't weak. He could, and he would deal. No way was he going to sit on a psychologist's couch and talk about his *feelings,* or listen to a shrink speculate on whether he'd been toilet trained too early.

Gazza had offered to talk. Had he had similar experiences to Riley?

Riley fished out his phone, went into his received calls and pressed dial. "Hey, Gaz," he said when his friend answered.

"Dude! Still living the dream?" Gazza's consonants were slurred and he spoke overloud. There was a hubbub of voices and clinking glasses in the background.

Riley stared at the school. With the blinds drawn against the setting sun, the windows looked like closed eyes. "Yeah, it's paradise, man. How are you doing?"

"Not bad. Jus' at the pub with a few mates. What's up? You booked your flight for ANZAC Day yet?"

"Not yet. But I've been thinking about Afghanistan lately. I was wondering—" A burst of raucous male laughter made him hold the phone away from his ear.

"Sorry about that." Gazza chuckled. "Hang on, I'll go somewhere quiet so we can talk."

Riley pressed two fingers between his eyebrows and waited.

"I'm back," Gazza said a few moments later. "What were you saying?"

"About the explosion that sent me home. Where it happened, what caused it—"

"It was a school for girls. You used to go there a lot, take them pens and stuff. That's all I know. Pete could probably tell you more. He was with you on patrol that day."

A school. Well, that explained the panic attack. "Where's Pete these days?"

"Don't you know? He's still over there. Secret ops on the border with Pakistan. I sent him an email a week ago. I'm hoping he'll be on leave for the ANZAC Day march."

"If you hear from him, tell him to get in touch." Riley hung up and drove through the leafy side streets of Summerside in the warm twilight with the windows down. A girl's school. So Nabili, the Afghani woman—was she a teacher?

Still mulling this over he turned onto Lexie's street. Cars lined the narrow road and muted sounds of conversation and laughter came over the fence from her backyard.

He felt like bailing on the party—God knows he wouldn't be good company. But this past week had been awful. His nightmares had been worse and he'd spent most evenings working alone on his kitchen. He simply couldn't take another long night in his own gloomy company. He should at least try to act normal. Things had been awkward with Paula ever since she'd confronted him. She'd said nothing more but the squad car felt smaller, as if a big fat elephant was sitting between them. The tables had turned. He'd been watching her, now she watched him.

And the hell of it was, his attraction to her hadn't gone away. If anything, it had become more intense.

He parked a block away and tucked a six-pack of beer under his arm. The front door was open but instead, he walked through the carport to the gate. Out of long habit he assessed the lay of the land before entering. Several dozen people were scattered about, more in the house. Seated in deck chairs on the patio was a group he didn't know. By the barbecue stood a cluster of people who were friends. In his present state of emotional disrepair he wasn't sure which was worse.

The door to Lexie's detached studio was open for inspection of her artwork, mostly local seascapes and portraits. Her most celebrated painting, a portrait of her sister-in-law Dr Sienna Maxwell, was hanging in the National Gallery of Victoria.

No matter which group he joined he was going to have to talk. Wow. When had socializing become a chore for him? He pushed his warm beer bottles into the tub of ice at the edge of the patio and picked out a cold one.

"Riley," a brunette with a wide smile and a great figure called. She waved him over.

"Hey, Renita, looking good." He still couldn't get over how much she'd changed. When he'd left for Afghanistan she'd worn glasses and was a good thirty pounds heavier. Guys hadn't been very kind to her in high school, probably less for her appearance than being intimidated by her brains. It was nice that she and Brett—an ex-football player and Summerside's most famous son—had gotten together.

Renita made room for him in the circle between her and Sally. Kisses on the cheeks, greetings and exclamations, smiles all round. He'd known most of these people since high school, some since primary school. As well as Renita and Brett there was Lexie's brother Jack and his new wife, Sienna; Darcy from the pub; John and his current squeeze, Trudy…

They were friends with whom he'd shared countless social occasions. Yet tonight he felt oddly detached, flat. Making small talk felt like having all his teeth pulled, one by one, without anesthetic. Gradually he stopped saying anything and let the conversation flow around him. Eventually he wasn't even listening, aware only of a buzzing in his ears.

The next time he glanced up John had a hand on his shoulder and was peering into his face. "What's the matter, mate? You okay?"

"I'm fine. Just…" Riley gestured vaguely. "I'm going to go sit down for a bit."

"I'll keep you company."

"No, stay here. I…need a moment by myself."

Riley started for the chairs then veered away and retreated to the empty trampoline at the side of the yard. He perched on the edge sipping on a beer, watching the party from a distance.

Lexie, her blonde curly hair flowing around her shoulders, carried a plate of appetizers from group to group, her laughter ringing out above the buzz of voices. Rafe, her fiancé was grilling seafood on the barbecue. Every now and then Lexie would load up another plate of appetizers and steal a kiss in the process.

"Yo, Riley," a woman said. "I was kind of hoping you would be here tonight."

Riley dropped back to earth. A blonde in a cherry-red maxi dress stood before him holding a champagne flute. She took a huge gulp, draining half the glass, and scrunched her nose against the bubbles.

"Paula," he said, startled. It had taken him a moment to recognize her without her uniform.

"Got it in one." Her shoulders, bared by the dress's halter-top, were angular and toned.

"I haven't seen you with your hair down, so to speak." And he wished he hadn't. Now she wasn't just another cop, she was a woman with breasts and silky-looking blonde hair and a faint floral fragrance. Her mouth was a sexy red and her blue eyes enhanced by smoky shadow. It occurred to him to wonder if she used the uniform to mask the woman beneath. Even though she was showing all the skin he was the one that felt vulnerable. "How do you know Lexie?"

"I don't. My sitter, Sally, invited me." Paula looked around and nodded to a group near the koi pond on the far side of the yard. "The brunette in the capri pants with the little girl."

"I know Sally. She was in my history class in grade eleven." And now a pair of tiny fists gripped her fingers as her toddler showed off with a few unsteady steps across the grass.

"It must be nice living in a small town and knowing everyone. I had no idea you and Sally were friends or I would have mentioned you were my partner."

Paula took another swig of champagne and glanced over her shoulder. She did a complete three hundred and sixty degree scan of the yard, looking over Riley's shoulder before she glanced at him.

Man, he'd thought *he* was paranoid. Even off-duty she was tense. Riley glanced behind him, and saw only the fence and bushes on the other side. "What's wrong?"

"Nothing."

"Are you worried about Moresco coming after you?"

Her eyes widened. "Why would you think that?"

"Something's got you freaked."

Paula didn't answer right away. She sipped her wine, her expression troubled. "Jamie's father showed up at the house before I left to come here tonight."

Riley peeled the corner of the beer label with his thumb. "I presumed from things you said that your ex wasn't in the picture."

"He's not. I didn't invite him. And I told him in no uncertain terms not to come back."

Riley knew he should just let it drop. The last thing he wanted was to get embroiled in her domestic issues. But one thing he couldn't tolerate was a woman being abused. "What happened?"

Her chin rose. "Nothing I couldn't handle."

He searched her face, her bare arms. For what, bruises? She wouldn't have worn that dress if there were marks. Still he had to ask, "Is he violent?"

Paula hesitated, then shook her head.

Maybe he had an overactive imagination but Riley thought she'd left something unspoken, like, *not yet, at least.* "What did he want?"

She ran a blunt-nailed finger around the rim of her glass. "To see Jamie." Her smoky blue eyes flashed with a look he couldn't interpret. "Let it go. I just want to forget about it. There's nothing you can do."

So, now she was shutting him down the way he'd shut her down over the PTSD. He didn't like it, not one little bit. For a moment he imagined how it would be if they each dropped their guard, confided in one another, were on the same team.

He would have her in his arms in a heartbeat.

No, no, no. He'd made a conscious decision not to go there. Why couldn't he put it completely out of his mind?

"Nice dress," Riley said.

"No personal comments, Henning. I mean it."

She looked over at the group around the barbecue. "Why are you sitting here all alone? You grew up in Summerside. You must be one of the gang."

"I needed to get away for a moment. Sometimes all the talk of mortgages and footy and the latest app seems so…trivial."

"I know what you mean." Her blue eyes met his, full of understanding.

Again, he got a flash of how much common ground they had between them, if only they allowed themselves to admit it. Sympatico. The thought stole his breath.

"But if you're going through a difficult time, friends can be a support. You should mingle."

The moment of shared understanding evaporated. A formless anger welled in him, out of the blue and out of proportion. He didn't need her patronizing comments, or her compassion. Sympathy was for weaklings.

"Are you ordering me to socialize? I understood from John that we're equal partners at work. Anyway, we're not on duty, so kiss my ass." He'd intended to say it lightly, as a joke. It didn't come out that way.

Nor did she laugh. "Have you forgotten already what happened at the school?"

He almost told her then what he'd learned from Gazza. But he didn't. It would have sounded like an excuse. "How many ways do I need to say it? I'm fine. I'm not going through a *difficult time*."

"Really," she said flatly. "I understood from Katie that you're usually quite the gregarious fellow. I expected you to be the life of the party. But hey, she's only your sister. She's probably all wrong."

Katie didn't know him anymore, not this... angry confused person he'd become.

"Riley." Lexie approached with a platter of marinated grilled prawns and calamari. She gave him a one-armed hug. Traces of paint stained her slender fingers and silver earrings dangled among the tangled blonde curls. "What are you doing hiding over here?" She turned to Paula. "I'm Lexie."

"This is Paula, my partner." Riley took a prawn and popped the whole thing in his mouth.

"Partner?" Lexie exclaimed, her blue eyes widening as she grinned with delight. "Oh, my God. I didn't know you were dating anyone. Where did you two meet?"

His mouth full of sizzling prawn, Riley could only shake his head vigorously.

"We're partners at work." Paula took a napkin and some calamari. "Running into each other here is a coincidence."

Lexie smiled knowingly and wagged a finger. "There are no coincidences."

Riley exchanged glances with Paula. She stopped just this side of an eye roll. On this at least they were in agreement.

"Congratulations on your engagement," Paula said, changing the subject. "When's the big day?"

"August, after snapper fishing season," Lexie replied. "Rafe has a boat charter business and he can't miss the most lucrative fish run in the year. You'll have to come out on the bay with us sometime." She turned back to Riley. "I haven't seen Katie in ages. I was hoping she'd be here tonight but she had something else on."

"She's always extra busy during the first school term." The truth was, his sister avoided social occasions where she knew John would be there. "I'll have to leave soon, myself." Riley checked his watch. How soon could he go without being rude?

"Sally's told me so much about your paintings. Would you show them to me?" Paula asked Lexie. "Riley can pass out the rest of the appetizers. It'll give him a chance to mingle." She had the audacity to wink at him.

"Great idea. Thanks, Riley." Lexie handed him the platter. She linked her arm with Paula's and the two women strolled across the grass toward the studio.

Paula glanced over her shoulder, an ironic smile on her lips. Try to manipulate him, would she? Riley cocked a finger gun, aimed and fired. Then, while she watched, he deliberately tipped the plate and dropped it, prawns and all, into the rubbish bin.

Lexie turned just then and saw, too. Her eyes widened. Paula frowned, said something to Lexie and quickly led her away. Riley stared into the bin. What the— He felt like a jerk, wasting the food and Rafe's efforts in cooking it. He was acting nuts. He had to get out of here.

He slid off the trampoline, ready to make his escape. But Rafe called out that dinner was ready and Riley was pulled along with the group like a bit of flotsam on the tide. He found himself at a picnic table next to Sally. She heaped his plate with food as she filled her own, as if feeding a small child. She chattered about her and Rick's upcoming trip to Bali and didn't seem to notice that Riley barely responded.

Football, village gossip, even statewide news, as he'd said to Paula, all seemed so trivial. It was ironic considering these were all the things he'd craved when he was discharged and what motivated his move back to Summerside. He had enjoyed them for a time. Now he was in a blue funk, feeling as if he had nothing in common with these people. They undoubtedly thought that a warm summer evening sharing food, wine, talk and laughter with good friends was what life was all about.

Until recently he'd thought so, too. He watched the others enjoying themselves and felt half angry, half wistful, wishing he could recapture the connection.

Paula seemed to be having trouble keeping her

mind on the party, too. Seated at the far end of the long table she never appeared to be fully relaxed. Her gaze was alert, as if she was always looking over her shoulder. Her lovely bare shoulder with the smooth golden skin…

Who was she more worried about—Moresco or Jamie's father? The juxtaposition of the two men's recent appearance in her life led him back to his earlier speculation. *Were they one and the same man?*

The sky darkened. Over the trees rose a sickle moon. A bat flitted, a dark shape above the roofline of the house. Dessert was served. Riley checked his watch again. For three hours he'd pretended to have a good time.

Finally, the meal was over, the party was in transition. Sally was saying goodbye, Chloe asleep over her shoulder. Lexie, Jack and Sienna carried empty dishes inside. Rafe and John arranged chairs around the chiminea. Brett stoked the fire while Renita stacked the box next to it with more wood.

Riley couldn't see Paula so he assumed she'd already left. He'd drive past her place tonight, make sure she was okay and no one was bothering her. If her light was on, he would drop in for a chat. Maybe her private life wasn't any of his business but he wanted answers all the same.

Deciding he'd call tomorrow to thank Lexie and

Rafe for the party, he slipped out the gate unnoticed. A blue Honda was pulling away from the curb. He recognized the woman behind the wheel. Paula was making her own getaway.

PAULA SQUINTED AGAINST the headlights in her rearview mirror. A car had been following her ever since she left the party. She tried to identify the make and model of the vehicle but it was hopeless with the glare of the headlights.

All evening she'd been on edge, worried that Nick would follow her and lie in wait until she left the party to see if she picked up Jamie. She'd only come out of bravado because if she stayed home, then Nick would have beaten her. She felt for the gun tucked in the side pocket of her car door, hidden beneath the rag she used to clean the windshield.

Her cell phone rang. It was both illegal and dangerous to drive while speaking on a cell but she reached into her purse for it anyway. There was no name next to the number.

"Hello?"

"It's me following you," Riley said. "Thought I'd better let you know so you don't call the cops or something."

Paula quietly let out her breath, hoping he didn't hear her sigh of relief. "I was planning to shoot out my open window and take out your tires."

"You've been watching too many cop shows."

In the darkened car, his low amused voice in her ear sounded too much like banter. Banter with Riley was dangerous and no gun could make it any safer. "What do you want?"

"To make sure you get home safely."

"I appreciate your concern." She slowed, put on her indicator and turned into her street. "I'm a big girl now."

"Will Jamie be home tonight or are you alone?"

Another time, another man, and those words might have heralded a romantic rendezvous. She stifled a sigh. How long had it been since she'd even allowed herself to think about romance? Who she was, everything she did, was for Jamie. "Alone."

She pulled into the driveway, her headlights illuminating Jamie's two-wheel bike against the back brick wall. "Thanks for the escort. See you on Monday."

She was about to hang up when she saw him park behind her and kill his lights. "Hey—"

"We're not done," he said, cutting her off. "I'm coming inside."

CHAPTER SEVEN

PAULA GOT OUT of her car and all but slammed the door. She was tired, worried and exasperated. All she wanted to do was crawl into bed and, just for tonight, pull the covers over her head.

Riley's window was down so she called out, "Whatever it is you think you're doing, don't."

He got out and walked toward her, a lean dark silhouette against the glow of the streetlight. A second later a flashlight beam danced over the pavement at her feet, then over the bushes at the sides of the house.

"You should have motion-sensor lights," Riley said.

"Give me a chance. I just moved in a few weeks ago."

He moved past her, up the steps, and shone the beam on the door. "The lock hasn't been forced."

"This is ridiculous and totally unnecessary." She was getting annoyed. "My ex isn't going to break in." She hoped. Nick was both ruthless and unpredictable. And his parting words had sounded distinctly like a threat. "If he does, I can take care of him."

"I'm sure you can. Even so, we'll check the place out together." Riley waited while she fished out her key and fumbled it into the lock.

"Damn it, you've made me nervous with your old aunt routine. This is only Jamie's father we're talking about."

Except Jamie's father wasn't an ordinary man. He was an international drug dealer and criminal. The lie of omission was getting too big to sustain. She needed to tell Riley, sooner rather than later, that Nick was Jamie's father.

The key turned. She opened the door and flicked on the light.

Riley walked into the living room on the left, switching on a table lamp as he went. The red couch and glass coffee table came to life. He shone the light on walls covered with artwork, potted plants and her collection of blown-glass figurines on the mantel over the fireplace.

"For only being here a few weeks, you're pretty settled in."

"I've gotten good at unpacking." She'd moved three times in the past seven years, each time was an upheaval for her and Jamie. The first thing she did in a new place was turn the rented house into a home.

Riley checked the sliding door in the dining room and moved into the kitchen.

"This is silly. There's no one here but us." Her voice sounded too loud in the quiet house. Paula wasn't sure if she was trying to convince Riley or herself.

"Pays to be thorough." He opened the door to the laundry.

Paula was tired of following him around so she headed toward the bedrooms. Halfway down the dark passage loomed a tall black shape. Her heart skipped a beat until she realized she'd left the linen closet door open.

Feeling along the wall for the light switch, she flicked it on. With illumination, her fear was put into perspective. *Safe as houses*, the saying went. Not hers, she thought, recalling the flimsy lock on the laundry room door and the windows that could be jimmied open.

She went into her bedroom, flicking on that light, too. Spying the book on her bedside table, *Exploring and Loving Your Inner Self*, she tossed it into the bottom drawer. She hated to think of the ribbing she'd cop if Riley saw that.

She peered into the closet then crouched to look under the bed. Hearing a noise behind her she scrambled to her feet. Riley stood so close she almost bumped into him. So close she could smell the night air on his skin. He could probably hear her heart thumping. "Don't sneak up on me!"

"Backyard's clear. You need to get a better lock on the—"

"Laundry room door. I know." She pushed her hair out of her eyes and brushed past him, heading to the spare room next door which would likely be his next destination.

She stood in front of the bookshelf. Riley ignored that, and the table cluttered with scraps of patterned fabric, to check the closet. It was empty but for winter coats, empty hangers and her tennis racket that she hadn't used since Jamie was born.

Across the hall she flicked on the light in the bathroom. In her hurry to leave for the barbecue tonight she'd left cosmetics strewn over the counter. It smelled like a bordello.

"Nothing to see here, folks." She snatched up her underwear and one of Jamie's discarded socks from the floor, and stuffed them in the wicker hamper. "Move along."

She crowded Riley out of the bathroom. Partners on the beat was one thing, him seeing her mess and dirty lingerie was quite another.

In front of Jamie's room, she paused, reluctant to enter. Nick had been here, handling her son's things. Tomorrow she would do a thorough clean, wiping everything with sanitizer.

Riley pushed the door, which was ajar, fully open.

"Let's make this quick. I'm tired." Paula strode past him into Jamie's bedroom. "There's nothing—"

But there was. Another shiny red remote-controlled car, identical to the first, sat in the middle of the floor.

Her stomach heaved. Her hand went to her mouth. Her knees threatened to buckle. Nick was showing her how easily he could get to her son, with or without her consent.

"What is it?" Riley touched her shoulder. "Paula?"

Her hand shaking, she pointed at the car.

Her ambivalence about Nick and his rights as Jamie's father crystallized in the heat of her anger. This wasn't how a father behaved, breaking into a child's home. This was a violation. Here she'd been worrying about family values. Nick had made it clear he thought he was above the rules that governed ordinary society. Well, she should have known that already, shouldn't she? She'd been blinded by her own guilt and shame, by her fears she wasn't giving Jamie everything he deserved. No more. From now on she would move heaven and earth to keep Moresco away from her son. If he was engaged in illegal activities, she would use all her powers as a cop to catch him. When she did, she would lock him up and throw away the key.

"Tell me what's wrong." Riley took hold of her shoulders and turned her to face him, bending his knees to peer into her eyes. "Has Jamie's father been here? How do you know?"

"The toy car. It wasn't here when I left for the barbecue. He must have put it here while I was gone."

"He has a key to the house?"

"No." She picked up the car, wanting to crush it with her bare hands. Or beat it to scrap metal with Jamie's cricket bat. No one threatened her child's safety. "First thing tomorrow I'm going to install deadbolts on every door, nail all the windows shut."

"You need to see a lawyer, take out a restraining order," Riley said. "You're already potentially in danger from Moresco, you don't need to be hassled by Jamie's father, too."

TO RILEY'S SURPRISE, Paula, furious only a moment ago, crumpled. She dropped the toy car and it fell with a thunk to the carpet. Covered her face with her hands, she spun away, shoulders bowed.

Riley shifted uneasily. What had happened to his tough cop? This woman was in a world of hurt, anger and confusion. He wanted to fix it for her but didn't know how. So he did the only thing he could think of. He put his arms around her.

"It's going to be okay," he murmured next to

her ear. She shook her head and his nostrils filled with the scent of her hair. He stroked her back, listened to her choked sobs and wondered what to say. "Have you got full custody?"

"Yes," she said on a hiccup.

"Then everything's fine. It's just a toy. He hasn't hurt Jamie, that's the main thing. I'll help you change the locks, make this place secure. Then you won't have to worry." As a cop he knew enough about domestic problems to know that things could get messy and possibly she did have to worry. There was no point in dwelling on that right now. He held her close, very aware of her in his arms, of her heat and the shape of her. He touched his mouth to her temple, feeling her pulse beneath his lips.

Naturally, being Paula, she didn't want comfort for long. She pushed him away, blinking her eyes dry. "I have to tell you something."

Then instead of speaking, she paced, moving restlessly around the room, straightening the bed, and picking up toys.

"So spit it out. I'm listening."

Her grip tightened on the T. rex in her hands. "Nick Moresco is Jamie's father."

Riley blinked, the crash of disappointment rendering him speechless. He'd known it in his bones and yet had somehow hoped beyond hope that he was wrong. Hearing her confirm it, the only surprise was how intensely betrayed he felt that she hadn't confided in him earlier.

"I beg your pardon?" Even though he'd heard, he wanted her to deny it.

"I said—"

"Never mind, I got it." He didn't want to hear it again. He struggled with the enormity of her admission. It was one thing to speculate, to have a theory. Another thing to know for certain that his partner, the woman he'd fantasized about sexually, had slept with a known drug dealer, a high-level criminal under her investigation. It went against everything he stood for. Everything he thought *she* stood for.

"I knew you must have done something pretty bad to warrant losing your detective stripes. But I never once thought that the guys at the station were right."

"Right? What do you mean by that?"

"That you're a bent cop."

"The hell I am!"

"You slept with a drug dealer. What else did you do? Did you sell drugs for him, too?" Riley didn't know why he was being so antagonistic, but he knew damn well he couldn't pat her on the back again and say, *there, there, everything's going to be okay.* "Why didn't you tell me before this?"

"It's none of your business."

"You've got to be kidding me. All the time we

were searching Timothy Andrews' car, looking for a link to Moresco, you were withholding vital information."

"Information that wasn't relevant to the case."

"And tonight, I'm checking out your house thinking you're worried about some dweeb pencil pusher who wants to take his kid out for a movie and a hamburger on Sunday when in reality, you're dealing with a freaking drug lord with body guards and gunmen ready to do his bidding."

"I told you, I can deal with him."

"You *slept* with him." Riley couldn't get over it. The knowledge rankled somewhere really deep, somewhere beyond the inherent wrongness of it in relation to being a police officer. It bothered him down deep where he was a man. If he didn't know better, he would have thought he was jealous.

Maybe he was jealous. Great. That was all he needed, to be falling for his partner.

"You don't know what it was like going undercover for over a year," she said. "I lived and breathed my role—"

"Yeah, yeah, you told me already. Therapeutic massages, my ass." At her scoff, he amended, "Okay maybe your massages were legit but female cops don't trade sexual favors for evidence. There are rules."

Her chin went up another notch. "You don't understand."

"You're right." Riley held up his hands. "I don't understand."

"And you have no right to judge."

"Don't I?" He walked over to her, the better to get in her face. Even though he'd considered this possibility he'd secretly wanted to believe she held herself to the same high moral standard that he did. Because if she didn't, what did that say about him, the guy who did everything right, that he could fall for a "bad" girl. Hell, he was still attracted to her. It was wrong, wrong on so many levels.

He didn't know how to handle his feelings so he turned his confusion into aggression. "You demand to know what went wrong in my past that's screwing me up. You tell me to see a shrink. Try to manipulate me into socializing."

"I was doing all that to help you—"

"All the time, you've been holding back."

"I'm not the one having panic attacks outside a primary school."

Riley took her by the shoulders, wishing he could shake some sense into her. "*Hello!* Nick Moresco is gunning for you."

She brought up her arms between his and pushed outward, breaking his hold. "Step *back*. You're too close. And don't be a drama queen. Nick's not like that. He wouldn't hurt me, or Jamie."

"You're defending him?" Riley said incredulously. "After he broke into your house?"

"No, of course not. But I don't need you telling me off." She walked to the door. "You'd better go."

"Damn right I'm going." He strode out of the bedroom and out the front door, not bothering to close it behind him. She'd played him for a fool. Lied to him. Made him feel protective of her, worried for her. And all the time she'd been holding on to this secret. Well, screw her.

Partners? Hardly.

He threw the flashlight onto the passenger seat and slid behind the wheel. Feeling in his jacket pocket for his keys, he started the Audi. Paula appeared in the lighted doorway. Savagely he turned the key and the engine started with a low rumble. The tires squealed as he burned out of the driveway in Reverse, did a two-point turn and peeled out of the cul-de-sac.

Jealous, him? No bloody way.

He roared down the side street toward the main road that led to the village business district. Just before the T intersection a white cat leaped out of nowhere. He slammed on the brakes and swerved to miss it. The cat streaked into the bushes. Riley brought the car to a halt and rested his forehead on the wheel between his clenched hands.

What the hell was wrong with him? He was

overreacting again. *Overreacting?* Hell, he was acting just plain crazy. He barely recognized himself.

Paula was his partner. So she'd made a mistake seven years ago. Big deal.

But it was. It was a doozy of a mistake. What kind of woman, let alone a cop, slept with a drug lord?

He started driving again—at the speed limit—through the commercial district, all two blocks of it. At midnight on a Saturday all the shops were closed except for the fish and chip take-out, a couple of restaurants and the pub.

She'd kept secrets. Well, who wouldn't keep a secret like that? She must be embarrassed and ashamed.

He headed for the cliff overlooking the beach. The moon shone over the bay. He sat in the parking lot, motor idling and watched the golden light ripple over the water.

She'd jerked him around. He wasn't going to be forgetting that in a hurry.

Still, she was in danger from that asshole drug dealer—even if she didn't realize it.

Riley turned the car around and drove to Paula's house. If he went home, he'd probably spend another sleepless night anyway. He might as well be doing something more useful than roaming the dark rooms of his subconscious.

All the lights were out at Paula's except the one over the porch. Good. He didn't want to talk to her again tonight. He cut the engine and coasted into her driveway. Pulling his jacket collar around his neck, he put his seat back as far as it would go and closed his eyes.

PAULA LAY AWAKE in bed, alternately replaying the shock of seeing the toy car in Jamie's room, and the warmth of Riley's arms around her. It bothered her how good his embrace had felt, and not only for the comfort factor—

A car approached then cut its engine right outside her house. What was that? She propped herself on her elbows, ears strained, waiting for the engine to start up again, or a door to shut. It almost sounded as if the car had come into her driveway.

What if it was Nick, even now silently moving toward the house? Maybe he'd waited until he'd seen her come home and Riley leave before returning.

She took her gun from the drawer and got out of bed. The hall floor was cold beneath her bare feet as she stole through the dark to the living room. With the barrel of the gun she pulled the curtains back a fraction of an inch and peered through the gap.

Riley's black Audi sat in the middle of the driveway.

Wonderful. Any minute he would knock on her door with some patronizing bullshit about how she should go to a friend's house. She would tell *him* where he could go.

She opened the curtain a little farther to get a better look. He was slumped behind the wheel, not moving. What did he think he was doing? Should she go out there and send him home?

He'd been a jerk about Nick. It was really disappointing. She'd hoped he might be different. Instead he was like all the other male cops who couldn't understand that she'd only slept with Nick because she had to, to crack the case. They all thought she was some kind of slut. It wouldn't be long before sly remarks and innuendo slipped into casual conversation in the locker room. Then would come the sidelong looks, the sniggers and even outright disgust, depending on the sensibilities of the cop.

She was tempted to order Riley off the property. Who did he think he was, camping out in her driveway? Just because he'd been SAS and was used to acting on his own initiative he thought he could override her wishes.

But she wasn't up to another argument tonight. Not when she was so jumbled inside over how she felt about him. Did she want his arms around her or did she want to tell him off? Both, if she was honest.

If he wanted to freeze his butt off sleeping in his car after she'd told him she could look after herself, that was his problem.

She would curl up in her warm bed and, yes, probably sleep a little sounder knowing Riley was keeping watch.

Not that she would ever admit that to him.

PAULA POURED A CUP of coffee and stirred in one sugar, the way she knew Riley liked it. What was the protocol for uninvited guests who camped in your driveway—invite them in for breakfast? She was feeling a little more charitable this morning, thanks to a good night's sleep.

Yes, definitely breakfast. Such devotion to duty deserved a reward. Now the question was, bacon and eggs or her special apple-streusel muffins?

Simple. She would ask him.

Carrying the peace offering she checked herself in the hall mirror and opened the front door.

Riley's car was gone.

The sunny morning lost a bit of its shine. She'd been anticipating ribbing him about his "stake out."

She was about to go inside when her mother's pale green Ford sedan turned into the cul-de-sac. Karen motored slowly down the street, peering left and right, as if she expected someone to leap out of the bushes.

Whoops. Paula hadn't called her mother back last night and explained what had happened.

The car turned into the driveway and came to a halt. Jamie flung open the back door and charged toward Paula. "We watched *X-Men* and played Uno and had popcorn…" He paused, running out of breath.

"Wonderful." She gave him a big hug. "Run inside. I need to talk to Grandma."

Karen approached, wearing the knee-length shorts and polo shirt she played golf in on Sunday mornings, Jamie's overnight bag in hand.

Paula walked down the steps to meet her. Jamie had shut the door, but she didn't want to risk him overhearing. She hugged her mother and took Jamie's bag. "Thanks for looking after him last night."

"Are you all right?" Strands of Karen's light brown hair blew across her eyes. She brushed them away to search Paula's face. "I've been so worried."

"Sorry, I should have called last night but I got home late. I didn't want to wake you."

"What's going on?"

Paula put the bag down at her feet. "Nick Moresco came to the house. He was here when you called."

Karen put a hand to her mouth. "What did he want?"

Paula gave mother an abridged version of the night's events, telling of Nick's wish to meet his son and, after some internal debate, the part about him leaving a toy car. Once again, the car was safely tucked in her trunk, ready to go to the thrift shop.

"Don't worry," she finished. "I've called a handyman to change all the locks and improve security on the windows. I'll get you a new key cut."

Karen shook her head, dismayed. "Jamie should stay with me until you catch that creep and put him back behind bars. I'll take some time off work. Jamie and I can drive up to Sydney and visit my sister—"

"No." Paula stopped her with a hand to her arm. "I need time to think this through. Nick hasn't done anything illegal—"

"He broke into your house! He should be arrested for that alone."

"Nothing big, I mean. He would get a slap on the wrist for a break and enter. Besides, if Nick can find out where I live, he could locate you at Aunt Lily's. I wouldn't feel easy with Jamie so far away."

"If only your father were alive," Karen fretted. "He knew how to talk to addicts."

"Nick isn't an addict. He's too smart to ingest his own poison." She gestured to the house. "Come in. I've got coffee."

"Thanks, no." Karen checked her watch. "I'm meeting the girls at the golf course in half an hour—" She broke off as Paula's gaze shifted to the street.

Riley's black Audi drove up for the second time in less than twenty-four hours and squeezed into a spot to the right of Karen's car.

"Who's that?" her mother asked.

"My partner. I wonder what he wants now."

Riley's faded jeans had tears in the knees but his white T-shirt was clean beneath an unbuttoned blue and green flannel shirt. He was carrying a toolbox.

"Well, I guess that answers my question," Paula said. "He thinks he's come to help me change the locks." Mr. Fix It to the rescue. She ought to be put out by his assumption—she *was* put out—but she was also grateful that he cared enough to help her, especially after their argument last night.

"I'm going." Karen hugged her, giving her an extra squeeze. "Call me if you need me. Anytime. Promise?"

"I promise. Thanks."

"Have you got enough room to get out?" Riley asked Karen as she passed him on the way to her car.

"I'll manage. I'm Karen, Paula's mother." She

shook his hand then glanced at Paula on the steps. "Thanks for doing this. She doesn't accept help easily."

"I can hear you!" Paula rolled her eyes.

"Don't worry, I'll take good care of her," Riley said in a loud stage whisper, clearly intending to piss her off. Karen got in her car and he came up the path.

Paula stood in the middle of the steps, blocking his access. "What do you think you're doing?"

He met her hard-assed glare with one of his own. "I'm here to change your locks. And don't give me any grief."

"I've already called a handyman. This is above and beyond, even for partners."

Riley mounted the steps till he was on the one below her, putting them at eye level. He was disconcertingly close. "When is the handyman coming?"

"Not till Friday," Paula conceded.

"Let's see, that's—" he counted off on his fingers "—five full days and nights for Moresco to waltz in and out of your house as he pleases."

She had no answer to that. He was right, damn it. It was one thing to reassure her mother, another to fool herself into thinking she had nothing to fear. Nick was getting more aggressive. He might very well do her harm if she continued to keep him from Jamie.

"The man is a criminal," Riley went on. "Whether he plans to harm you or not, breaking into your house is illegal."

"As I told my mother, and you know very well, a B and E doesn't carry significant punishment and might make him angry rather than deter him."

"And as I'm sure your mother told you, *keep the bastard out*. Now are you going to let me help you, or am I going to call her and tell on you?"

He surprised a laugh out of her. Damn it, they were right and she was being stupid and stubborn. Paula stepped aside. "Sorry to be ungracious. I'm not used to people doing stuff for me."

"So I gather." He followed her inside. "I'll make a list of what I need and then take a trip to the hardware store. The laundry room seems to be the weakest spot. I'll concentrate on that first."

He was brisk and businesslike as if determined to ignore last night, both the embrace and their subsequent fight.

She glanced over her shoulder as she led him through the kitchen. "I'm paying for the materials."

"Too right you are. Did I mention I charge forty-five dollars an hour?"

"Any discount if I give you a hand?"

"You?" he said skeptically.

"Hey, I'm not helpless. I can put up bookshelves

and change the oil in my car. I can change a washer in a tap and unclog a drain."

"Can you change a lock on a door?"

"I could learn."

She hoped he wouldn't take her up on the offer. He looked too good and smelled too male, as if he'd bathed in testosterone. And there was something about a low-slung tool belt over jeans-clad hips that brought out her inner slut. At the same time she was still pissed about his attitude toward her with regard to Nick. If they worked closely together, the attraction and the conflict were bound to spark off each other and who knew what might happen.

Jamie ran in from the backyard, carrying his water pistol to refill. His T-shirt, hair and face were wet, as if he'd been spraying himself—which he probably had.

"You remember Riley, don't you?" Paula said, speaking to Jamie but watching Riley for signs of stress. Since his panic attack at the school she'd wondered if young children triggered his symptoms of PTSD. But seeing Jamie didn't change his demeanor. He only looked tired, as he was bound to after spending the night in his car.

"Hey, champ." Riley crouched and gave Jamie one of those complicated handshakes that only guys knew. Jamie didn't quite get it but by the time Riley had taken him through it twice the boy's eyes were shining. "Want to give me a hand fixing some stuff?"

"Okay," Jamie said. "What stuff?"

"Come with me and I'll tell you as we go." Riley laid a hand on the boy's shoulder. "First stop, laundry room. Have you ever used a hammer or a screwdriver?"

"No." Jamie's hand crept to Riley's hip and rested there.

"It's time you learned, don't you think?"

Jamie nodded, his young face eager.

Paula's chest suddenly felt too small for her heart. She did the best she could as a mother but it didn't take a genius to see that her son needed something she couldn't give him—a father.

She stood in the doorway unable to take her gaze away from Riley and Jamie. And it wasn't only because Riley had taken off his flannel shirt and draped it over the washing machine, revealing tanned, well-muscled arms below his white T-shirt.

Her day-dreamy, easily distracted son paid rapt attention to Riley as together they examined the door lock. Riley explained how it worked and tested the sturdiness of the facing jamb.

"We should be able to switch this old lock with a deadbolt without resorting to serious carpentry," Riley told Jamie. "I think with a chisel and a hammer we can make the necessary adjustments. What do you think?"

"I think…yes?" Riley nodded and Jamie's face was suffused with a self-conscious grin of importance he couldn't have contained if he'd wanted to.

Paula smiled, too. Her little boy knew squat about deadbolts and chisels. But he, too, could learn—if he had someone to teach him.

Riley got out a pad of paper and made a few notes. "Hold that for me," he said, handing the pad and pen to Jamie. "Right, then, let's have a look at the windows."

He clucked his tongue over the old-fashioned swing-out window with a simple sliding bolt. He glanced at Paula. "I recommend replacing these with the wind-out type that lock with a key. How many other windows do you have like this?"

"I'll go around and count. How do you know all this stuff? You've been in the army for years."

"Before I joined up I started an apprenticeship as a carpenter. Almost got my trades papers, too."

"What made you change your mind?"

"Long story short, I was twenty years old and looking for excitement. Working on construction sites wasn't doing it for me. So I applied for the SAS."

He made it sound like child's play but Paula had seen a documentary on the SAS training. It was brutal, ending in hospitalization for some of the potential recruits. Out of three hundred men fewer than fifty made the cut.

Riley turned to Jamie. "Can you get me the measuring tape out of my toolbox?"

Jamie squatted before the box as if opening a treasure chest. He scanned the contents, fists on his knees.

"That's it on the right," Riley said. "The square metal thing."

Jamie handed it to him, earning a nod of approval. Riley measured the window's dimensions, stretching on his toes to reach the top far corner. He came down with a wince, pressing a hand to his back.

"Sore?" Paula said.

"The front seat of an Audi doesn't make the best mattress. I'll be fine."

So he kept saying.

He made a few more notes then closed the pad and tucked it in the back pocket of his jeans. "Jamie and I will go to the hardware store now. Is that okay?"

She opened her mouth to say yes then stopped. What if Riley had a panic attack while her son was in his care? Who knew what else might trigger his symptoms? Staple guns? Ladders? Okay, that was probably crazy...

"Please, Mum?" Jamie begged. "I'll be good."

Paula tugged on her ponytail. She could go with

them… Or she could show some trust to the man who was going out of his way to help her. "Okay." She ruffled Jamie's hair and spoke to Riley. "You won't be gone long." It was a statement not a question.

"I'll be back as soon as I can." With a show of nonchalance he pulled his cell phone out of his pocket. "We can exchange numbers if it will make you feel better."

"Good idea. Jamie knows how to use a cell. And he knows that if the person he's with can't get to their phone then in an emergency he's allowed to use it to call for help."

Jamie, oblivious to undercurrents, ran out of the room. "Yay, we're going to the hardware store."

Riley paused, his gaze meeting hers, as if seeking to reassure her. "It's only five minutes down the road."

Paula chewed on her bottom lip. "Have you had any more episodes?" He shook his head. "If you start feeling weird, stop the car and call me right away."

His mouth flattened. "I'm not an idiot."

Okay, so she'd gone a step too far. Too bad. "No one said you were an idiot. But I'm Jamie's mum and I'm entitled to ask, especially in light of what happened last night."

He stepped closer, looming over her. "In light of

which happening? Nick breaking in or you throwing yourself into my arms?"

"I did not throw myself into your arms." But God help her, she wanted to do so now. Instead she pushed on his chest. "Go, before I change my mind."

CHAPTER EIGHT

PAULA LET THEM go. She felt she had to. But as she watched Riley drive away with her son she wondered what had possessed her to allow Jamie out with an unstable man. Riley was brave and smart, humorous and caring and if it wasn't for the PTSD, she'd have had no trouble letting Jamie go anywhere with him.

Was she that anxious for her son to have a male role model that she would risk sending him off with a man with undiagnosed mental health issues?

She needed to keep busy while they were gone, to stop fretting. Opening the blinds in her sewing room to let in natural light, she spread the half-finished quilt over the table, smoothing out the creases with her hands.

The patchwork was constructed of pieces of fabric of odd shapes, sizes and colors. A winding trail—or maybe it was a stream—of predominantly blue and green, meandered diagonally through a multicolored background. Where the trail or stream led she didn't know, she simply followed the twists and turns as fancy took her.

After studying where she'd left off for a few minutes, she up-ended her bag of scraps and sifted through them for suitable pieces. It was like doing a jigsaw puzzle. Piecing together the fabric occupied her mind and was soothing at the same time, almost like a meditation.

She was pinning a piece of green and blue paisley fabric to the trail when the phone rang. Her first thought was disaster. She snatched up the phone. "Is everything all right?"

"Everything is wonderful," Nick said. "Did Jamie like his new toy car?"

"*You.*" Paula paced the small room, one arm wrapped around her waist. "How dare you break into my house? I could have you arrested."

"But you won't," he replied silkily. "Why is that?"

Paula kicked aside the big plastic bag of fabric scraps. Because she knew he was too smart to have left fingerprints and because she couldn't prove he was the one who'd broken and entered. All of which he knew very well. "When you go back to jail I want it to be for a very long time."

"Have you thought about my request to see Jamie?"

"I don't need to think. The answer is still no. And always will be no."

"Is he there? May I speak with him at least?"

"He's not here. And no, you may not speak with him."

"I could apply to the Children's Court for an access visit. But it would be a pity to subject him to all the rigmarole unnecessarily. Why not let me come by one afternoon for coffee so we can meet?"

He made it sound so normal, so reasonable. She couldn't let herself forget who and what he was. If he wasn't a dangerous criminal, if he hadn't acted like a bully and broken into her house, she might have agreed. But he did break in because that was his mentality—he wanted something so he took it—and in doing so he'd threatened her son. No one threatened her son and still got what he wanted.

"You'll never get access. You're a criminal."

"I told you, I've turned over a new leaf. I bought a new restaurant—"

"Bully for you." She didn't believe for a second he'd cleaned up his act.

"—in Summerside."

Paula stumbled across the room on rubbery legs and sank onto the bed. "Which restaurant?"

"Not a restaurant so much as a café and ice cream parlor. It's on the main street, a thriving business. Kids like ice cream. What boy can resist a father who can give him unlimited access?"

Paula felt as if a net was closing around her. Nick had invaded not only her home, but also her town. She walked down the main street half a dozen times a week—at least half of those times with Jamie. Imagine Nick standing in the shop doorway, luring Jamie in with an offer of treats...

Not only that, he could use the shop to launder drug money.

That thought reminded her she wasn't just a mother—she was a cop and she had a job to do. And she had to prove to John—and Riley—she could be trusted. "Give me your number. I need to think about this."

Nick recited the digits. With tailor's chalk she scrawled them on a paper bag from a sewing shop.

"I'll get back to you." She hung up.

She tried to get absorbed in her quilting but she was too agitated to settle. The sound of the front door opening was a welcome distraction from her thoughts.

Jamie's excited voice rang through the house. "Mum, you should see all the stuff we got."

"Hey, kiddo." She caught Jamie as he ran past and gave him a fierce hug. Her little boy was always precious but even more so with Nick circling like a shark.

"Mum." He squirmed out of her arms. "Riley and I need to start fixing stuff." The gaps in his teeth meant he lisped on the last three words.

"What's that on your shirt, young man?" Paula wiped a fingertip through a wet stain on the front of his green T-shirt.

"We stopped for ice cream." Riley came in carrying bags that rattled and clinked with each step.

"At your stepmother's shop?"

"That's the only one in town. Why?" Riley paused on his way to the laundry room. "Is something wrong? You look pale."

She directed a meaningful glance at Jamie. "Later, when you've finished."

Riley smiled and squeezed her shoulder. "Hey, don't look so worried. It was only a small cone. It won't spoil his dinner."

"CAN I HAMMER?" Jamie asked.

"Sure." Riley helped the boy clamber onto the counter and held the nail while Jamie gripped the hammer with both hands and tapped the nail laboriously into the wood. After a moment he said, "I'll take it from here."

Jamie scooted back to the wall, crossed his legs and leaned forward to watch Riley. "Did you know velociraptors used to live in Australia?"

"Is that so?" The kid's lisp was too cute. Riley struggled not to grin inappropriately. If he had a son, he'd like him to be just like Jamie. Of course first Riley had to find a woman to settle down with. He had the home and once it was renovated, hopefully the rest would follow. But he wasn't rushing into anything. When he married he wanted it to be for life.

"They lived ninety-hundred billion years ago," Jamie went on earnestly. Riley bit the inside of his cheek to stop from laughing. "Scientists found their bones in a prehistoric billabong. My mum took me to the museum, that's how I know. We saw a model of a Stegosaurus as big as the house."

Riley's father had been lucky enough to find true love, twice. If cancer hadn't claimed his mother Riley was positive they would still be married. Sandra was a nice woman and she adored his dad so that was good enough for Riley. He hoped he would be half as lucky as his father.

He liked that both his mother and Sandra had their own careers. Whoever he hooked up with would be independent, too. Not at the expense of family, mind you, but he intended to be a hands-on father, with equal responsibility for the kids. Riley shook his head. Look at him, getting all clucky and domestic. Must be doing chores around the house, with a kid in tow. It reminded him of himself and his dad.

He gave Jamie the window locks and asked him to slot screws into each of the two holes in preparation for installing them. The simple task took all of the boy's concentration and kept him quiet for a couple of minutes.

Riley was more relieved than he would have liked to admit that he'd arrived safely home with Paula's son. If anything happened to Jamie while under his care… It was too dreadful to contemplate.

But maybe the panic attack was a one-off. Just because he'd freaked out and lost whole minutes that day at the school didn't mean it would happen again.

"How are you doing with those locks?" he asked.

"Just about…" Jamie slotted the last screw in a hole. "I'm done."

"Good on you. Oh, wait, here's a couple more. They were hiding in the bag."

Riley handed them to Jamie and proceeded to install the first lock, starting with hammering in the screw a little way so it bit into the wood.

It sucked that a nice kid like Jamie should have a criminal for a father. Paula was a great mother but the boy was clearly dying to have a man in his life to do guy stuff with. She needed to find a decent guy and marry him. She was smart, good-looking—okay, pretty damn gorgeous—and passionate, if that hot temper was any indication. She'd probably be terrific in bed.

An image of her naked flashed before Riley's vision as he brought down the hammer. It missed the nail and hit his thumb. Wincing, he blew on the tip.

"Do you need a bandage?" Jamie asked.

"Teaching my son what not to do?" Paula appeared in the doorway with two glasses of lemonade. She gave one to Jamie and handed the other to Riley.

"Thanks." He stuck his throbbing thumb into the icy liquid. Having just imagined Paula naked he couldn't look at her. Instead he pointed out the new deadbolt. "You'd have to be a professional lock-picker to get through that. Or else take an ax to the door."

"You guys did a great job." Paula twisted the deadbolt, testing the lock.

"Jamie's been a big help." Riley bent over to pick up a screw from the floor. Coming up, he twisted the wrong way. Pain lanced up the right side of his back. He grimaced. "I need to make a date with my chiropractor."

"Are you sure it's skeletal?" Paula prodded the muscles alongside his spine. "I can feel a knot." She pressed harder.

Riley jerked away. "Ow!"

"I can probably help you with that."

Right, because she was a trained massage therapist. Riley was tempted. He had occasional back problems where his muscles seized up and his mobility would be restricted for days. This seemed to be developing into one of those times. But stripping off his shirt and letting Paula move her hands all over his naked back? Massage definitely wasn't on the list of things partners did for each other.

"The kink will work itself out," he said. "But thanks, anyway. Jamie, let's tackle the windows."

Jamie's attention lasted another hour before he got bored and wandered away to play with his cars. Riley worked faster alone but he missed the boy's amusing chatter. When he was finished in the laundry room he moved on to the bedrooms. Paula had gone ahead of him and cleared the space in front of the windows for him to work. Another couple of hours went by. He finished up in the dining room where he added a top and bottom bolt to the sliding glass doors.

The aroma of roast lamb coming from the kitchen was making his stomach rumble. No wonder. It was nearly 7:00 p.m. He packed his tools in his box and dusted off his hands on the seat of his jeans.

He poked his head into the kitchen where Paula was putting the final touches on dinner. "All done." He hesitated. "I guess I'll see you at the station."

She set a bowl of salad on the table next to one of mashed potatoes. Three places were set. Two of them had wineglasses. "You're staying for dinner."

His hands went up. "I—"

"Don't even think about refusing. After all the

work you've done it's the least I can do. If you say no, I'll get Jamie in here to make you stay."

He kept his hands in the air. "I had no intention of refusing. I was merely showing you I need to wash my hands."

Her mouth twitched. "Bathroom's down the hall."

Riley took off his shirt to wash up, using the cloth Paula had left out to scrub the perspiration and dust from his face, neck and torso. He put his dirty T-shirt on, hoping it was true that women liked the smell of a man's clean sweat.

Jamie was already seated at the table. Riley dropped into a chair opposite. "I'm hungry enough to chew my arm off and eat it."

Jamie giggled and pretended to gnaw on his own arm, accompanied by horrific sound effects.

"Thanks," Paula said dryly as she handed Riley a glass of red wine. "Is that okay? Or would you rather have a beer?"

"This is great." He sipped the peppery shiraz.

Dinner passed in a pleasant blur despite the pain in his back. Second by second he could feel it seizing. Jamie was making the most of Riley's presence, showing off a bit and being silly. Paula gently scolded him but Riley could see she was pleased at his high spirits and protective of him.

Finally Paula rose. "School tomorrow, mate. You've talked Riley's ear off, but now it's time for your bath and pajamas." She turned to Riley. "Take your wine into the living room. I'll get Jamie settled then join you."

She and Jamie left. Riley tried to stand…and couldn't. His back was completely rigid. He made a second attempt and pain clouded his vision. Panting, he rested a moment. He couldn't sit here all night. Pushing his chair from the table, he did a controlled fall forward onto his hands and knees.

Inch by excruciating inch he crawled out of the kitchen, through the dining room and into the living room. When he reached the carpet he collapsed, face down. His watch was in front of his nose. The journey had taken him twenty minutes.

He was still lying there when Paula returned. "Sorry I took so long. Jamie would like to say goodnight— Oh, my God. What happened?"

"Just inspecting your carpet." He twisted his head enough to see her bare feet. She'd recently had a pedicure. Her nail polish was pearl pink.

"I'll tell Jamie you can't come tonight. Be right back." She hurried off and returned a few minutes later with a folded towel and a bottle of massage oil. "Put this under your chest and face. Can you get up on your elbows? I'll pull your shirt off."

Just the way he wanted an attractive woman to see him—lying helpless on the floor. Before he could protest she'd grasped the hem of his T-shirt and was tugging it over his head. He eased down. Might as well give in. He wasn't going to get far as he was.

"Try not to lift your head. Rest your forehead on your hands. That will keep your neck in alignment."

She left him for a moment to put on a CD, a soft slow duet of piano and bass, an unlikely combination that was deeply restful. "Are you warm enough?"

"Yes," he said, his voice muffled by the towel.

Her warm hands, slippery with scented oil, smoothed down from his shoulders to his waist in one long firm motion. Oh, man, that felt good. So good, he momentarily forgot the pain. Her fingers were magic, working his knotted muscles, kneading his tense, tight flesh, digging deep in the painful spots to find the twisted muscle fibers and loosen them with sure strokes.

She didn't speak. He couldn't. It had been a long time since anyone had touched him this way. While he was in the SAS he'd had women but never a girlfriend, not wanting to commit to a relationship when his life was in constant danger. One-night stands and good-time girls weren't known for administering tender loving care.

Paula's fingers explored him, seeking and healing, as if reaching into places he was afraid to go. To his dismay he found himself getting emotional. He had the affection of his friends and family, but there was a hole in his life, a longing for a woman to call his own, a life partner. The longing was all mixed up with a turbulent cloud of guilt and grief. There was anger, too, at himself for being weak. Where was this coming from? A tear squeezed out and trickled through his fingers. Shit. Was he crying? He couldn't let her see him crying.

"How are you feeling?"

"Good," Riley grunted. He hoped she couldn't hear the lump in his throat.

"Sometimes massage can bring out the emotions in people." She poured more oil on his back. "Just thought I'd warn you."

A little late for a warning. He grunted again, noncommittal, battling the feelings overwhelming him. The bass vibrated, adding fear to the swirling mix, and the blackest emotion of all... self-loathing.

"Unless SAS soldiers don't have emotions."

He didn't answer. Of course he had emotions. He had too many emotions. He was working damn hard to keep them all under wraps.

He squeezed his eyes shut, wishing this was only a simple massage, even a prelude to something romantic. But his subconscious or whatever, was ruining the moment. As she stroked away his physical pain, she was stroking his emotional pain to the surface.

"You really got chewed up over there, didn't

you?" She traced a ridge of scar tissue across his back, completely unaware of the effect her touch was having on him, or what he was going through right under her nose. "Are these from the explosion? That must have been horrible. Was anyone killed?"

Nabili. He'd seen her die, watched her blown apart. The realization came to him out of nowhere.

A groan was wrenched from the depths of him, way down in the solar plexus, so deep and so raw that it was agony to even make the sound.

"Sorry. Did I hurt you?" Soft hands pushed back his hair. Paula laid her head on the carpet trying to see his face.

He couldn't do this any longer. Riley pushed himself up, fighting his strained back to get himself to a seated position. Bare chested, his pants partly unzipped, he sat back on his heels.

"My mate from the SAS, who was with me in Kabul, told me the explosion was a suicide bomb attack on a primary school."

"Oh." Understanding dawned in Paula's eyes.

"But I didn't remember. Until just now. Some of it, at least. While you were working on me I—" He couldn't articulate all the feelings roiling around inside him. "That massage is powerful juju. You should be careful how you use that stuff."

"Massage heals. What do you remember?"

"The teacher was a young woman named

Nabili." He swallowed hard and his voice dropped to a whisper. "She and her whole class, twenty young girls, were…killed. Blown into pieces."

Paula's hand went to her mouth. "Oh, no."

"I was first on the scene. I had the suicide bomber in my sights. I—" He shook his head. Everything was blank after that. He couldn't remember firing his gun. "That's weird. I can't recall anything else after that."

"Don't try too hard. It'll come to you."

He wasn't sure he wanted it to. "Maybe. Anyway, I remembered the most important part."

He reached into his back pocket and pulled out his wallet and the photo inside. Even though he hadn't known its significance till now, he'd felt compelled to keep it nearby. "This is Nabili."

"She's beautiful." Paula studied the oval face draped in flowing blue cloth. The Afghani woman had even features, light skin and large green eyes framed in thick black lashes. Paula turned the photo over and saw the name written on the back. "And she was the teacher?"

"I believe so."

"Was she your girlfriend?"

He shook his head. "Does she look like she'd be allowed to go out with an Australian guy?"

"Secret romance? Maybe she got caught. Could she be the victim of an honor killing?"

"No, it was a suicide bomber, aimed at destroying a school for girls." No wonder he'd been so messed up. He'd seen the young woman die a gruesome death, along with all her young charges.

Paula studied the photo. "She looks like Katie."

Riley shifted next to Paula to look over her shoulder. He could smell her hair, her skin. He wanted to touch her. Instead he made himself stick to what they were talking about. This was important. "I thought so, too. It might be partly why I felt so bad seeing her killed."

Paula twisted her head. Her blue eyes searched his. "You think that explosion is the cause of your PTSD?"

"What else can it be? It's the worst thing that happened to me in Afghanistan."

"I guess it makes sense." With the tip of her baby finger, she wiped away the remains of a tear from below his eye. "Sorry about making you upset."

"It was worth it. I found out something important." He took the photo from her and tucked it into his wallet. Looked at Paula.

Conversation had ended. She wasn't moving away. Her deep blue eyes, her full pink lips, were so close. *Kiss her.* It wasn't so much a thought as an urgent desire. Kissing definitely wasn't something partners did. But it was what a man did when his attraction to a woman was so strong it overrode his personal code of conduct.

Leaning forward, he kissed her, softly at first, then with greater pressure. She moaned softly and his pulse quickened. Her lips were plump and delicious, her breath warm and sweet.

He took her shoulders and gently turned her to face him, seeking a better angle to kiss. Paula rose on her knees and planted her oiled hands on either side of his face, her mouth opening to his.

A few minutes ago Riley had been overwhelmed by negative emotions. Now a sweet hot rush of desire swept them away. He'd wanted to kiss Paula since the first day he'd met her. He'd held back for a whole lot of good reasons.

The reasons hadn't gone away.

Reason itself had disappeared.

He began to undo her buttons. She pushed his hands away. He was moving too fast. Hell, it shouldn't be happening at all. They were partners.

"You're right. This is inappropriate. I'm so—"

"Don't you dare apologize." She whipped her shirt off over her head. "We're going to have sex. It's going to be great. Then we're never going to speak about it again. Got that?"

"Uh...I guess." He shouldn't agree to anything while under the influence of his hormones. On the other hand, while under the influence of his hormones he would agree to anything—

There went her bra. The most luscious pair of

breasts he'd ever seen bounced free. Riley blinked and reached out to cup them in his palms. Best not to overthink.

PAULA FELT RILEY'S HANDS close around her breasts and her eyes shut on a sigh that came right from her belly. Inappropriate or not, she didn't care. His touch felt like heaven. His kisses were better than chocolate. She liked him, she liked what he was doing to her. And she wanted more.

She was tired of being cautious. Tired of examining every feeling and idea that came into her head to see if she should act or if she should clamp down on her desires. She was tired of keeping herself wrapped up tight as a drum in case she inadvertently let loose with "inappropriate" behavior. For seven years she'd kept her nose clean. For what? Last she looked, no one was handing out medals for being Miss Goody Two-shoes.

Riley was an honorable man. He liked her kid, and if that bulge in his jeans was anything to go by, he was hot for her. So what if they gave each other a bit of release this once? It didn't mean they were in a relationship. She wasn't ready for that. Neither was he. But if they were adult about this, they could have sex without it interfering with their work.

He was hot. Literally hot. His skin felt like it was burning up. All the time she'd been massaging him, feeling his corded muscles and broad shoulders, she'd imagined what it would be like to have her breasts pressed against his chest, skin to skin. Now she knew, and it was good. So very, very good.

Her hands were still slick from massage oil. She moved them across his pecs, tracing the outline of his flat nipples, threading her fingers through the dusting of dark hair that narrowed to a line down his belly. Then he claimed her mouth again and the jolt of heat turned her brain to mush.

He rose, pulling her up with him. Then he winced.

She eased away. "Is your back up to this?"

Riley twisted his torso experimentally. "My back does what I tell it to."

She laughed. "Yeah, right. You're such a hard ass."

"Okay, credit where it's due. You are some sort of miracle worker. My muscles have loosened up."

Her expert eye assessed the degree of movement. He might still be in a bit of pain but what she had planned wouldn't hurt him. In fact, she'd make him forget all about his back.

"Come with me." She took his hand and led him to her bedroom. "You're going to lie down and do exactly what I tell you to do."

"You're turning me on." Riley brought her into

his arms for another kiss. He whispered in her ear, "I have my handcuffs in the car."

"If we run out of ideas, we'll get them." It was a good thing no one from the station could hear them. "I have something special I want to try on you."

"What about what I want?" He stroked her breast with just the right firmness, holding up the nipple for a quick and devastating suck. "Are we going to have a battle for control in the bedroom, too?"

Paula unzipped him and pushed her hand down his pants. *Oh, yes, he has one helluva package.* "What battle? I'm in control."

"You think?" He flipped her onto the bed and moved over her. Holding her wrists together over her head with one hand, he trailed his fingers down her breasts, touching, tormenting.

Paula thought about ways she could break his hold.

And rejected them.

She moved her hips instead, her legs parting in invitation. Riley brought his mouth down to hers, kissing her as he slid his hand up her leg, beneath her skirt. His thumb brushed between her legs where she could already feel the moisture seeping through her cotton panties.

Then his mouth followed his hand, kissing his way up her inner thigh while he tugged down her panties and flicked them away. He released her wrists but she was too limp to struggle. She found enough strength to pull his boxers down to his thighs. He sprang loose.

Come to Mama. "Hang on." She fumbled in her bedside drawer for condoms—and flipped over her self-help book, hoping he hadn't seen the title.

He did get an eyeful of her revolver. "Is that a gun in your drawer or are you just happy to see me?"

She winced. "Oh, that's bad."

"Hey, there's not a lot of blood circulating upstairs." He stood up to drop his jeans.

He put on a condom and she pulled him on top of her. He took her mouth with his, cupped both breasts in his hands and nudged her legs apart, sliding home.

They made love sharp and fast, bodies slick with sweat and massage oil, hips pumping, breath coming in pants. There was no more talking, no joking asides. Paula concentrated on Riley's face inches away, and his hard, scarred body moving against hers. Their rhythm wasn't perfect—she was too needy and he was in too much pain. But every thrust built the ache inside her to a higher peak. Her teeth ground together in the effort to get closer.

A bead of sweat dripped off his brow onto her

cheek. Was he tiring because of his back? No, please no. Not when she was so close....

She gave a heave and flipped him over, straddling his hips. His hands moved up to trace the dip of her waist and flared again to push up on her breasts. The heat in his eyes lit a fire in her belly. She paused to catch her breath then lowered herself onto him, holding his gaze. One thrust, two... and she broke. Riley, rigid and drenched, gave another pump of his hips and came, too.

Paula collapsed on top of him. If this was a mistake, she would take her lumps.

CHAPTER NINE

RILEY BLINKED HIS eyes, squinting against the sunlight coming through the cracks in Paula's bedroom curtains. He stretched cautiously, not wanting to wake her. His body felt rested, with a sense of physical ease he hadn't experienced for weeks.

No headache, no backache. He'd slept through the night. Whether it was the massage or the sex or spending time with Paula and Jamie he didn't know, or much care. He felt good.

Only a corner of the sheet covered his hips and thighs. Paula had pulled the covers over her, tucking them in around her neck. Not used to sleeping with someone. Well, he was out of practice, too.

He turned on his side to look at her. Her blonde hair was spread across the pillow, her mouth was swollen from kissing, her chin lightly burned by his beard. A slight frown drew twin creases between her eyebrows. Even in sleep she worried. Not good. He wished he could wipe away that anxiety and make her feel safe.

He remembered the book he'd glimpsed in

her bedside table. *The Courage to Be Yourself.* Why did she need a self-help manual? He'd never known a woman so gutsy.

Her lips twitched and curved up. Ah, that was better. He smoothed back a strand of hair that had fallen over her face and leaned in to kiss her cheek.

Her eyes, a dreamy blue, opened, and took a moment to focus. "Oh, my God." She twisted to look at the clock. "We're going to be late for work."

"Who cares?" He stretched luxuriously. Then rolled onto his side, gathering her into his arms, twining his legs with hers. His mouth sought the spot behind her ear. She liked to be kissed there.

"No time for this." Paula struggled to break free.

He released her. She shot out of bed, reaching for her dressing gown on a hook on the closed door. "Jamie will be up any minute. If you want a shower, have one now. Then you need to get going. Quickly."

"What time is it?" Like he gave a damn. Riley stretched again, revelling in his pain-free back and head. "You are a miracle worker, you know that? Come here and give me a kiss."

She threw his shirt at him. "Get out of bed. And remember, as far as Jamie is concerned, last night never happened. Got it?"

Ouch. She was serious. His smile faded. "I got

it." He rolled out of bed and started dressing. "I'll shower at home."

She yanked on her underwear drawer so hard that it came clear out of the dresser. Bras and panties fell in a heap on the carpet. Riley started to help her gather up her underwear.

"I'll get this. You just go." Lingerie clutched to her chest, she pleaded, "Please?"

"You don't want your son to know I've spent the night." He nodded. "I get it. It's too soon."

"I don't want *anyone* to know we spent the night together. Not the guys at the station, either."

Okay, now that really hurt. Even though he, too, was of the opinion that smart cops didn't get involved with work mates. In Paula's case he was willing to make an exception. "Why not?"

"Because..." She blew a wisp of hair off her forehead. "Just because."

"Not good enough."

"We're partners. It's not professional. We have to behave normally around the station. No flirting, no stolen kisses, no sidelong glances—"

"Were you being professional when you slept with the criminal you were investigating?"

Her head jerked. "That's a low blow."

"It's a valid question."

"I've learned from my mistakes." She got to her feet and stuffed the underwear in the drawer. "I needed to talk to you about something important last night. We got distracted. Now we don't have time."

Standing behind her, he took her by the shoulders and pressed a kiss on her neck. "Just tell me you don't regret making love."

Her shoulders slumped. "No, I don't regret it." She met his gaze in the mirror and sighed. "Sorry, I'm being a bitch." She turned in his arms and cupped his jaw in her hands. "Thank you for all the work you did on my house. I feel safer thanks to you. My son is safer thanks to you."

"Then I've fulfilled my purpose in life." He spoke lightly but he meant every word.

Protecting people was what he did. It was why he'd gone into the SAS. It was what he was trained for. And it was what gave his life meaning. He'd struggled when he came out of the army until John had recruited him for the Summerside P.D.

He pulled on his jeans. "Will I see you again?"

"In less than an hour we'll be on patrol together. So I think that's a yes."

"You know what I mean."

Paula hesitated. "We really don't have time for this conversation right now."

"Twenty-five words or less."

"Okay, it's not just the moral code thing. I like you. I like you a lot. But you're not stable." She said it bluntly, looking him in the eye. "You've been amazing with Jamie and you've helped me enormously. But for my son's sake, hell, for my own sake, I can't get involved with a man who has unresolved emotional issues. Mental issues. Whatever they are."

"I feel different this morning, honestly." Riley twisted his torso, touched his toes a couple of times. "Not just physically but mentally, too. Lighter. I think I've made a breakthrough, no doubt thanks to you and your massage."

"Massage is good but it's not that good. I doubt your recovery is going to be that easy."

He tried to kiss her again. "You wouldn't want me to have a relapse because you rejected me, now would you?"

"I don't know if you're cured but you're definitely back to being chatty." She rose on her tiptoes and kissed him. Then placed a finger over his mouth. "One-off."

"Mum, I can't find my school shirt." Jamie, still in his pajamas, trailed after her down the hall as she carried the clothes hamper to the laundry room.

"Did you look in your dresser drawer?" Even the obvious wasn't necessarily obvious to a six-year-old.

"I'll go check." His footsteps thudded lightly as he ran to his room.

Riley had tiptoed out of the house ten minutes ago, seconds before Jamie came out of his room.

Paula had showered, dressed in her uniform and fixed her hair. On the outside she looked every inch the cop. On the inside she was a woman who ached in all the right places. She could still feel Riley's lips pressed to her breast, his hands moving over her body. How was she going to face him in the Incident Room and pretend they hadn't had awesome sex?

Paula transferred clothes from the basket to the washing machine. She grabbed the blue flannel shirt lying on top of the machine and started to push it in with the rest of the laundry. The unfamiliar feel of it stopped her. Riley's shirt. She crushed the soft fabric between her fingers and a smile came unbidden. Then she sighed. She was so used to fending for herself, to being strong for Jamie, that she wasn't certain how to react to Riley's protectiveness. She wasn't his girlfriend, she wasn't even a friend, really. And yet, they depended on each other, at work and at home, too. And now they'd had sex, further complicating their partnership.

If he was a different sort of man, if she wasn't so worried about Nick, they might have a chance together. But Riley had too many problems. And she couldn't relax until Nick was out of her and Jamie's lives for good.

She turned the shirt over in her hands. Should she wash it before returning it? It didn't *look* dirty and he hadn't worn it to work in. Feeling a bit odd, she raised the shirt to her nose. It smelled clean, like laundry detergent and fresh air. And Riley. She breathed in again and caught a faint tang of spicy aftershave…and the indefinable scent that came from contact with his skin. It was a good smell.

"What are you doing?" Jamie asked, now wearing his shirt. His hair stuck up in tufts from pulling it over his head.

"Nothing." Flustered, she pushed Riley's shirt into the washing machine, shut the door and added detergent. "Go start breakfast. I'll be right there."

She punched a few buttons, twirled the dial and pressed start. Jamie hadn't moved from in the doorway. A frown wrinkled his forehead. "What's wrong, mate?"

He dropped his gaze. Pushing at the groove between the tiles with his sock-covered toe, he said in a small voice, "I want to see my father."

My poor baby. She crouched to give him a hug. "We've been through why you can't, sweetheart. What started this again?" Please don't let Nick have gotten to him somehow.

"Nothing. I just don't get it. Why is he bad?"

Paula took a deep breath. "He sells drugs."

"Like at the pharmacy?"

"No, *bad* drugs. Illegal, harmful drugs that are against the law to take or to sell."

"But…you're a cop. You wouldn't…" Jamie's nose scrunched as he tried, and failed, to come up with the words to express what he only vaguely knew his mother and this bad man must have done to produce a baby.

Lord help her. How did she explain to her child that she'd had sex with a man so she could arrest him? It sounded sleazy and it was. No fine words about "serving the greater good" could whitewash her actions in the black and white view of a child. And telling her son she'd made a mistake was tantamount to telling him that *he* was a mistake.

She crouched before Jamie and looked him in the eye. "Sometimes, out of bad things, good things come." She hugged him hard and tears pricked her eyelids. "The good thing—the best thing in my life—is you."

Jamie still looked unhappy. Maybe she'd told him that once too often without delivering what he really wanted.

"I wish I could give you a father, baby. I wish—" She broke off and had to swallow. She wanted to give Jamie the sun, the moon and the stars, the whole world. Instead, as the son of a convicted criminal, she'd given him a social handicap that would affect him for the rest of his life. She didn't have the words to express how sad and ashamed that made her feel.

So she thrust her feelings aside, gave him another hug and got to her feet. "Let's go. It's time for school."

SLEEPY SUMMERSIDE POLICE station was buzzing with activity when Paula finally got to work. John's office door was closed but through the glass she could see him in earnest conversation with a tearful woman in her late forties. Crucek and Jackson were talking volubly as they worked together at a computer. The phone in Dispatch was ringing off the hook. Patty could only say, "Hold please," before picking up another line and repeating the request.

Three teenage boys wearing the local high school uniform were waiting in reception. They looked about fifteen and all had gelled hair styled in elaborate waves that stood out in different directions. Two boys wore sullen expressions. The third boy sat a little apart, looking terrified.

"What's going on?" Paula whispered to Patty.

"They were caught with drugs at school," Patty murmured. Then she spoke into her headset. "Summerside Police Department. Hold please."

Paula walked through the bull pen into the locker room. Riley stood at his locker with his back to her. One glimpse and she went soft all over.

Damn. This was exactly why she hadn't wanted

to get romantic with a fellow officer. How could she be a tough cop if she was obsessing about her partner—thinking about sex, wondering if he really liked her, speculating about where it was leading?

Last night she *had* wanted to get busy with Riley. She'd wanted him so badly she'd gone against her better judgment.

He reached up to the top shelf in his locker and his shirt stretched across his shoulders, reminding her of his naked back, scarred and muscled and beautiful. Should she run away before he saw her or should she say something? She hated that she'd suddenly turned cowardly and indecisive.

Delinsky came out of the shower room, shrugging into his shirt. "Drummond. Did you hear the news?"

Riley turned. Their eyes met.

"Something about school boys and drugs." She dragged her gaze away from Riley. "Did they get caught smoking a joint?"

There, she'd done it. She'd acted cool, as if Riley was merely the guy she regularly exchanged snarky insults with. She risked another peek at him. His expression was a complete blank. Even though she was getting exactly what she'd asked for, it cut her to the bone. Again reinforcing why she didn't get involved. Relationships messed with her head.

"Crystal meth," Riley answered for Delinsky. "Someone sold it to them on the way to school this morning. A teacher saw the boys talking to an older man and got suspicious when money changed hands."

Meth. Not again.

"Do we have a description of the suspect?" Paula hoped it was Nick so she could arrest him. But he never did the dirty work himself.

"Jackson and Crucek took the boys' statements," Delinsky said. "John wanted you and Riley to work with the drug-liaison unit, but you were both late." He smirked. "Whatcha been doing? Something the rest of us would like to know about?"

Paula bent down, pretending to retie her bootlace. She didn't trust herself to speak.

"Delinsky, get your mind out of the gutter," Riley drawled. "Drummond, get your ass ready for work."

He walked past her, close enough for her to feel the breeze of his passing. Close enough to hear his barely whispered, "Your very hot ass."

She stifled a gasp and kept her red face down till Delinsky had left the locker room. How dare Riley? He was unbelievable, in control of himself and the situation, and completely disregarding her express wishes. Leaving her floundering with embarrassment and, yes, feeling a little flattered but totally off balance.

The door swung shut behind him. She quickly buckled on her vest and went out to the bull pen.

Patty pointed to the Incident Room. Paula hurried inside. John stood before a whiteboard and the other officers were seated on metal chairs arranged in three rows. "Glad you could join us, Drummond."

"Sorry, boss." She took a seat on the opposite side of the room from Riley. And instantly realized her mistake. Prior to last night she would have sat next to him as a matter of course. Instead she'd swung too far in the opposite direction. Maintaining a neutral attitude was going to be even harder than she thought.

John briefed them on the morning's events. "Crystal methamphetamine has become a presence on Summerside streets. Sixteen ounces was recovered from the vehicle of Timothy Andrews, deceased, with an approximate street value of $12,800. This morning at 7:55 a.m. the principal of Summerside Secondary College called police in to question three boys about the alleged purchase of the drug on school grounds. Five grams of crystal meth was discovered in one of the boys' lockers. Crucek, did any of those kids give you a name for who sold them the drugs?"

"No, boss." Crucek consulted his notepad. "Warren Tipman, aged fifteen, alleged he'd never seen the man before. According to his description, corroborated by the other boys, the suspect was approximately thirty-five years old, with light brown hair, indeterminate eye color. He wore a black jacket, blue jeans and running shoes. Distinguishing features—he chewed his fingernails."

Paula's lungs deflated. It wasn't Nick. Of course not. It wasn't going to be that easy to get him behind bars and out of Jamie's life.

Feeling someone's gaze on her she glanced sideways. Across the room, Riley was watching her, wondering perhaps, if she knew more than she was letting on. She did, in fact. But could he still doubt her loyalty to the force after last night? She shook her head slightly and faced front.

"Anything else?" John asked.

Jackson lumbered to his feet and smoothed back his sparse hair. "Prints have been obtained from the plastic bag containing the ice. We're awaiting a computer check with known drug dealers in the local area. A report is being prepared for a joint investigation with the Frankston Drug Task Force."

"Thank you, Jackson. Good work."

"Boss," Jackson said, still standing. "Crucek and I think we know who this guy is. He's been nabbed before for pushing ecstasy. Shall we pay him a visit?"

"Wait for the print results. For now, everyone be alert," John said. "Officers Drummond and Henning, stay behind. The rest of you, dismissed."

The other officers filed out, talking among themselves. When they were gone Riley was left sitting on one side of the room and Paula on the other with rows of empty chairs between them.

"What's with you two?" John demanded. "Have a lover's tiff?"

She froze then realized he was joking. "That's right. He hogs the covers." She picked up her hat and moved to the chair next to Riley. "What's up, boss?"

"Moresco has been sighted locally," John said.

Her fingers tightened around her cap. "Where?"

"In the Grand Hotel in Frankston." John gave her a hard stare. "Has he made contact again?"

"As a matter of fact, he did. Yesterday." Paula could feel Riley start. She turned to him. "I was going to tell you but…something else came up."

A faint wash of color appeared in his cheeks. So, he wasn't quite as cool as he seemed.

"He called while— He called yesterday around noon." Paula left Riley to figure out the timing. She wasn't ready to tell John she and Riley were seeing each other off duty, even just as friends. It might lead to questions. And besides, there were more pressing topics to discuss. She glanced at John. "I need to tell you something. Possibly I should have mentioned it earlier but I didn't think it was relevant to the case, if there is a case, against Moresco."

"What is it, Drummond?" John said. "Spit it out."

"Nick Moresco..." She took a deep breath. "Is the father of my son."

John quietly laid the marker he'd been holding in the tray of the whiteboard. "You're right. I should have been informed of this earlier."

Was this going to affect her promotion? John was the best sergeant she'd worked for since going back to uniform. He listened and actually considered what his officers suggested. He didn't ask them to do anything he wouldn't do. And he didn't play favorites or pick on anyone. She liked him as a person and hated knowing she'd let him down. "As I said, I didn't think it was relevant—"

"Of course it's relevant." John shook his head. "Whether he's involved in these particular crystal meth incidents or not, he's a known criminal and you're an officer belonging to Summerside P.D. You're also a member of the community and one of us. I haven't known you long but I'd like to think we could become friends. Your safety and well-being are my concern."

"Yes, boss." Paula blinked, blindsided. Being part of a community, having friends, even taking a lover were luxuries she hadn't allowed herself for a very long time. First Riley taking the time to secure her home, now this declaration from John. She was touched. "Thank you, boss."

"Now that that's out of the way, let's get down to business," John said. "What did Moresco want?"

"To see Jamie." She hesitated. "He also informed me he bought a business in Summerside." She turned to Riley. "The ice-cream shop."

Riley's jaw literally dropped. He looked hard at her as if to make sure he'd heard right. "My stepmother works there. You had this information since yesterday and you didn't tell me?"

Paula tried not to squirm. She should have found the time to tell him but she'd forgotten all about it once she'd started his massage. "As I said, I was preoccupied."

"Some things are more important than—"

"Really?" she said coolly. He hadn't thought so last night. In fact, she'd rarely seen a man so eager. And he knew damn well neither of them had been thinking about anything except getting their gear off.

"Settle down. This is no time for one of your spats." John eased himself onto the edge of the table. "What else did Moresco say?"

She cast her mind back. Then shook her head. "Nothing really. He claims he's not manufacturing or distributing drugs. He claims he returned to his religious roots while in prison."

Riley snorted. "Yeah, right."

"Do you believe him?" John asked Paula.

"It's possible he's become religious. I know members of his family are strong believers."

"Unfortunately religion isn't inconsistent with criminal activity," Riley said. "A leopard doesn't change its spots."

"We could bring him in for questioning," Paula suggested. "Make up your own mind."

People *could* change. If she didn't believe that she wouldn't have fifteen self-help books on her shelf. On the other hand, she'd never found the magical formula that led to self-actualization. She wasn't even sure what that meant in practical terms.

"All crims are liars," Riley said. "Or didn't you know that?"

"We're trained to detect when they're lying," she shot back.

"How are you going to bring him in?" John asked, ignoring Riley's comment. "Do you know where he's living?"

"No, but I now have his mobile phone number."

"You friend him on Facebook?" Riley asked.

"This is serious." Paula turned to John. "Calling him is no good now that I think of it. Nick wouldn't come in voluntarily for questioning. And there's no point tracing his call to my house. He always uses prepaid phones so there's no record of calls or contact details."

"If he owns the ice-cream shop there will be

records of his residence and other details," Riley said. "I'll look into that."

"He usually puts his property in a family member's name," Paula said.

"You say he wants to see his son…" John mused.

"Oh, no." Paula got to her feet. "I'm not using Jamie as bait. The kid is messed up enough about not being allowed to see his father without being promised a visit only to find his dad being questioned by the police."

"Jamie doesn't need to know about that," John said. "He wouldn't even need to know Moresco is his father if you made that stipulation. We could save a lot of time tracking him down if you arranged to meet with him. Find out as much as you can about his current circumstances then leave it to the Frankston detectives to pull him in for questioning."

Paula paced through the row of chairs, kicking one out of her way. "I don't want Moresco in the same town as my son, let alone in the same room."

"Summerside never had hard drugs until…recently," Riley said quietly.

Paula stopped short. He wasn't being snide. He was simply telling the truth. Crystal meth had found its way to Summerside because of her relationship with Nick. The evidence was circumstantial but that's undoubtedly what Riley and John believed. She believed it, too.

"If I'm the cause of the problem, I will fix it. Somehow." She pressed a hand across her forehead. The creases between her eyes felt as if they were becoming permanent.

Riley and John exchanged a glance.

"What?" she said. "I will do something."

"*You* are not why Moresco is dealing drugs, here or anywhere else," Riley said. "He's doing it because he's a criminal."

"No one's blaming you," John added.

They didn't need to. The fact was obvious, despite what they were saying. True, she wasn't responsible for Nick choosing to pursue illegal activities. But if she hadn't slept with him, he wouldn't be in Summerside looking for his son. She had to make this right, for Jamie's sake. Even if that meant putting his father behind bars again for a very long time.

But how would she catch him? Nick was motivated by two things—money and family. She didn't have enough money to interest him. All she had was Jamie.

No, she couldn't use her son, an innocent child. She wrapped her arms around her waist, feeling sick. Did she really have any choice? By the time they gathered enough evidence to charge him with something he could distribute crystal meth all over the peninsula.

Paula approached the two men, keeping enough

distance that she could watch both their faces. "Why stop at questioning him? Let's go one step further. What do you say to a sting operation?"

"What are you suggesting?" John asked.

"I make Nick a business proposition. I pretend I'm leading a new drug task force. All information and evidence will pass through me. I'll say I will turn a blind eye to methamphetamine distribution in my area in exchange for a kickback."

Riley and John were silent, absorbing the implications. Paula had only thought of the plan this minute, but it could work.

"Nick lost all his cash and most of his assets in the last bust," she went on. "He's starting from scratch again. This will be a boost for him."

"How will you get him to come to the party?" Riley asked.

She paced some more, tugging on her ponytail. "There's only one surefire way. Jamie. You're right, boss, he doesn't have to know Moresco is his father." She met John and Riley's gazes. "I'll use him once and once only, as the initial lure to gain Moresco's confidence."

"What makes you think he'll buy your proposition?" Riley asked. "You're a cop. You put him away last time."

"I'm also the mother of his son." Paula avoided Riley's gaze. "I'll pretend that since my demotion I've become disillusioned with the police force.

I'll pretend I've missed him and I want him to be part of Jamie's and my life. That we'll be together, as a family."

CHAPTER TEN

RILEY KNEW SHE was talking about a ruse not reality, but her plan to form a family with Nick Moresco hit him like a kick in the gut. Which was nuts. He'd known her only a short time and slept with her exactly once. An encounter never to be repeated, according to her.

"He'll flay you alive when he finds out he's been duped," Riley said.

"By that time, he'll have been arrested and be safely behind bars," Paula replied. "If all goes according to plan."

"If you're sure about this, I'm on board," John said. "We'll need to run it by Frankston P.D. Get their assistance. We don't have the resources to handle it all by ourselves."

"No, it's too risky," Riley said. "I looked up the guy's case files. He's had people kneecapped, bashed, even killed."

That's the guy Paula had slept with. And now Riley was involved with her, a woman capable of crossing a moral boundary he wouldn't ever consider—sleeping with a criminal under her investigation. He scrubbed his hands over his face. She deserved so much more than Moresco. Like a crazy ex-soldier, perhaps?

No, he was over the PTSD. Cured.

"I agree, it's risky," John conceded. "But it could work. She would wear a wire the whole time. You would be her backup, make sure she's safe."

"A backup needs to be fit for the job," Paula said.

Riley felt her gaze on him, willing him to speak. Or *she* would? Was this tit for tat? He kept his mouth shut. Maybe he had had a bout of PTSD but he felt fine now.

"What do you mean?" John glanced between them.

Still Riley said nothing. If John knew about the incident at the school, he might take Riley off Paula's case. Jackson, Crucek and Delinsky were good cops but they didn't have Special Forces training or his ability to instantly size up a threat and act accordingly, even if it meant letting the situation play out a little longer. Bottom line, Paula needed protection and he was the best man for the job.

"Are you going to tell John or am I?" Gently, briefly she touched his knee. "The fact that you haven't already talked about this with your old friend suggests to me that you're in denial."

She wasn't badgering him, she was…caring. That's what undid him.

"All right." Riley raised his palms. "I've been having migraines, nightmares, insomnia."

"Don't forget the panic attack outside the primary school," Paula prompted.

Okay, caring was one thing, squealing on him was another. Riley bristled. "While we're at it, maybe you should fill John in on the break and enter Moresco did on your house over the weekend."

"Whoa, slow down. Panic attack? Break and enter? You first." John pointed at Paula. "Why didn't you report it?"

"There was no damage. Nothing to report."

"Break and enters still need to be filed. All the more reason since it was Moresco."

"He left a toy for Jamie. That's all."

John just looked at her and shook his head.

"You see," Riley said to her. "You're the only person who doesn't think that's sinister."

"I think it's downright creepy," Paula protested. "But what's the good of being a cop if you can't take care of yourself?"

"We don't tolerate mavericks at Summerside P.D.," John said. "File a report, Constable."

"Yes, boss." Paula threw Riley a dark look.

"As for you," John said, turning to Riley. "What's all this about panic attacks? I've noticed you haven't been yourself lately. Why didn't you say anything?"

Riley sat to attention like the strong soldier he wanted to believe he still was. "I was dealing with it in my own way."

"I'm your superior officer," John said, then added in a softer tone. "And I'm your friend, you dope. Tell me what's going on."

Riley was silent, his jaw working. The last thing he wanted was for people to worry about him. Maybe he and Paula had something more in common besides chemistry.

"We think it's something to do with what happened in Afghanistan," Paula said. "We think it's post-traumatic stress disorder."

"*You* think," Riley shot back.

"What's your diagnosis?" Paula demanded. "A bad case of the collywobbles?"

Despite his annoyance, he wanted to grin at *collywobbles*. It was something his mother might have said back in the day.

Riley quickly filled John in on what he knew of the explosion in Afghanistan and what he remembered about witnessing Nabili's death.

"But I believe I've turned a corner," Riley said. "Talking about it with my army mate and remembering other things on my own has helped me understand. My migraine has disappeared. I slept like a rock last night."

"That's all good, but it's too soon to call yourself cured," Paula insisted. "I used to work with a cop who suffered from PTSD after being shot in the chest while on duty. He had good days and bad days but in the end he had to get treatment. Trauma victims don't get better by themselves."

"I agree," John said. "Riley, if you want to play a role as backup to Paula in a sting operation, then you need to have a session with the police psychologist, Simone Richards."

Riley wanted to protest more—he had no time for shrinks—but between the two of them, they had him boxed in. "Okay, I'll see the psychologist. No big deal. I'll have a chat with her and she'll pronounce me sane."

"Good." John rose. "Paula, write up a proposal for your sting operation and we'll set up a meeting with Frankston to keep them apprised of events."

"Boss." Paula stood, too, and cleared her throat. "If I'm going to lead this operation, I should have detective status."

"We talked about that—"

"Temporarily. Make me Acting Detective."

A grudging smile tugged at John's mouth. "I guess the budget could stretch to a stint of Acting."

"Thanks, boss. It'll look good on my record."

"I'll put in a requisition." John nodded to them both and left the Incident Room.

"You've got balls, I'll give you that," Riley said.

"At least we're off traffic patrol." Paula led the way to the bull pen. She glanced at Riley. "Hope my being detective won't put your nose out of joint."

"I'm sure it will have no effect whatsoever on our working or personal relationships." He just wished he'd thought of it first. But he hadn't put in the time and he didn't have the detecting chops that she had. He hoped all that authority wouldn't go to her head.

"I'm glad you're being mature about this." She sat at a desk and brought the computer out of sleep mode.

Riley leaned against a neighboring desk. "Do shrinks really make you lie on a chaise longue and tell them about your childhood?"

"How should I know?" Paula opened a Word document to type up a draft before she put it into official format.

"I thought you would have had your head examined after sleeping with a hard-core criminal." Riley rapped his knuckles on the desk and pushed off. He took a few steps and waited. What, no smart-aleck comeback? Was she already above their bicker-banter?

He glanced over his shoulder. She was giving him the finger. He started to grin, then sobered. She wasn't laughing. And he got that. Something he held against her couldn't be turned into a joke. Was it because she was officially his boss that he was trying so hard? Was he so small a man he could feel threatened?

He got coffee for both of them then pulled up a chair by her desk. "Sorry about the crack. That was out of line under the circumstances." He paused. "But I didn't appreciate you telling John about my panic attack."

"Somebody needed to say it."

"All right. We were both keeping things quiet that we didn't want people to know about. But after last night we're beyond sniping, don't you think?"

She sighed and looked at him. "I want the best for you."

"Same." He got lost for a few seconds in her eyes.

Paula pulled herself together first. "You left your flannel shirt at my house, by the way. I put it in the wash."

"The cuffs are frayed and it's missing buttons. Just throw it out."

"Sure? Because it's no trouble to bring it in."

"You'd be doing me a favor." He sipped his coffee and grimaced. The stuff was foul. "If we're going to do this sting, you need to tell me about Nick Moresco."

Paula glanced around. There was no one within earshot. "What do you want to know?"

Why you slept with him.

"What he's like. How your relationship evolved. How it all came down."

"I told you already."

"Tell me again, in more detail. You were undercover?"

She hit Save on the computer and leaned forward, twining her fingers together. "He had a shoulder injury from a bullet wound that hadn't healed well. I posed as a massage therapist. I did a crash course, intensive one-on-one for six months and received a special dispensation to get my license. I got a job in the spa where he went for his daily massages. Eventually we worked out a deal where I would come to his home."

Riley's eyebrows went up.

"For therapeutic massages," she added, her eyes flashing. "I was wired the whole time. Look, if you're going to be like that, I'm not talking."

He held up his hands. "Sorry."

"This is strictly between you and me." Color appeared high on her cheekbones and she couldn't look at him. "Don't even tell John, not as your sergeant or as your friend."

She *was* ashamed. All her bluster and defiance was a front. Riley almost felt sorry for her except that mingled with his pity there was the niggling feeling that she was right to be ashamed. Or was she a victim? He didn't know who was more conflicted over this, him or her. Keeping his expression neutral, he said, "I won't."

Paula narrowed her gaze at him as if trying to decide whether he could be trusted.

"I promise." He held up three fingers next to his head. "Scout's honor."

She relaxed a fraction. "Gradually Nick got used to having me around. I could tell he liked me. He'd flirt with me. We'd talk."

"What did you talk about?" What could she possibly have in common with scum like that?

"All sorts of things—art, music, European architecture. It doesn't matter." She dismissed that with a wave.

"The guy's a real Renaissance man."

Paula sat back. "Okay, that's it."

"I'll stop." He mimed zipping his lip.

She rolled her shoulders and took a sip of coffee. "One rainy winter day I went to his apartment. His shoulder was aching badly. It always got bad during the wet weather. But that day he couldn't relax enough for me to massage. I asked him what was bothering him. He wouldn't answer. He was edgy, almost nervous which was unusual for him. Usually he was cool and in control. I gave up trying to massage him. We had a drink together instead. Finally he told me he was meeting an important business associate that evening. Right then I knew this was the mega deal we'd been waiting for."

"What deal?" Riley asked.

"Our investigations so far had revealed he was negotiating a partnership with a local biker gang who were cooking crystal meth. He didn't trust bikers, thought they were thugs. But he figured if he provided them with the facilities to expand their production then he could expand his distribution."

"Don't the biker gangs have their own turf?"

"Nick wasn't interested in their turf. He had his sights on national and international trade. Like I said, he saw himself as a businessman."

Riley swirled his coffee and downed the dregs. He was going to have heartburn for sure. "So where did you come into all of this?"

"He wanted me to stick around to act as his hostess during the dinner meeting."

"And you agreed?"

"Of course. It was the break I'd been waiting for."

"Go on. Who was there?"

"In our camp was Nick, myself and Nick's right-hand man, Bruno. The guests were Al, the leader of the bikies, and his main man, a brick shithouse named Tony."

Our camp. Interesting that she'd aligned herself with the drug dealer. It was ridiculous to feel a twinge of jealousy. But he did. Art, music, European architecture... Could he converse intelligently on those subjects? Music, maybe—

"Hello, Riley." Paula snapped her fingers inches from his nose. "You asked about this. Are you listening?"

"Yep." He set his cup on the desk. "What happened next?"

"Nothing." She threw up her hands. "We ate a catered dinner, nothing too fancy. The guys played pool. They started drinking heavily. Then Al brought out a pipe and they all had a hit of crystal meth."

"Did you?"

"No." Paula was very firm on that. "I'd told Nick early on I had asthma so I couldn't take anything into my lungs. Plus I told him I had a phobia about needles so that let out shooting up. He was fine with that. He didn't do drugs himself. Bruno did the sampling for quality control."

The entrance from the parking lot opened. Jackson and Crucek entered, accompanied by a boy of about seventeen wearing the local private school uniform.

"In here." Jackson ushered the teen into an interview room.

Crucek headed for the coffee room, passing Paula and Riley. "He was spotted on the security camera, kicking in the liquor store window. He was going to a party and his parents refused to buy booze for him."

Paula mimed playing the world's smallest violin, eliciting a chuckle from Crucek.

As he left, Delinsky came through the door from reception. Patty followed, also looking for coffee.

"It's like Grand Central Station around here," Riley said. "Let's grab something from the deli and have an early lunch away from the station."

"I have to finish my proposal," Paula protested.

"I happen to know that John's got meetings all afternoon with divisional station heads. He won't be asking for it till tomorrow, earliest. Come on."

Riley rose and led the way to the parking lot. He held out his hand for the keys.

"Where are we going?" she said, handing them over.

No argument for once. "You'll see."

They bought a couple of sandwiches and some decent coffee to take away. Riley drove through the winding leafy streets to a small gravel parking lot atop the cliff overlooking the bay.

A single wisp of cloud rode high in a crystal blue sky. White sailing dinghies bobbed on the sparkling water.

Riley cut the engine. Theirs was the only car in the lot. He checked the rearview mirror for dog walkers. The street was clear. Houses on the opposite side of the road had their blinds closed against the afternoon sun.

He twisted in his seat and leaned over, sliding his hand into Paula's hair to gently drag her head closer.

"Hey…" She resisted, her gaze darting wildly.

"There's no one around. All through the briefing this morning I was thinking about you." He punctuated his comments with kisses either side of her lips. "Imagining you naked."

"Riley—"

He captured her mouth in a bold kiss, plunging his tongue between her parted lips. She returned the kiss, one hand on his shoulder, then the other, straining to get near.

Abruptly she pushed away and touched her glistening mouth with the back of her hand. "This isn't a good idea. I've got an opportunity to be Acting Detective. I don't want to screw things up. You brought me out here just to kiss me, didn't you?"

"So sue me." He grinned. "Better still, bite me." Whatever she said, she couldn't hide the fact that she'd kissed him back, with interest.

"I mean it, Riley. Last night was a one-off."

"I know. I'm cool with that."

"But you just admitted…" She flounced back into her seat. "It's not easy pretending nothing's going on. I look at you and I—"

"You what?" he asked, interested. "You want me all over again?"

Paula eyed him. "Is this where you brought girls in high school to make out?"

"One of several spots. I could give you a tour."

She rolled her eyes. "Do you want to hear the rest of my story, or not?"

"Yes, I do, tough girl." Riley passed her a brown bag and opened his own, taking out a foil package. He opened it, releasing the aroma of hot corned beef and melted Swiss cheese on rye bread. "Start talking."

"Imma mimma," she mumbled, her mouth full of turkey and lettuce. She chewed and swallowed. "I'm starving. Didn't realize how much."

"Confessing is hungry work."

"Who's confessing?" she countered sharply. "I'm telling you how I busted Moresco."

"Right. Carry on."

"Where was I? Oh, yeah, the guys were getting wasted, fooling around playing pool. I was wondering, where was the big drug deal? Then Nick started…" She took another bite of her sandwich.

"Started what?" Doing the hokey pokey? Raping her?

"Playing romantic music. He asked me to slow dance."

"While the biker thugs watched him grope you? Sounds *very* romantic."

"We went into the living room." Paula gazed out at the bay, her voice faraway. "He had a penthouse with floor-to-ceiling windows overlooking the Botanical Gardens and the lights of the city beyond. I asked him, didn't he need to do business? He said there was no rush. He sent them all away, even Bruno, his own guy. He said something didn't feel right. He had a sixth sense that someone was trying to pull a fast one on him."

"You?"

She nodded with an expression of sick awareness. "I didn't realize it at the time. I thought Nick meant Al, who was a really dodgy character. Or Bruno. He'd voiced concerns about his bodyguard's loyalty before. Nick could be quite paranoid, understandably in his situation."

She certainly identified with her criminal and his problems. There was a term for that, something long-term hostages felt for their captors. Then a thought occurred to Riley that almost made him open the car door and purge himself of his lunch. "After he'd gotten rid of everyone. Did he…hurt you?"

"No, just the opposite." She laid her half-eaten sandwich on the paper in her lap. "He asked me to stay the night. Said I was the only one he trusted." She glanced up. "I'd never done that before, gone that far with him. It felt like a test. Or a profound compliment. I'm not sure. In hindsight, I must have been pretty confused."

"You were wired, you say?" Riley prompted.

She nodded, averting her gaze. "You don't want to hear the details."

No, he didn't want to hear how Nick paid her compliments and she lapped them up. But he'd asked for it, and if he was going to be of real assistance in dealing with Moresco, he needed to know how the man operated. Riley had to forget that he'd made love to her last night and simply be a cop, assessing intel.

"I can handle it." Even if it killed him. "Go on."

"When he asked me to go into his bedroom, I told him I'd like to take a shower first."

"He didn't want to join you?" he asked, torturing himself.

"No, he was always good about letting me have space." She took a breath. "He presented me with a negligee. He made it seem as if he'd planned to give it to me anyway, whether I stayed or not. Said his cousin had a boutique or some such thing. For all I know that's true. Whatever. I showered and changed. When I came into the bedroom, he had champagne on ice and canapés. He must have seen I couldn't eat much at dinner. He didn't know I was a bundle of nerves, too." She paused. "Or maybe he did."

Romantic music, dancing, danger and compliments—she'd been seduced by a pro, Riley thought bitterly. He could imagine the bastard feeding her caviar, clinking glasses, all the clichéd romance moves.

"All I know is that he behaved like a gentleman."

Riley had assumed she'd been coerced, made to feel she had to put out or she'd lose her place in his entourage. The notion made it easier to excuse her, to blame the circumstances instead of her. Instead, what he was hearing was that she'd gone willingly, even eagerly, to Nick's bed. For some reason that made him feel like a fool. For the thousandth time, how could he be falling for a woman who could sleep with the enemy?

"You enjoyed it, didn't you?"

"No," she said sharply. Her hands crumpled the paper holding her sandwich. "You *are* jealous."

"Of a drug lord?" He snorted. "You've got to be joking."

And yet, unbelievably, he *was* jealous.

The air in the patrol car was hot and thick with tension. Now he could see why they shouldn't have slept together. How could he respect himself if he couldn't respect her?

Except that he would do it all over again, given the chance. Maybe he *was* nuts.

Riley lowered his window and sucked in the fresh sea breeze tangy with salt. This was getting too intense. Needing a distraction he focused on the small figures walking along the curving strip of sand to his left. It worked for only a moment before his mind returned to chewing over his relationship with Paula. Whether he wanted to sleep with her again or not, was moot. She'd made it clear there was to be no repeat of last night. Maybe he should be happy about that.

"So what happened after you had sex with him?" he asked, wanting to cut to the chase.

"I slept for awhile, maybe an hour. It had been a long day and I was exhausted." She frowned. "I wondered later if he'd put something in the champagne, something slow-acting." She shrugged. "I woke up and he was gone."

"What if he'd looked through your clothes while you were asleep? If he'd found the wire, things could have gotten ugly."

"I hadn't planned to sleep," she said. "I'd tucked the wire in my evening bag and put that on the bedside table next to me. I took note of the exact position so I'd know whether it had been tampered with. It hadn't.

"Anyway, I was lying there, wondering where he'd gone when I heard voices coming from the living room. I got up, wrapped a sheet around myself, and peeked out. Al had returned, by himself. He was shaking hands with Nick. The deal was done." She dropped her gaze to the remains of her sandwich.

She didn't need to spell it out. She'd literally

been asleep on the job, her wire off so she could have sex with the crim under investigation. What evidence she'd gathered had been enough to put Moresco away for only seven years instead of fifteen or twenty.

No wonder she felt ashamed.

Poor Paula.

"You've spent the last seven years beating yourself up over that night," he said. "Do you think you deserve a longer sentence than Moresco got?"

CHAPTER ELEVEN

PAULA PACED HER bedroom, steeling herself to make the phone call to Nick. Strength was the only way to deal with him. Strong wasn't how she was feeling, though.

Riley's grilling this afternoon had stirred up memories she'd been trying for seven years to forget. All day she'd been eaten up with guilt and shame.

Riley was right, she didn't deserve to suffer more than Nick. He was a criminal. She was a cop, on the side of law and order. Right now she had to put her past behind her and concentrate on the plan to take Nick down.

Picking up her phone, she dialed the number. "Hello, Nick?"

"Paula." Nick recognized her voice instantly. "I've been waiting to hear from you."

"I've thought about your request." She softened her voice. "In fact, I've been thinking a great deal about you. And Jamie." She let a beat go by. "And me."

She paused again, letting that sink in, and

crossed the hall to Jamie's room to double-check he was asleep. Sure enough, he was on his back, eyes shut, limbs sprawled over the twisted covers. His breathing was regular and deep. He was safe.

"You intrigue me," Nick said. "Go on."

Quiet jazz played in the background on his end of the line, reminding her of late nights and smoky bars. Where did he live now? At the trial it had come out that his penthouse apartment was registered in his mother's name, as were most of his assets. The penthouse, she knew, had been sold.

"I'd like to talk in person," Paula said. "We can meet at the little park next to the shopping strip in Summerside. You come alone. I'll bring Jamie."

"I'll be there. What day and time?"

"Tomorrow afternoon at four-thirty. On one condition," she warned. "Jamie isn't allowed to know you're his father."

Nick let loose a few words in Italian. He'd come to Australia in his late teens but he conversed with his family and friends in Italian. Paula had studied the language as prep for her undercover role. She'd forgotten most of it, but she didn't need to be fluent to tell that what he'd said wasn't complimentary.

"Take it or leave it." She yawned to make herself sound bored. "I don't want to hear you whine." Soft then hard, keep him guessing.

"I'll take it," Nick said. "You and Jamie only. No one else."

Paula clicked her phone off and sank onto her bed. Perspiration bathed her underarms and adrenaline had left a sick feeling in her stomach. Yet at the same time she was charged up, excited. She was a detective again, finally getting a chance to redeem herself.

Riley's final words of their conversation came to her. *Do you think you deserve a longer sentence than Moresco?* Why was she so wracked with guilt? She'd made a blunder, sure, but screw-ups happened all the time during undercover crime investigations. She hated that Riley despised her for sleeping with a crim. Thing was, she didn't blame him. As for his accusation that she'd *wanted* to sleep with Nick, well that was plain absurd. She'd been playing a role. She was glad Nick wasn't a troll—that would have made it a lot harder. But she hadn't been in love with him.

She was too agitated to sleep or watch TV or even read a book so she went to her sewing room and sat down with her quilt and pieces of fabric.

She studied the edge of the quilt then sifted through the fabric scraps for a yellow patterned piece. Ah, there was a sleeve from a dress she had years ago. It was cotton blend, a yellow background covered in tiny red strawberries. She'd worn this dress to accompany Nick to his box seat at the Grand Prix.

For a moment she hesitated, wondering whether to use the scrap because of its associations. Then she thought about Jamie asleep across the hall.

Like it or not, Nick was already woven into the fabric of her life.

She measured the gap in the quilt, marked the scrap with tailor's chalk, then cut out an irregular shape. While the iron was heating she found a reel of yellow thread in her sewing box. She turned back a narrow hem on the scrap and pressed it flat then sat down again to pin it to the quilt.

With the needle threaded, she shone the goose-neck lamp on her work and began to sew the scrap to the quilt with tiny even stitches.

With Riley she hadn't needed to pretend. She'd wanted him. She still wanted him. Sex wasn't the problem. If it was only lust, she might have had a discreet affair.

No, the problem was, she was starting to fall in love with him. She loved his keen intelligence coupled with the lame jokes, how handy he was with a hammer and screwdriver. The way he never let her get away with bullshit. She loved his battered soldier's body, and that he'd befriended an Afghani teacher and cared about girls getting an education.

The way Riley related to Jamie was the icing

on the cake, like a dream come true. She could almost see a piece of blue flannel taking its place in her quilt.

The needle pushed through the layers of cloth and pricked her finger. Paula sucked away a tiny bead of blood.

Riley was wonderful in many ways. Except…

She hated feeling as if she was always looking over her shoulder, waiting for him to flip out over some trigger he hadn't seen coming. She'd taken a chance sending Jamie to the hardware store with him and it had turned out fine. Next time they might not be so lucky. If anything happened to Jamie… She couldn't contemplate such a thing without feeling hollow.

There was an old joke—how many psychiatrists does it take to change a lightbulb? Only one, but the lightbulb has to want to change.

Riley was a troubled soul. He had problems he wasn't addressing without coercion. When—if— she got serious about a man, he would have to be a stable father for Jamie.

RILEY'S GAZE FOLLOWED the small green light flashing from left to right, then back again, every two seconds. He was seated in a comfortable chair in a light-filled room, holding the photo of Nabili loosely in his hands. Tears streamed over his cheeks, trickled under his jaw and down his neck. He made no move to wipe them away.

Simone Richards, a calm middle-aged woman with shoulder-length brown hair, sat opposite him on a straight-backed chair. A psychotherapist with twenty years experience, Simone had asked him many probing questions about his life since being discharged from the army. Sleep patterns, physical health, relationships, general state of mind, et cetera. To Riley's chagrin, she confirmed Paula's amateur diagnosis of post-traumatic stress disorder.

Simone hadn't bought his belief that he was cured, either. She'd said positive reinforcement could have caused his symptoms to go into remission but that the root cause of his problems hadn't been addressed. Or some such psychobabble mumbo jumbo.

Now she was employing Eye Movement Desensitization and Reprocessing or EMDR to treat him. Damned if he could see how following a green light with his eyes while talking about the explosion in Kabul would fix his panic attacks.

"Where do you feel it?" Simone had her pen poised above an open notebook.

She meant the unpleasant sensations triggered by looking at Nabili's photo and remembering how she'd died. The idea was to invoke the stress response—occurring in a primitive part of the brain devoted to emotion—and at the same time focus the thinking part of the brain onto the flashing green light.

Apparently this somehow defused the emotive power of the trigger. So far, it wasn't working.

"In my chest. It's tight. It…hurts." He flinched as a shaft of pain pierced his right temple. "And my head. My eyes. Everything hurts."

"What do you see?"

Riley stared at the flashing green light, but his mind's eye was focused inward. "It's bright, blinding. Like looking into the sun."

"What is happening?" Simone asked.

"There's a loud noise, an explosion. People are screaming. Children are—" Riley broke off, sweating. His heart raced. His arms and legs felt heavy. He needed to run but he couldn't. Something was flying toward him.

Oh, good Lord. It was a hand.

He shut his eyes, taking refuge in blackness.

"Keep looking at the light," Simone reminded him. "Go back to the moments before the explosion. What's happening?"

"I can't." Eyes still shut, he gripped the chair arms, breathing hard. "I can't remember."

"We'll stop there for today," Simone said. "Take a moment. Just relax. Go to your safe place."

Before they'd started the treatment Simone had gotten him to think of a safe place, somewhere he felt happy, comfortable and at ease. Riley sat with his eyes closed, blocking the final image with his safe place—Paula and Jamie around the dinner table. The laughter, warmth and acceptance were a balm to his pain. Gradually the visions and sounds receded. His heart slowed.

He opened his eyes. The green light was off. Simone was writing in her notebook.

Seeing him stir she glanced up. "Okay?" He nodded. "Can you tell me more about what you experienced in Kabul? What was your last recollection of Afghanistan?"

"Waking up in the hospital with a broken pelvis, three broken ribs and a punctured lung. Lacerations to the face and hands."

Simone tapped her pen against her notebook. "There must be records of where you were that day, what you were doing. Was anyone else injured?"

"My partner, who I was on patrol with that day, is still in Afghanistan. He knows what happened. I believe Nabili is dead, as are most, if not all, of her students."

"You believe. Don't you know?"

Riley unclenched his hands from the arms of the chair and flexed his fingers, getting the blood circulating again. "I never asked."

"Why do you think that was?"

"I don't know."

"Maybe you didn't want to know."

He moved his palms over his jeans. "What I don't understand is why the PTSD symptoms didn't come on right away," he said. "I've been out of the army nearly twelve months and I only just started getting headaches and nightmares."

"That's not uncommon. PTSD can occur years or even decades later in some cases. Usually an incident triggers the return of the memories. Think back over what you've been doing since you left the SAS. Has something different happened recently?"

"I was working at a nightclub in Frankston for the first three months. Then I trained for the police force and joined Summerside P.D. and moved back to Summerside."

"Are you living on your own or with family?"

"On my own, in my childhood home."

"There's no tension between you and other members of your family?"

He shook his head. "We all get along. I'm close to my younger sister. I see my father and stepmother regularly. They helped me move in. My dad is coming over this weekend to help me install new appliances." He smiled wryly. "It's going to be great to have a working stove again. I'm renovating."

I tore down my mum's kitchen.

"What is it?" Simone asked.

"Nothing." He shook his head. His mother had died twenty plus years ago. He'd come to terms with his loss. "I'm thinking ahead to stuff I have to do. It has nothing to do with Afghanistan."

Simone regarded him seriously. "Yet you thought about it now. There are no coincidences."

He glanced up, startled. "I beg your pardon?"

She glanced at her watch. "Our time it up for today."

"Who said that about coincidences?"

"I think it was Agent Mulder." She thought a moment. "Or it could have been Scully. Neither of them would have liked coincidences."

"I thought you were going to say Freud, or Jung."

"Do you want to schedule another session? I can do Tuesday, same time."

"I'll have to get back to you on that."

"Whatever it is you're blocking, you should search for it." Lightly she added, "The truth is out there."

Just what he needed, a shrink with a penchant for sci-fi. Riley shook her hand. "Thanks, doc."

Simone walked him to the door. She touched his shoulder. "Riley, this treatment often works quickly, with only a few sessions. But you have to be prepared to re-experience some painful memories. Possibly come up against some things you might not be expecting."

Yup, she was really making him want to come back.

"We confirmed the source of the PTSD, didn't we? Witnessing the Afghani pupils and Nabili getting blown up was the trauma. Then seeing the children at my sister's school was the trigger for my PTSD."

"Maybe," Simone said. "It could lie deeper."

Riley walked out of her clinic and put a hand up to shield his eyes against the bright sunlight. He'd done what John and Paula had asked of him, but he had no intention of repeating that experience. As far as he was concerned, he was in working order. If he was blocking something, it was probably the gory details of dying children. Who wouldn't block such a memory?

As he walked past the pub he looked through the big bay window. Darcy Lewis was pulling beers for a couple of tradesmen wearing overalls and sitting at the bar. Now there was therapy, a pint or two to decompress from what he'd just been through.

He pushed through the door into the brass and wood bar. "Hey, Darcy. What have you got on tap?"

Darcy angled a glass under the tap and pulled. "Try this Tassie lager. It's pretty good."

Riley slid onto a stool and reached for the foaming glass. He took a long deep draught. He'd met the beast within and faced up to it. Finally, he could stop thinking about it all and just enjoy a beer with a mate.

"THE MEETING BETWEEN me and Moresco is arranged for this afternoon," Paula told the group assembled in the Incident Room the next morning.

John, Riley and Detectives Leonard and Cadley from Frankston P.D. Drug Unit Investigation were present. She passed around a photo of Nick she'd taken one day when they'd walked along the pier at St. Kilda.

"This picture is seven years old. He's got more gray around the temples and a few more wrinkles but looks otherwise the same."

Paula had eaten a banana at 6:30 and nothing since. Riley had chosen today to bring in a box of goodies from the bakery. The smell of the warm pastries was making her salivate.

She ignored her stomach. John was going over the arrangements with the detectives from Frankston. "We'll have a wire on Constable Drummond. You two will be set up in an unmarked van in the Safeway parking lot half a block away, listening in."

Riley spoke up. "What's my role?"

"You'll be off duty." John scanned the room. "Any other questions?"

"My understanding was that I would be part of the team if I fulfilled your...requirements," Riley said. "Officer Drummond needs backup. She won't be packing so she'll need someone to protect her if things turn ugly."

Paula glanced at John. They'd discussed this privately and she'd asked that Riley not be present, in spite of his session with the psychologist. She didn't want to worry about him having an episode when all her attention should be focused on Nick. It wasn't just the delicate negotiation involving the sting that she needed to concentrate on. She also had to make sure Moresco didn't renege on his bargain not to tell Jamie he was his father. After witnessing her ex-colleague at the Melbourne police station grapple with the randomness of his episodes and the devastating impact on those around him, she didn't want anything like that happening to Riley in a situation where her son could potentially be harmed.

Riley saw the exchange and stiffened, clearly recognizing he was being sidelined but unable to do anything about it. Nor could he say anything in front of the Frankston detectives. Paula felt badly, but Jamie was too important. She couldn't afford to take chances.

"Things won't turn ugly," she said. "Whatever

else Nick is, he's not violent to those he considers part of his family. That includes Jamie, naturally, and also me, as Jamie's mother."

"You think?" Riley said, skeptically.

"Moresco is more likely to get nasty if he thinks he's under surveillance," Paula insisted.

The meeting broke up shortly afterward, with Detectives Leonard and Cadley heading off to organize the stake-out van. John walked them out, leaving her and Riley.

"Almond croissants, my favorite." Paula reached for a pastry and took a bite. She swore she could feel the sugar go straight to her bloodstream. "Bribery will get you five to ten."

Riley was silent. Stormy emotions played across his face. Undoubtedly he was offended, hurt, angry and bewildered.

She'd done that to him. Paula set her croissant down carefully and licked the sugar off her fingers. "How did your session with the shrink go?"

"Yeah, good." His fingers drummed the table, a frown dragging at the corners of his mouth.

Paula sipped her coffee. She wanted to get going but she couldn't leave Riley like this. "It's for the best."

"I care about Jamie, too."

She'd expected to hear about how he was her partner and a cop, too, how his PTSD wouldn't interfere with his job. How he was part of this sting and she shouldn't cut him out. She hadn't expected him to want in on the operation because he cared about Jamie. She knew he liked her son but that much?

Paula reached for a napkin. She blotted her mouth as a pretext for blowing her nose. And swiftly dabbed her eyes. "The sugar went up my nose."

"You're meeting with a ruthless criminal," Riley said, ignoring her clumsy attempt at covering. "I want you and Jamie to be safe. A couple of middle-aged dicks playing around with electronics in a van aren't going to do squat if Moresco takes it into his head to snatch your son."

Paula felt the blood drain from her face. "Don't say that." She sucked in a breath. "It'll be broad daylight, right next to a busy shopping strip and the main street. Nick is not going to do anything stupid."

"He might not regard taking custody of his son as stupid. I know if I was a father and had a child I wasn't allowed to see, I'd do anything to spend time with him."

"Except break the law."

Riley made a small shrug, suggesting he would consider it. He was a soldier, used to obeying orders. But he was also ex-Special Forces, trained to think for himself. Would he be willing to break the law for her son?

Paula did a quick rethink. The plan was already in motion but John had left Riley out on her recommendation. If she talked to the Sergeant again...

"What if you were in the van, listening in. If things sounded dicey you could stroll by." John had already arranged for a uniformed cop to do that but an extra pair of eyes and hands could be a comfort.

"I'd rather be in the park, walking my dog."

"Your non-existent dog?"

"I've been thinking of getting a pooch. I could stop by the shelter and pick one up."

"You would do that?" Too late she realized the unspoken implication. *For me.* "To crack a case, I mean."

"I would do anything," Riley said simply. He leaned forward and wiped a thumb across the tip of her nose, taking off a smudge of icing sugar.

Paula felt the warmth of his touch, of the look in his eyes. She glanced away. She couldn't allow emotions to cloud her judgment.

"Wouldn't work," she said, shaking her head. "Jamie would recognize you and Nick would immediately suspect something was up."

"Baseball cap, dark glasses..." he suggested. She shook her head. "Parks worker uniform?" She kept shaking her head. "Clown makeup? Astronaut?"

Her mouth twitched. "The van. That's my final offer."

"Deal."

"You do realize I'm going to be playing up to Nick, don't you?" Paula said. "Flirting a bit to get him onside. It's all part of the act."

"Is it an act?" Riley asked.

"You know it is."

"Do I?"

"Quit asking dumb questions." Paula jumped up and started stacking the used coffee cups. "I've got to go. I'll talk to you later."

Riley reached out to touch her arm. "Be careful."

She moved her arm out of his reach. "Naturally."

RILEY WAS GIVEN a set of headphones and told to stay in the passenger seat of the van and keep quiet. He checked his watch. Ten minutes until meet time.

They were parked in a short service road outside the post office with a view of a two-block stretch of Main Street, traffic lights at one end and a roundabout that led to the park at the other end.

If Riley leaned forward he could just see the ice-cream shop where his stepmother worked, now owned by Moresco.

In the back of the windowless van, Detectives

Leonard and Cadley went about the business of setting up their surveillance equipment. He could hear them testing the wire with Paula, adjusting the volume and sound balance. Her voice through his headphones sounded curiously close, despite the slight static.

Then he heard Jamie's voice in the background and smiled, straining his ears to hear what the boy was saying. Something along the lines of "Watch me." Riley could picture him clambering over the monkey bars.

Movement down the street to his left drew his attention. A man in a suit was entering the ice-cream shop. Not unusual in itself, but something in the cut of the clothing made Riley bring out the photo of Moresco Paula had passed around this morning. He had dark hair going gray with a lean and handsome face.

It drove Riley nuts that she'd had a relationship with this guy. In the *past*. Why couldn't Riley let it go? Why did he doubt her story? Probably because he thought she was lying to herself. What exactly were her feelings for Nick Moresco?

A few minutes later Moresco emerged carrying a tray of three ice-cream cones—chocolate, vanilla and pistachio nut. He knew Paula's favorites, too.

He moved with natural grace, his gaze watchful. If Riley didn't know every cop in the area, he might have thought he was looking at a detective. Besides police officers and soldiers, the only people who had that level of hyper-alertness were up to no good.

Riley slumped deep in his seat and watched the man pass. Yep, there was a resemblance to Jamie in the olive skin, the angle of the jaw and the set of his eyes. The unwelcome image of Paula having sex with this creep flashed through Riley's mind.

He swiftly thrust that thought away and turned to the guys in the rear. "Suspect passing directly in front of us. He'll be at the park in approximately two minutes."

"Roger that." Detective Cadley looped his headphones over his ears and flicked a switch to allow him to speak to Paula. "Drummond, do you read me?"

"Loud and clear," Paula replied.

"Perp is on his way from south side of Main Street. All systems go."

There was a static-filled pause. Then Paula said, "I see him. Two-way communication ceases from...now."

Riley adjusted his headphones and prepared to be tortured.

PAULA STOOD BY THE monkey bars, one eye on Jamie crawling among the brightly colored steel maze, one eye out for Nick. Behind her were the public washrooms and a barbecue area with a picnic table. Tall pines bordered the small park.

She'd told Jamie they were meeting an old friend of hers from the city. He took it in one ear and it went out the other. Typical of what didn't concern him.

After Detective Cadley's warning she glued her eyes to the street. Sure enough, she spied Nick strolling up the path, a tray of ice-cream cones held casually, almost negligently in one hand.

"Hey, Nick." She painted on a smile. "Over here."

Jamie, hanging upside down, twisted his head up to see his mum's friend. "Ice cream!"

"Ciao, bella." Nick kissed her lightly on both cheeks, giving her a whiff of expensive cologne. He presented the tray for her to take the pistachio. Then glanced at Jamie as hungrily as the boy was eyeing the ice cream. "I didn't know what your son liked. Jamie, is it?" He crouched down. "Would you like chocolate or vanilla?"

"Chocolate." Jamie edged closer.

"Manners…" Paula murmured.

"Please?" Jamie looked at Nick with big dark eyes.

"*Si, bambino.*" Nick handed over the cone with an Italian word of endearment. "How old are you, my friend?"

"Six," Jamie replied, lisping a little. "Six and

a half." He licked, turning the cone to catch the melting ice cream.

"Almost a grown man," Nick said, laughing. He turned to Paula, including her in his delight.

She felt sick and tense. She didn't want to align herself with Nick. She was afraid he would say something that would give Jamie a clue to his identity.

Jamie tugged on her skirt. "Mum, will you push me on the swing?"

Nick held up a hand to stop her and bowed to Jamie. "I would be honored to push, if you permit?"

"Okay." Jamie shrugged and ran off to the swings.

Nick handed Paula his cone and followed. He grasped Jamie's swing and pulled back. "You like to go very high?"

"Yes." Jamie giggled, his legs dangling as Nick held him poised in the air.

"I give you one big push. Then you must pump your legs." Nick pushed hard, then slipped sideways, out of the way of Jamie swinging back.

Paula chuckled. Then she realized what she was doing. While Nick was occupied she discreetly felt for the wire beneath her top. The tape was in place.

Nick gave Jamie another push then glanced at Paula. "I will speak to your mama now. Remember, pump your legs."

Paula wondered what Riley was making of what he was hearing. Nick didn't come across as the big bad drug dealer. He was good with children. He had a big family with lots of nephews and nieces.

"Jamie is a charming child," Nick said, returning to where she stood by the picnic bench. He removed a big white silky handkerchief from his breast pocket and laid it on the bench of the picnic table. He gestured for her to sit. "Now, you and I can have a chat."

CHAPTER TWELVE

THE CLEAN WHITE linen against the scarred and dirty picnic bench reminded Paula of Nick himself, an elegant facade for grubby dealings. She planned to use both the handkerchief and the man without getting soiled herself.

Lowering herself to the handkerchief, she glanced at him beneath her eyelashes. "Are you living in Summerside?"

Her flirtatious glance was wasted. Nick's gaze was on Jamie, energetically swinging. "I'm never far away. He's a handsome boy. He looks like me when I was that age."

Nick's egotism was so boundless he probably didn't even realize what he'd said. "You're looking well."

He rested one polished Italian boot on the bench and leaned an elbow on his knee. "I'm glad you think prison agreed with me."

"You always outshine your surroundings." She let a beat go by. "Nick."

He glanced at her, the smile lingering. "Did I

even outshine my penthouse apartment? You enjoyed that place, didn't you?"

"Who wouldn't appreciate the best views in the city?" Outwardly she smiled, maintaining an aura of calm. Inside, her heart was tripping over itself. With Nick you never knew when a light conversation would take a darker turn.

Nick twisted his torso, rolling his shoulder then rubbing it. "Prison wasn't good for my bad shoulder. I've been so stiff lately." His smile turned suggestive. "Do you still have the magic touch?"

Paula flashed to a late afternoon in winter, a few weeks before the investigation came to a head. He'd insisted Paula join him for a glass of wine, saying it would help him relax for therapy. Cozy on a love seat before the fireplace, they'd kissed for the first time. She'd initiated the kiss. It had seemed necessary at the time, a way of gaining his confidence for the final push. She couldn't do that again, not for the job, not for anything. Not now that she'd made love to Riley.

"I'm out of practice," Paula said apologetically. "Let's not dwell on the past. Let's talk about the future."

"The future? Do you mean Jamie?" Nick asked. "I am pleased you agreed to allow me a relationship with my son. It's so much easier than going through the courts."

"You wouldn't have had a hope if you're still engaged in illegal activities."

"I told you, I'm not."

This was the opening she'd been looking for. With the right touch of quiet regret, she looked him in the eye. "Pity."

He stilled, his gaze sharpening. "What do you mean?"

But it was too soon. She'd only wanted to plant the seed. "Oh, nothing." With a judicious brief touch of his knee, she changed the subject. "Who in your family knows about Jamie?"

"Mama, my brothers and sisters, the aunts and uncles, *touti mondi*. Everyone wants to meet him."

Paula had a vision of Jamie disappearing into a vast sea of Morescos, never to be seen again. Nick had three brothers and dozens of cousins, some of whom had worked for him. His little brother Rico was an expert forger who could easily doctor a passport.

Despite her plan, the anxious mother overrode the cop. "Jamie will grow up on the right side of the law."

Nick chuckled. "You should see yourself, the fierce mama bear protecting her cub. Don't worry, *cara*." He stroked her hair, sliding his fingers slowly through the loose strands. "I have only Jamie's best interests at heart."

His touch made her skin crawl. She forced herself to continue the charade. "He needs a father."

"You know I want to be part of his life."

"Then perhaps," she said slowly, "you'd like to provide for him."

"You want support payments? I would have offered, but I didn't think you'd accept *tainted money.*"

He'd guessed correctly. Paula would starve before she'd accept a penny of drug money. "I thought you had legitimate businesses now—the restaurant, the ice-cream shop."

"I do. I'm working my way back from nothing. It takes time to build a clientele again."

Did he mean drug users or ice-cream customers? They were dancing around, talking of two things at once. "I'm in a position to help build your client base."

"Oh?"

"I think I told you there's been an influx of crystal meth into the area." Paula strove to sound casual. This was the critical moment when she had to convince him she was being upfront. It wasn't going to be easy given that, until now, she'd been hostile every time she'd encountered him. She watched his face carefully. He didn't so much as bat an eyelash. "I'm in charge of the new Drug Investigation Unit at the department. I've initiated a task force looking into the local trade."

"I thought you'd been busted back to uniform." Nick sounded equally casual.

"The sergeant in charge reinstated my detective stripes. He wanted someone experienced on the job."

Nick stroked his jaw. "And this would help my ice-cream business, how?"

"Everything goes through me. All the intelligence reports, evidence, drug hauls, you name it. I decide what to act on, where to send my men, what information to send up the line."

"Why are you telling me this?"

"I missed you. I'm sick of being a cop. The police never treated me as well as you did. We— you, me and Jamie—could be a family someday."

Nick's gaze narrowed. "That's not what you said when I first contacted you. You didn't want me to have anything to do with my son."

"I've had time to think, to remember our times together. I hated turning you in. I'd like to make up for that. I could help you. With your businesses."

He smiled, then his gaze drifted to Jamie. "We'll talk more in a while. My son is playing by himself."

He strolled over to the swing set. "Show me how high you can go, Jamie."

Paula propped an elbow on the picnic table and covered her mouth to speak into the microphone in her cleavage. "Are you getting all this? He's being cagey, but I think I can get something useful if I keep at him."

"Roger that," Detective Leonard said.

In the background she heard Riley say, "Tell her not to let the prick touch her."

"Tell Henning he can go jump. Quiet, he's coming."

Nick wandered back. Paula adjusted her blouse and leaned her head on her hand, smiling at him.

He crouched at her feet and placed his hands on her knees, looking into her face. "Did you really miss me, *cara?*"

She met his gaze square on, calling upon all her acting skills. "Yes, Nick. Very much."

"And you can see a future for all of us together."

"You, me…and Jamie." The catch in her voice was real when she added, "He needs a father."

She just didn't want that man to be Nick. Riley's rugged features came to her. His strength combined with tenderness that was so appealing. How could she ever have fallen for Nick's oily sophistication?

"I need a son, to carry on the family," Nick said. "Shall we tell him now?"

"No," she said quickly. "You couldn't have any association with me or Jamie while I'm still on the force…helping you. But that won't be forever. Two years tops, I reckon."

"You would make this sacrifice for me?" he

said, turning his mouth to kiss the palm of her hand. "You would betray your principles, break the law, for me?" He murmured the words as if they were endearments.

Paula took in a breath. "I would do anything for you. You're the father of my child. That means something. And I love you. I've always loved you—"

Nick rose to his feet, so swiftly and unexpectedly Paula rocked forward before she caught herself. Gripping the bench she looked up.

"You love me? You want to help me make money?" His voice dripped with bitter sarcasm. A flash of his dark underbelly showed in his glittering black eyes. "What kind of fool do you think I am? You betrayed me."

All Paula's instincts and her training told her to get to her feet, to be prepared for a contest of strength. With an effort she stayed seated, tried to pretend she wasn't bothered by his outburst. "I was doing my job."

"Was it your job to sleep with me?"

Paula was aware that Riley was listening. But she was playing her role. She would say what she had to say. "No, that was my choice. I wanted to."

"You're lying," Nick said harshly. "This whole business proposition is a lie. You're trying to set me up. But it won't work because I'm clean."

"Nick, calm down. I was only joking." Her voice had a tremor. She prayed he didn't notice.

He planted a foot on the picnic-table bench and stroked his booted ankle, drawing her attention to the secret pocket where he kept the stiletto. "You know I can't abide traitors."

Paula got to her feet, all her senses on alert. A quick glance at the playground showed Jamie pushing a toy car through the sawdust at the base of the climbing apparatus. She glanced back. Nick had taken out the thin blade and was using the tip to clean his perfectly manicured nails.

"Where's the wire?" Nick's gaze dropped to her blouse.

"Put away the knife before your son sees you and misunderstands," she said calmly. "You don't want him to think you're a bad man."

Nick hefted the blade loosely in his palm. He took a step toward her.

"Stop," she said, moving backward. "You know you won't hurt me. I'm the mother of your child."

He affected a negligent shrug. "Actually, that means nothing to me. The boy is all that matters."

All she could think about was Jamie's safety. She had to remain calm and not inflame the situation. Nick had vulnerable points. She had to tap into them. She could talk him out of this, she was sure.

"Jamie adores the remote-controlled car you sent him," she said. "I let him keep it this time."

"Really? He liked it?"

"Yes." She swallowed. "He plays with it all the time."

Nick hesitated then slid the knife inside his boot. "What else does he like? I wish to give him another present."

Paula slowly let out her breath. There was still a chance she could turn this around. Nick was fond of playing games. Chances were he'd been merely trying to scare her. "Dinosaurs. They're his favorite things after cars."

PUT AWAY THE KNIFE, was the last thing Riley heard before he tore off his headphones and leaped from the van.

"Wait!" Detective Leonard called after him.

Riley ignored the summons to stop. He raced down the sidewalk, dodging a man pushing a stroller and almost ran over an elderly woman who'd stepped off the crosswalk.

She shook her cane at him. "I've a good mind to call the police."

Visions of Paula stabbed and bloodied, and Jamie in the clutches of the criminal filled Riley's mind with a red haze during the short stretch of street between the van and the park. Ahead, he could see Moresco standing too close to Paula. Jamie kneeled in the dirt, oblivious to the danger, alone and vulnerable.

"Paula!" Riley put on a burst of speed.

She waved her hands, shaking her head at the same time. The message was unmistakable. *Stop! Go away!*

Riley didn't process that. He barreled up to her and Moresco, grasped Paula by both arms and set her aside. He wedged himself between her and Moresco.

Breathing hard, he flipped out his badge. "You're under arrest for threatening a police officer with a deadly weapon."

Behind him Paula groaned. "He didn't threaten me."

"I heard him." Riley gripped Moresco's wrist and twisted his arm up behind his back. "You're coming with me, down to the station."

"Riley!" Jamie came running over. Then stopped to glance uncertainly from Riley to Nick. "What are you doing?"

"He's playing a very silly game." Scowling, Moresco tugged on his arm.

"There are no grounds for arrest," Paula hissed at Riley. "What are you doing here?"

Reluctantly he released Moresco's arm. "No grounds? But I heard—"

"Is this the type of person you work with these days?" Moresco brushed his suit sleeve fastidiously. "I suppose this ridiculous setup was his idea." He reached for his handkerchief from the picnic-table bench, shaking it out with a snap.

"Don't go, Nick," Paula said, pushing a hand through her hair. "It wasn't a setup, honestly. I don't know why Riley burst in on the scene. Please, stay and chat a little longer. Riley was just leaving." She glared at him. "Weren't you?"

Adrenaline was still pumping through Riley's body. His hands were fisted at his side. "I heard—"

"You're imagining things." Paula gave him another fierce look—*shut the hell up*—then turned to Moresco. "He was in Afghanistan. He has PTSD. It makes him do crazy things."

"He was listening to the wire taped to your lovely body," Moresco said. "Nobody fools Nick Moresco twice, not even you, *bella*."

Riley sat on the picnic table, confused. Had he imagined Paula's fear, her words about a knife?

"Show me your cars before I go." Nick put an arm around Jamie and guided him toward the playground.

Riley jumped up and started to follow.

Paula grabbed his arm and restrained him. "Nick was briefly hostile when he figured out I was wired," she whispered fiercely. "But I was talking him around. If you hadn't come charging in here like some bloody Keystone Kop, I might have gotten some useful information out of him."

Out of the corner of his eye Riley saw Nick pick

Jamie up. The red haze returned, blurring Riley's vision. Pain seared through his right temple.

Paula was wrong. Moresco was taking the boy hostage.

Riley's heart began to palpitate. Sweat broke out on his forehead and under his armpits.

Do something. Act, you coward.

He couldn't move. His legs felt as if they were made of lead. Paula's voice faded to a tinny distant sound. Colored flashing lights obscured his vision. He heard the explosion, saw the blood and the flying hand coming at him. He clutched his head with both hands, trying to stop the pain by pressing on his skull. He fell to his knees, collapsing forward, his arms curled over his head.

The next thing he knew, Paula was shaking him. "Riley, snap out of it. Everything's all right."

Slowly he uncovered his head, pulled himself upright on his knees. He looked around. Moresco had gone. Jamie's eyes were wide, his mouth slack. Paula peered into Riley's face, frowning. "Are you okay?"

"I thought..." His throat was dry, his heart still pounding. "I thought Moresco..."

He'd thought Moresco was a suicide bomber who had grabbed Jamie as a hostage.

"He was hugging Jamie goodbye," Paula said then spoke into her cleavage. "It's all over."

Riley wiped a hand across his sweaty brow. He

was going insane—if he wasn't crazy already. The worst thing was, if Jamie had been in real danger, Riley wouldn't have been able to do a thing about it.

"Are you okay, Riley?" Jamie touched him on the shoulder, his small face troubled.

He hated the boy seeing him like this. He managed a shaky smile. "I had a bad turn. I'm fine."

"Mum's friend, Nick, gave us ice cream," Jamie said. "He even knew that chocolate was my favorite."

"That's terrific, mate." Riley clambered unsteadily to his feet. The migraine throbbed but at least it wasn't affecting his vision anymore. He felt like the worst kind of fool. He couldn't even look at Paula. "Sorry," he mumbled.

"Yeah, whatever."

Detectives Leonard and Cadley were walking over from the van to see what was going on.

"Stay with Riley," she said to Jamie and went to meet them.

Jamie stood with Riley, watching him unhappily as if standing guard on the lunatic. Riley ran a hand over his face. He couldn't go on like this.

PAULA PULLED RILEY'S blue flannel shirt from her scrap bag and spread it out on her ironing board. It was threadbare but the muted blue-green plaid would look perfect pieced into her quilt.

It was late, nearly midnight. She should go to bed but she knew she'd lie awake, wondering how Riley was and thinking about how next to tackle Nick.

She ran the iron over the soft fabric, remembering how it had felt covering Riley's strong shoulder. What would he think about her using his shirt this way? Well, he'd thrown it out. It was hers now.

Her anger had faded. He couldn't help himself. He'd been doing what he thought necessary to save her and Jamie. Too bad Riley couldn't save himself.

Paula took the shirt to her worktable and cut out the back of the garment. She spread it out, glancing at her quilt to see what shape would best fit into the whole. Taking up her scissors again, she carefully cut out an irregular polygon about the size of her palm.

Was Riley awake right now, too? She was tempted to call him, see how he was doing. She'd phoned after dinner but got his voice mail. Hopefully the reason he hadn't called back was because he was working on his renovations and not because he was having another attack.

Paula pinned the fabric to the quilt on three sides then threaded a needle with blue cotton. Using the sewing machine would be easier and faster but part of the therapeutic effect of quilting was the hand sewing.

Today had been bad on so many levels. Riley had screwed up her encounter with Nick. He'd freaked out Jamie—her, too, to be honest. Seeing Riley, whom she thought of as strong and confident, reduced to a trembling mess was plain scary.

He'd frightened off Nick before she could get anything useful out of him. A few more minutes and she might have gotten Nick to agree to her plan—

Get real. Nick had her numbered long before Riley had burst onto the scene. She might have talked him out of his hostile mood but the sting operation was a hopeless cause. She should have known better. Nick was too smart and too wary to fall for something so ham-fisted.

Was he responsible for the crystal meth coming into Summerside? He kept denying it. She took that with a grain of salt, but he had to know that if he seriously wanted to be part of Jamie's life he couldn't risk getting caught manufacturing or dealing in drugs.

Was Riley right? Leopards don't change their spots.

How much did Jamie mean to Nick—enough to make him go straight? Seeing him interact with her son at the playground had almost made her believe. On the other hand it was impossible to envisage Nick running an ice-cream shop in a small town and being a soccer dad.

A noise behind her made her glance around. Jamie stood in the doorway, his pajamas twisted, rubbing his eyes and yawning. "What are you doing up, mate? Did you have a bad dream?"

Jamie nodded and ran to her. Paula put the quilt aside and held out her arms. He crawled into her lap. She cuddled him, stroking his hair. He was too big to sit comfortably in her lap but she held him anyway.

"It's all right now. You're safe with me."

"A dog was chasing me." He burrowed his face into her shoulder. "A big black dog with sharp teeth."

"Shh, it's okay." She hummed a lullaby she used to sing when he was younger. Gradually he relaxed against her but when she tried to release him, he squirmed back into her arms. "Do you want to look at my quilt?"

Jamie sat up, sniffing. "Okay."

They sat on the bed with the quilt spread out, Jamie tucked in close. "Watch out for the pins. See this piece?" She pointed out a dark red with thin navy blue stripes. "That was your Grandpa's favorite shirt. He wore it when I was going through police training. I was making my first quilt then. When Grandma threw out the shirt I took it. A piece of it is in every quilt I've made."

Jamie tapped the other side of the quilt. "Here's another bit of it."

"I put lots of pieces in this quilt." Stupid to get sentimental about scraps of fabric but she couldn't help the lump forming in her throat. "He would have liked you, kiddo. Do you see any more of Grandpa's shirt?"

Jamie leaned closer. "There! I found another one. It's like *Where's Waldo.* And another!" He twisted his face, with its gap-toothed grin toward her, seeking her approval.

"You're good at this." She stroked his hair off his forehead.

"Well, there are a lot," Jamie said modestly.

"I wanted there to be lots. So that even though Grandpa's passed away, he's still in our life."

"Is there any of me?" Jamie asked.

"Of course. This piece is from a T-shirt you wore when you were three years old." She pointed out a yellow and green scrap. "And this bit with the bunnies is from your sleepers when you were a baby."

"Tell me more." Jamie was wide awake now, his nightmare forgotten.

She should get him to bed—he had school in the morning—but she relished these quiet times together. "This is from Grandma's blouse. And this is from curtains we had when I was a teenager. This was from one of my dresses." She knew the origin of every piece of fabric. Looking at them brought back happy memories and positive emotions of days past. "It's like a story of our life."

"What's this piece from?" Jamie asked, touching the blue and green flannel she was sewing in tonight.

"Riley's shirt. He left it here when he was changing the locks."

Jamie whipped his head around to see if she was joking. When she nodded, he gave a shocked giggle. "Won't he be mad that you cut it up?"

"It's so old and frayed he told me to throw it out. He said I'd be doing him a favor getting rid of it because he couldn't bear to throw it out himself."

Jamie smoothed down the raw curling edge of the flannel. "Now Riley's part of our story."

Paula wanted to deny it, but her heart wouldn't let her.

Jamie had gone quiet. "Why did Riley act weird in the park?"

She'd already explained it that afternoon, but post-traumatic stress disorder wasn't something a six-year-old comprehended easily. She tried again.

"Riley got injured in an explosion in Afghanistan. Sometimes his mind flashes to things he saw and he starts to feel scared, just like he did when the bomb went off."

"But there was no bomb today." Jamie scrunched his face up. "I don't get it."

"To be honest, I don't fully understand it myself. I don't think Riley does, either." She sighed. "We don't always know why we do what we do."

"Do dogs know why they do what they do?"

Paula laughed. It always astonished her how her son's mind flipped from subject to subject. "Maybe. It would be fun to know what a dog is thinking."

"He's thinking, 'I'm going to find a bone,'" Jamie said, wide-eyed. "He'd dig and dig and dig..."

Paula started to stand. "Come on, matey, it's time we both got some sleep."

Jamie resisted moving. His smile faded and he frowned. "I'm worried about Riley."

"Don't worry." Paula hugged her son, holding him close. "Riley is going to be fine. He's a soldier. He's big and strong."

She led Jamie to his bedroom and tucked him under the covers, kissing him good-night again. She went out quietly but didn't close the door all the way in case he woke up.

She tidied her quilting materials and went to bed. But she didn't sleep. She was worried about Riley, too.

CHAPTER THIRTEEN

"I HAD ANOTHER panic attack," Riley said to Simone Richards two days later. It was humbling to have to admit, especially when he'd been so cocky and dismissive of therapy. But after his meltdown in the park he could no longer deny his condition was serious. "I didn't think that would happen again, not after our last session when I relived the bomb explosion and Nabili and her students getting killed."

Simone had a desktop waterfall trickling in the background. It was undoubtedly meant to be soothing but in his present state the noise was annoying. He didn't want to be soothed. He wanted to be cured, damn it.

"I did tell you the trauma might lie deeper than your Afghanistan experiences," Simone reminded him. "Can you think of any other past event that affected you in a strongly negative way?"

He spread his hands. "I've seen nothing as bad as witnessing dozens of innocent people blown apart."

"It doesn't have to be a violent trauma," Simone said. "Just something that affected you deeply."

Riley shrugged. "My mother died from breast cancer when I was twelve. I took that pretty hard."

"Let's explore that. Often children feel abandoned when a parent dies. They can feel angry as well as bereft."

Riley thought back. He'd started his first year of high school. His excitement and nervousness had been overshadowed by his mother's illness and death. "I don't recall feeling angry. I was in turmoil, for sure. Grieving and confused."

"At that age you might not have recognized your emotions as anger." Simone made a note in her book. "How did your father handle her death? Did he talk to you about your feelings, encourage you to remember your mother? Or did he shut down emotionally?"

"Dad's ex-army and old-fashioned. Very stiff upper lip and get-on-with-the-job," Riley said. "He didn't talk about what he was going through, but he didn't stop my sister and me from remembering her."

"Were you close to your mother?"

Again Riley shrugged. "She was my mother. I loved her but I took her for granted. I was twelve years old, remember?" He shifted restlessly in his chair. "With respect, where's all this going?"

"Let's try approaching this from another angle,"

Simone said. "When did you first experience symptoms of PTSD? Those might include headaches, sleeplessness, depression, panic attacks..."

Riley leaned forward, planting his elbows on his knees. "It was the night before I was supposed to give a talk at the primary school. I came down with a vicious headache that I attributed to dust from the renovations. In hindsight I think it must have been brought on by the thought of going to a primary school and associating that with Afghanistan."

"Possibly. You mentioned renovations. What exactly had you been doing that day?"

"I think I told you I recently moved into my old family home."

"The house you grew up in?" Simone tilted her head. "Was this where you were living when your mother died?"

"Yes." Riley stood and paced to the window. His stomach felt funny. He glanced at his watch. It was only 11:00 a.m. He couldn't be hungry.

He turned to Simone. "I get it. You think tearing out my mother's kitchen triggered the panic attack, not the primary school."

"The renovations and the explosion in Afghanistan could be linked in some way. Can you think of any association between the two?"

He shrugged helplessly. "The only link is myself."

She folded her hands on her notebook and regarded him over her half glasses. "The answer is rooted in your emotional response to the two events."

Riley shook his head, drawing a blank.

"Could you have been angry at yourself for some reason, perhaps for not being able to prevent either your mother's death or the suicide bomber?"

"How could a kid stop someone from dying of cancer when a team of doctors couldn't do a damn thing?" The anger came from nowhere, welling up in him, making his hands curl into fists. Riley felt like punching something, like the blow-up clown in the corner of the office. Was that what the clown was there for? He'd assumed Simone kept it around for any children she was treating. He paced the other way, away from the grinning red mouth.

"What are you feeling right now?" Simone asked.

"You're the shrink. You tell me," he said, scowling.

She regarded him dispassionately. "I think you had a strong emotional response to the idea of not being able to prevent your mother's death. Clearly, from an adult's point of view that isn't possible. But a child might believe differently." She paused a beat. "Could you have done something to stop the suicide bomber?"

"I don't know." Riley dropped into the chair and put his head in his hands. "That's the hell of it. I don't remember." He looked up as tears blurred his eyes. "If I'm blocking some memory, I need to find out what it is."

Simone touched his knee. "You will."

PAULA SHIFTED THE gift-wrapped package into her other hand and rang Riley's doorbell. She couldn't hear any walls being broken down. Hopefully that meant she was catching him at a good time. She checked that her skirt was straight, feeling the back to make sure it wasn't tucked into her panties.

Why the hell was she nervous? He was her partner. Sure, she felt bad about yelling at him yesterday but anyone in her position might have been frustrated.

The door opened.

Bleary-eyed Riley ran a hand through his already mussed hair. His shirt was wrinkled, as if he'd slept in it. His skinny jeans sat low on his hips. "Hey."

Even disheveled he looked hot. The condom in her purse was suddenly burning a hole through the leather. Her self-help books were always telling her to be honest about her motivations. Okay, she was nervous because, in spite of what she'd told him about their night together being a one-off, she still wanted him.

"I hope I didn't wake you."

He glanced at his watch and his eyebrows rose. "Four o'clock already. I guess I fell asleep on the couch." He opened the door wider. "Come in."

"It's your day off. You're entitled." She entered the foyer and held out the gift. "A housewarming present."

He took it gingerly as if afraid it might explode in his hands. "What is it?"

"The usual response is, 'You didn't have to.' Open it and find out, dummy."

"I'll put on the kettle." Tucking the package under his arm, he led the way through the living room and dining room and into the kitchen.

Paula stopped in the doorway. In place of the construction zone she'd seen last visit was a gleaming brand-new kitchen in blond wood and dark green tiles with cream-colored appliances. It was sleek and modern yet warm and homey. "Wow. When did you do all this?"

"I didn't do it all myself. My dad and his plumber friend helped me install the appliances. A cabinetmaker built the cupboards."

"But you're Mr. Handyman." She walked closer to the U-shaped workspace, running a hand over the dark green countertops. "I'm disillusioned."

"Every time I worked on it, I got a migraine." He put her gift on the table. "Today at the shrink's office, I got an idea why."

"Spill."

"In a minute." He carefully picked the tape from the ends of the present.

"Oh, you're not one of those people, are you?" She hovered over him. "Just rip the paper off."

"No way. I re-use it."

"So, cheapskate, you're going to wrap my birthday present in my own paper?"

"Who says I'm giving you a birthday present?" He slid his finger carefully beneath the edge, lifting off the tape without tearing the paper. He pushed away the paper, revealing the box showing a picture of the contents. "You got me a ceramic rooster. Cool."

He peeled back the flaps and pulled out a twelve-inch ceramic rooster. The rooster had his black wings flung back, his head tilted, red crest splayed and beak open as if letting loose a full-throated crow. Around his feet were clustered grapes, apples and other fruit.

"It's a French cock. Country-style decor," she said. "It's supposed to be good luck."

"Thanks." He set the rooster on the end of the counter next to the toaster. "This place needed something homey."

"So what happened at your appointment today?"

Outside, a lawn mower started. Instead of replying Riley carefully folded the gift wrap. And kept folding till it was a small square. "I have nothing left of my mother in here. Nothing."

"The house is fifty years old," Paula pointed out. "I'll bet your mother would have loved this new kitchen."

"Her eggcup collection used to sit above the stove on that narrow shelf." He stared at the square of paper as if not knowing what it was. Then he gazed at the empty shelf. "I thought of putting spice jars there, but it wouldn't be the same."

"What happened to the eggcups? Does your father have them?"

"No, Katie does. It wouldn't be fair to ask for them back. She misses our mum, too."

"You could start a new eggcup collection."

He looked askance at her. "You do think I'm a girl."

"No." She slid her arms around his waist and leaned back to look into his face. Maybe sex would take his mind off whatever was eating him alive. "I think you're very much a guy."

Riley put a hand beneath her jaw. His tortured gaze held hers for a heart-squeezing moment then he lowered his mouth to hers. He kissed her hungrily, his hands moving over her shoulders and down her back to cup her hips and pull her in close.

She wanted him even though he couldn't be the man she needed him to be. At least he couldn't be right now. He thought he was weak but he wasn't. Latent strength ran all through him, as taut and hard as the muscles beneath her palms. Troubled, yes. Unstable as a loose cannon...whoo, boy. But he was solid at his core. He only needed to believe it.

He pulled her blouse over her head and took her breasts in his hands, raining kisses over them. She tugged at his shirt buttons, ripping off a loose one in her urgency. It clattered to the floor and rolled beneath the table. "Oops."

The window curtains were pushed back. In the next yard the neighbor's head bobbed above the privacy fence as he mowed the lawn. "We should go to your bedroom."

Riley hoisted her into his arms. She wrapped her legs around his waist. He carried her through the house to the far end of the hall to an irregularly shaped room, containing a dresser, a desk and a single bed with the covers tucked in tighter than a drum.

Odd that he wasn't using the master bedroom...

He laid her on his bed and started pulling the rest of her clothes off and soon she couldn't think anymore.

SLOW DOWN. Don't go after her like a rutting bull.

It was tempting to lose himself in her sexy body and her beautiful blue eyes. Here in his room she

wasn't the boss carrying a torch for her criminal
ex. And he wasn't some screwed-up soldier who
crumpled like a paper doll when he was needed
most. They were just a man and a woman who
couldn't get enough of each other.

She thought she was bad. She wasn't.

"You're one of the most honorable people I've
ever known." He kissed his way down her flat
stomach.

"What—" she pushed her fingers into his hair
and lifted his head "—did you say?"

"I…said…you…were…honorable."

"If that's your way of angling for a wedding
proposal, think again." She sucked in a breath as
he dipped lower, between her thighs. "Oh, my."

Her pleasure spurred him on. Her soft moans
made him harder, tense with the urgency of un-
consummated need. He made her come quickly
then while she was still limp and moist he dragged
himself up to lay beside her, stroking her, fon-
dling her breasts, kissing her, waiting patiently,
watching for that moment when the light in her
eyes rekindled.

"You're beautiful." His body was humming, no
screaming, for release but here at least, he was in
control.

She stirred and turned into him, wrapping her
leg over his hip. Taking him in her hand, she
guided him to her. "You're like a live power line

that's been cut, snapping with electricity. I can feel the energy running through you."

She closed around him, so hot and tight he could barely breathe. "Here I thought...I was being so... controlled."

"Don't hold back." Slowly she began to grind her hips against his. "Show me Riley unleashed."

He didn't need to be told twice. He flipped her onto her back and drove into her. Pleasure flooded his body, lack of blood made him light-headed. He was operating on pure instinct. He held her breasts in his hands and her gaze with his eyes, thrusting fast and hard. He was hanging on by a thread, wanting her to come again. When he couldn't last another second, she climaxed with a shriek that sent chills down his spine. A moment later he came, too, powerfully, explosively.

Panting, Paula grinned up at him. "Your neighbor must wonder what's going on in here."

Riley grinned back, unabashed. "He can't hear over the lawn mower."

"What lawn mower?"

He cocked his head to listen. Silence. "Oops. Oh, well, who cares?"

He kissed her, slow and lingering. He didn't know when he'd had such great sex. Paula was fit and strong enough to match him. The sex was athletic and jubilant.

He shifted to look at her, stroking a lock of hair

behind her ear, suddenly assailed by doubt. Was he trying to make himself feel like a man? Was that what this frenzied coupling was about? How much did he really like her? How much did she like him?

"What are you thinking?" she asked.

What did a guy like him have to offer a woman like her? Unable to give her the truth, he offered her a smile. "Nothing."

Paula lifted herself onto her elbow. "We should talk about it."

"About nothing?" Even as he teased, a filament of fear inserted itself in what passed for his spine.

"About the elephant in the room."

"Which elephant?" It seemed to Riley they had a herd of the beasts following wherever they went.

"How you feel about me being Acting Detective and you having to take orders from me."

"Ah, *that* elephant."

"So you admit that sometimes you find it hard working with me."

"When I see you I want to rip off your clothes and make love to you on the station floor."

Her nose wrinkled. "Pardon me if the setting doesn't appeal. Even though the act might."

"Okay, the locker room, then." He ducked, grinning as she hit him with the pillow. When she'd settled back in a huff, he said quietly, "What I find hard is thinking of you with Moresco."

"So don't think about it. That's in the past."

He hoped so. "Do you find it hard working with me?"

"Yes," she said eagerly, as if dying to get it off her chest. "I'm always expecting you to question my orders so I come down on you too harshly at the start. Then I feel bad and do the opposite only to end up despising myself for being too lenient."

"You're cute when you're conflicted, you know that?" He touched her nose with a fingertip, deliberately trying to get a rise out of her. She was so easy that way.

She swatted his hand away. "I don't want to be critical or question your judgment but sometimes, like yesterday, I have to."

"I promise you, that won't happen again." He'd had enough of this conversation. He didn't want to talk about how he wasn't good for her. "I'm hungry. Let me cook you something in my new kitchen."

"I'd love to but—" She glanced at the bedside clock and swore. "I have to pick up Jamie from school today. He's bringing home the class guinea pig overnight and I don't want Sally to have to deal with the cage and all the food." She rolled out of bed and began to dress.

"So where do we go from here?" Riley knew where he'd like to go—into a real relationship, out in the open, with the possibility of a future together.

"Continue our covert op." Paula fastened her bra and reached for her jeans. "You haven't told the other guys, have you?"

Riley gave her a twisted smile. Nope, they weren't on the same page at all. "No, and I'm not going to."

"Good, because sex is fun but it doesn't solve anything."

IF ANYTHING, WHAT SHE had going on with Riley made her life more complicated. Paula entered the briefing room the next morning and hesitated. John was seated at the head of the table with Detectives Leonard and Cadley to his left, Riley to his right. She had a split second to choose—the seat next to Riley or the one opposite John.

The last time she'd been with Riley they'd been naked in each other's arms. Worse than baring her body, she'd revealed her self-doubts and the way she second-guessed herself. All eyes turned to her as she dithered over where to sit. Heat tinged her cheeks. What had happened to the decisive, assertive Paula Drummond?

She dropped her notebook on the table and slung her purse over the back of the chair farthest away from Riley, deliberately creating space. They were here to discuss illegal drugs in the community and how to stop them. She had to focus.

"Detective Leonard was just filling me in on your meeting with Moresco," John said. "The sting obviously won't work. We're back to square one."

"I still believe Moresco's the key to the crystal meth we've been seeing in Summerside," Paula said. "We'll just have to tackle him from another angle."

"I've gone over the transfer of ownership of the ice-cream shop," Riley said. "He's using a post-office box for an address." He paused half a beat. "I got the paperwork from my stepmother late yesterday afternoon."

After she'd left his house, in other words. "Good. Can you follow that up with the post office today?"

"Boss." Riley gave her the tiniest wink.

She ignored him and turned to Detective Leonard. "Have you found anything in your database that matches the description the high school kids gave us on the dealer they bought the crystal meth from?"

"We've got three possibilities," Leonard said. "Two have priors for dealing, one is a junkie who's been arrested for theft and breaking and entering. We'll chase down those leads—"

U2's "It's a Beautiful Day" suddenly blared from Paula's purse.

"Bloody hell." She fumbled open the zip on her bag and rummaged for her phone. "Sorry. Forgot to put it on silent." She was about to turn it off when she noticed the caller ID.

"It's him. Moresco." The bar of music started to play again. She glanced at John. "Should I take it?"

John nodded. Riley stopped doodling and put down his pen. Detectives Leonard and Cadley leaned closer.

"Hello?" Paula punched a couple of buttons and put the cell on speaker. "Nick?"

"You're on speaker phone. Why?"

"I'm washing dishes and my hands are wet." She rolled her eyes at the flimsy excuse. A sound-effects machine would have been good right now.

"Is anyone else there?"

"No." Paula glanced around at the four men around the table, so quiet you could hear a pin drop—or Nick's voice through the phone. "Look, I'm sorry about the other day. My sergeant had this dumb idea for a sting. I told him it wouldn't work. That you were too smart."

Sorry, she mouthed at John.

"Never mind that. My grandmother is visiting from Palermo. She is eighty-five. Her health isn't good. I want Jamie to come to her birthday party on Saturday afternoon. It's from one to six."

Three heads around the table nodded yes vigorously. Riley frowned and shook his head.

He was listening, no doubt, to the way she spoke to Nick. Listening for the emotional connection he insisted was there no matter how much she denied it.

"I admit, I was fudging the truth the other day, about us being a family," Paula said. "But if you really are going straight, then I will consider you having a role in Jamie's life. But you have to prove yourself before that can happen."

"How do I do that?" Nick asked.

"Well, you could start by giving me your full contact details, where you live. Then you could come to the station and have a chat about the crystal meth that's on the streets right now. If you're not involved, you have nothing to hide. If you help the police in our enquiries, you get brownie points from me."

"First off, I have no address yet. I'm staying with family and friends and you're not getting those details. After your stunt yesterday, I don't want them hassled. Secondly, I've done nothing wrong so I see no reason why police should question me. I do not know who's responsible for the drugs in Summerside so I would be of no use to you."

"You don't wish to earn my trust?"

"It's you who needs to earn my trust. Let Jamie

come to the *festa di compleanno*. His great-grand-mama is old—this is likely her last visit to Australia. All his cousins, his aunts and uncles, and his grandpapa will be there." He paused. "Like it or not, my family is his heritage. They are not all criminals."

She could imagine the scene, a huge boisterous Italian gathering, everyone doting on Jamie. Her son was an only child. All he had were two cousins in Sydney, her brother's kids, who he saw maybe once a year. She experienced a fleeting moment of temptation on Jamie's behalf. Then she remembered who she was dealing with.

"Give me the address," she said. "I'll bring Jamie by for a couple of hours."

"My family would not welcome you," Nick said. "You must trust me with our son."

John was writing something on a piece of paper. He passed it to Paula. *Say yes. You'll have full back-up.*

Paula pushed the paper away. "No deal." She spoke to Nick but was looking at John. "Jamie doesn't go anywhere without me."

Detective Leonard groaned. He quickly clamped a hand over his mouth.

"What was that?" Nick said. "Is someone else there?"

"Jamie. I've got to go." Paula hung up.

She faced down the hostile stares around the

table. "Back-up or no, if Nick gets Jamie inside a house full of his relatives, I might never see my son again."

"While we waste time locating Moresco's residence more teenagers will be sold crystal meth," Detective Cadley said. "We put a tail on our man, a SWAT team at the ready, and your son would be recovered before he even set foot in the house."

"No," Paula said.

"Without evidence linking him to the drugs we got nothing," Detective Leonard said. "If we know where he lives, we can get a warrant to search the premises."

"No," Paula said, louder.

"I agree with Paula," Riley said. "It's too risky."

"Thank you," she said fervently.

Despite Riley's support the tension in the briefing room was thick as she turned her phone off and dropped it in her purse.

She knew she'd done the right thing. But although John hadn't explicitly stated that her future at Summerside P.D. hinged on her cracking this case, she knew the chances of her making the leap from Acting Detective to permanent Detective would be a lot higher if she did. He could find a way around the budget clampdown if he really wanted to.

It mattered. A lot. She had planned to move on

to a larger police department once she got her detective stripes. Now Summerside was where she wanted to live and raise Jamie.

CHAPTER FOURTEEN

"I JUST WASTED four hours of my life I will never get back." Riley entered Paula's temporary office without knocking. He was hot and sweaty from the long drive to the other side of Melbourne through rush-hour traffic. To top things off, the patrol car's air-conditioning had conked out half way.

Copies of the files of her original investigation of Nick were spread across her desk. She was marking places on three different reports with fingertips. "You broke my concentration," she snapped.

"Bite me." The words slipped out before he could stop them.

"I beg your pardon?" Her frown deepened.

"*Boss.* Don't you want to know why I wasted my time? The address the post office had for Moresco belongs to his great-aunt."

"At least you tied up that loose end."

"Bully for me."

The entire drive back, all he'd thought about was seeing her, the two of them sinking a couple of cold ones in his backyard or maybe taking

Jamie to the beach. Instead she was giving him grief for not kowtowing and tugging his forelock. The investigation was stalled. They had no leads whatsoever on Moresco. And ever since the day she'd come to Riley's house with her housewarming gift their relationship had taken a step backward. She wouldn't let him kiss her or even take her hand within four blocks of the station. Claimed her feelings for him made her a lousy cop.

"I'd better go," he said, rising. "I'm in a foul mood, not fit to be around people."

"Wait," Paula said. "I spoke to Katie yesterday when I picked up Jamie and the class guinea pig. We got to talking about your new kitchen and I mentioned the eggcups."

"You shouldn't have. It's really no big deal." He ran a hand over his head, feeling the damp hair and hot scalp underneath. He hated that Katie knew he was being a sook over the eggcups. He didn't want her worrying about him.

"She said she wasn't using them. They were collecting dust in the back of her cupboard."

"Yeah?"

"She brought them around for you." Paula stood and picked up a cardboard box in the corner of her office. "She says they belong in your house. The only reason she took them was so they wouldn't get thrown out. You were in Afghanistan on your first tour of duty or something. Your father was getting married again and was purging, making room for Sandra's things."

Riley opened the box and took out the top cup. It was ceramic with vivid purple and yellow stripes. He remembered eating out of it when he was a kid. "I'm surprised Katie even gave a thought to the eggcups. She was so sick at the time."

"She mentioned she was sick years ago. Was it serious?" Paula delved into the box and came up with an eggcup in the shape of a baby duck. She handed it to Riley.

"Breast cancer. When she was only twenty-two. She almost didn't survive."

"Thank goodness she did. But what an awful thing to go through so young."

"The worst part was, her fiancé couldn't deal with it. He cancelled the wedding and took off on a surfing safari that lasted two years." Riley hadn't been much more support for her. His company had been called to Afghanistan when Katie was in her second round of chemotherapy

"That's terrible. What a jerk."

Riley wasn't about to tell her she was talking about their sergeant. When John had abandoned Katie he'd burned Riley, too. They'd repaired their friendship, but it had been a long slow process that had taken years and a lot of persistence on John's part.

Riley thrust thoughts of the past aside. Something was happening to him right here and now. His hands were shaking, making the ceramic egg-cups he was holding clatter together. Sweat trickled between his shoulder blades. His heart started to race. Spots danced before his eyes.

It was happening again.

The eggcups were like frickin' Kryptonite.

He dropped them into the box, grabbed the one out of her hand and stowed it, too. He had to get out of here before he fell apart in front of her a third time.

Riley folded the flaps on the box and tucked it under his arm. "I need to take off early today. Personal business. I'll make up the time tomorrow."

Paula followed him to the door. "What's going on? Talk to me."

"Later. I'll call you." Riley forced himself to walk, not run, to the exit. As soon as he hit the parking lot he broke into a jog.

He put the box in the trunk of his car, slid behind the wheel. Pain throbbed in his right temple like an enemy beating on the gate.

He punched Simone's number on his cell. The call went to voice mail. Hell. "Simone, this is Riley Henning. I need an appointment. It's kind of an emergency—"

"Hello, Riley," Simone said, picking up. "I had a cancellation. You can come in right now if that suits."

Simone's calm voice had never been so welcome. "I'll be there in five minutes."

A short time later Riley was seated in front of the EMDR machine holding a brightly colored eggcup in each hand. He felt like a dick, but he'd had enough of this post-traumatic stress crap.

"How does this work again?" he asked. "I understand that I felt guilty as a kid over my mother dying. But as an adult I also understand I couldn't have saved her. Why isn't that enough to cure me?"

"It's not that simple. Other factors may be acting upon your subconscious," Simone explained. "EMDR works without you necessarily knowing the exact cause of the trauma."

"You mean I may never know what's at the bottom of the panic attacks?"

"With time we may get a better understanding. At the moment the main thing is to reduce your symptoms. We can explore your feelings about your mother's death at the same time."

It was all mumbo jumbo to Riley but he respected Simone's expertise. "Whatever you say."

"I want you to think about the last few weeks or months of your mother's life," Simone said, in her pleasant, hypnotic voice. "What was it like at home? Was your routine interrupted by hospital visits? Were you scared? Possibly you resented her for not having time for you, for her illness turning your life upside down."

"I don't know," Riley said.

"Take a good look at the eggcups. Turn them over in your hands. Can you picture your mother using them? Perhaps washing them, putting them on the shelf."

Riley gazed at the one in his right hand. The purple and yellow striped cup had been one of a pair. His mother's favorites. "I broke one just like this. I dropped it on the floor."

"Did your mother scold you?"

"No, she was understanding. If something went wrong, she always assumed my sister and I had tried our best. She rarely got angry." He scrunched his eyes shut against a piercing pain in his frontal lobe. "My headache is getting worse."

"Why do you think that is?" Simone asked.

"I—" Shame flooded him. "I broke it on purpose. I was angry with her. I can't remember why— Wait, I can. She'd refused a third round of chemotherapy. Her prognosis wasn't great. She wanted quality of life for her last months. I thought she was giving up. Giving up on her family. On me." Thinking back now, he felt like a selfish child. "I thought breaking the eggcup would be the best way to hurt her."

"Did it?"

He recalled her face, soft with love, raddled with pain. "Yes. I think she knew I did it on purpose but didn't want to make me feel badly because she had so little time left."

Simone flicked on the green light. It flashed on the left, then the right. "Follow the light with your eyes. What else?"

He leaned back in the chair and fixed his eyes on the sliding green light.

"The next day, I went to football practice after school. I wasn't supposed to. I'd been told to come straight home and make sure she was okay, see if she needed anything. But I was still angry." That anger welled up in him now, making his voice hoarse and raw. "She *wasn't* trying her best!"

"So you got home late that night," Simone said evenly. "Keep watching the light. Did something happen?"

"An ambulance was in our driveway as I turned into the street." Flooded with anger, guilt and grief, for a moment he couldn't speak. He could see the ambulance in his mind. "It was dusk. The lights weren't flashing so I knew it wasn't an emergency. But that was worse because it meant there was nothing they could do. She was taken to the hospital. I went with my dad and Katie in the car."

"Did your father make you feel guilty about not being home?"

"No. He barely registered I was there. He was worried about my mother." Riley's breath caught in a sob. Tears blurred his eyes. "I—I wanted to say I was s-sorry to Mum."

"Were you able to apologize at the hospital? Keep watching the light."

He tried but it was like watching a traffic light through a rain-soaked windscreen. Pressure built in his chest. His words came out in short gasps. "I couldn't... tell her anything. She was in a coma. She died the next day." Riley broke down, hands over his face. "I couldn't tell her I was sorry. I couldn't tell her I loved her. I never in my entire life told my mother I loved her."

"You were twelve, Riley. And a boy. In many families boys are raised not to show their emotions. Your father was emotionally reserved. Am I right?"

Riley nodded. He wiped the tears from his eyes with his sleeve and kept his eyes focused on the flashing green light. It seemed to help distance his mind from what he was feeling. "We knew he loved us though even if he didn't express it in words."

"Just as your mother knew you loved her," Simone said gently. "Mothers know that without being told."

"I guess." He took a long breath. Having reached a peak, the overwhelming emotions began to subside.

"She forgives you, Riley. Do you forgive her?"

Fresh tears leaked out. He felt Simone thrust a box of tissues into his hands. He grabbed a wad and blew his nose. "There's nothing to forgive."

"I'm sure that's what she would say about you. It's okay to cry. It's a sign of healing."

With the tears he felt drained, exhausted. The pressure in his chest had eased but he still ached, as if he'd run a marathon.

Simone gave him a few minutes to compose himself, then said, "I think we made considerable progress today."

Riley blinked, mopping at the last of the moisture. "Does that mean I'm cured?"

"Patience. Time will tell. But I believe you're getting there."

So he might or might not have another panic attack.

Riley booked another appointment for the following week. The process was painful but it was better than the alternative.

As he walked to his car he thought over how he'd behaved with Paula earlier. He should have simply told her about his symptoms. But she already thought he was too unstable for a long-term relationship. If he came clean, she might cut things short right now. He'd never get the chance to be the man he wanted to be with her. The man she and Jamie needed.

Hiding his symptoms was dishonest. It disconnected him from her. He wasn't ready to talk about his treatment—not until he was sure his panic attacks were under control—but she deserved an apology for *bite me* and for the abrupt way he'd left.

He sat on the wrought-iron bench beneath the gum tree in the town square and called her cell. Her voice mail came on, so he dialed her office phone. When she didn't pick up he started counting the rings. Seven, eight… He was about to hang up when she answered.

"Hello?"

"It's Riley—"

"I can't talk. I'm on the other line with Sally. She's at the hospital emergency ward." Paula sounded breathless and something else he'd never heard from her—scared out of her wits. "Chloe's been attacked by a dog. Jamie's been snatched."

"SLOW DOWN, SALLY, I can't understand what you're saying." Paula paced her tiny office, picking up and putting down objects at random. Sally was hysterical and Paula could barely contain her own panic. "Take a deep breath, then let it all the way out. Start at the beginning and tell me exactly what happened."

Sally sucked in a long lungful of air. Her words released in a rush on the exhalation. "We were in the front yard. I was weeding the garden. Jamie was playing with his cars. Chloe was on her ride-on toy in the driveway."

"Keep breathing." Paula pressed a hand to her diaphragm as a reminder to herself to do the same thing. Dizzy from lack of oxygen she sat, surprised to see a stapler in her hand. She set it down and picked up a pen. Taking notes made more sense. "Go on."

"A car drove slowly by and parked halfway down the block. A man got out and started walking his dog, coming our way. I thought it was a bit odd to come to our street to walk a dog, but thought maybe he was visiting someone. Then I forgot about it because Jamie was telling me about the parking lot he was making and I told him not to drive into the flowers—" Sally let out a choked sob.

"It'll be okay." Paula heard the tremor in her voice and fought for control. "What happened next?"

"Suddenly the dog—a big black vicious looking thing—was loose." Sally's voice was high-pitched and thready. "H-he charged at Chloe. He attacked my baby. Oh, God, Paula, I was so scared. I thought she was going to be torn apart in front of my eyes. I ran at it with my trowel and hit him on the head and kicked him as hard as I could. He wouldn't let go." She broke down, crying. "He wouldn't let go of her leg."

"Sally, is Chloe all right?"

"The bite wasn't deep, more of a scratch, really." Sally sucked in another shuddering breath. "It's a miracle she wasn't killed. Her leg has been bandaged. We're waiting for someone to give her a tetanus shot and take a blood sample for rabies."

"Thank goodness she wasn't hurt badly." Paula heaved a sigh of relief. "And Jamie?"

Sally started weeping again. "While I was busy trying to get the dog off Chloe, the man must have grabbed him. He whistled for his dog. It let go of Chloe immediately and hopped into the rear of the station wagon. I yelled at the man, demanding he come back and see what his dog had done to my child. That's when I saw Jamie in the backseat."

Paula dropped her head and fought for breath. "Did you get the license plate number?"

"No. He just drove away. Fast."

"Make and model?"

"It was white with one of those cages separating the backseat from the trunk area. It might have been a Ford. Or a Holden. Oh, Paula I'm so sorry."

"It's not your fault."

"I ran after the car with Chloe in my arms. But it was going too fast. I—I saw Jamie turn his head and look at me."

Having a child snatched was every mother's nightmare. Being a cop made it worse. Paula had read reports and seen graphic images of the horrible things that kidnappers did to their victims and knew the terrifying statistics about pedophilia rings. She knew things that would make her violently ill if she thought about them being done to her son.

But her gut told her this wasn't a random kidnapping.

"What did the man look like?"

"He wasn't tall but not short, either. He had dark hair. I didn't get a good look at his face. His clothes were kind of…I don't know, they looked out of place. Like city clothes, not small-town clothes, if that makes any sense."

It did to Paula.

"I believe the man who took Jamie is his father."

"Oh!" Sally processed this. "You were worried about something like this happening. But this is better than a stranger, right? You can contact him."

Paula was dialing Nick's cell number on her landline even as Sally spoke, the receiver tucked between her ear and shoulder. She waited impatiently, but all that met her ear was silence.

He'd already destroyed that phone.

"I don't have a number for him," she told Sally with a sinking heart. "I'll send an officer to the hospital to make sure you're okay and to get a statement. I would come myself but I need to find Jamie."

"I understand." Sally sniffed. "I'm so sorry."

"Don't worry. It's going to be okay," she said with a calmness she wasn't feeling. "What time was he taken, as near as you can tell?"

"It was around four o'clock. I had the radio on in the garage and the news had just come on."

Paula looked at her watch and noted the time. Twenty minutes had elapsed since Jamie had been snatched.

She hung up and put out an all-points bulletin on white station wagons. She thought a moment then extended that to airports. For Nick, obtaining a fake passport would be child's play. He could spirit Jamie out of the country and she would never see her son again.

RILEY WENT STRAIGHT to the station. Paula was in the Incident Room, setting up a whiteboard. He pulled her into his arms and hugged her, not caring who saw. "We'll get Jamie back, don't worry. Tell me what happened."

She hugged him briefly, then eased away. Her eyes were dry and she was in control but she was strung tight. Quickly she brought him up to speed. "I'm almost positive Nick took Jamie."

"When I get hold of that bastard—"

She held up a hand. "Don't. We need to focus on police procedure."

"Where's John? Where's everybody?" Riley

looked out into the office. They had a kidnapping and the place was deserted.

"Delinsky and Grant are off today. Jackson and Crucek are on traffic. I've put a bulletin out for a white station wagon. Our first priority is to find out where Moresco is staying. The dog might be useful in tracking him down. He used to own a Doberman pinscher. I don't know if it's the same dog or another like it."

"Vicious dogs. At least they can be. I'm surprised Chloe's injuries weren't worse."

"That struck me, too," Paula said. "It's almost as if the dog was holding Chloe in place without harming her, like he'd been trained to do that."

"While Moresco grabbed Jamie." Riley sat on the edge of the table. "He wanted your son to go to his grandmother's birthday party."

"That's why I don't believe Nick means to harm Jamie. Whether he plans to give him back after the party is another question."

"What do you want me to do?"

"Work on finding Nick's residence. You can check motor-vehicle registrations for white station wagons."

"Needle in a haystack stuff."

"Got a better idea?"

"No." He eased off the table and headed for the door. "I'll get started right away."

"Riley, wait. I thought you had personal business today."

He paused in the doorway, just wanting to get away. "I had an appointment with the psychologist."

"How's that going?"

It was still too raw for him to talk about. "I had a breakthrough."

Of course he'd thought that before and then he'd cracked when Moresco had picked up Jamie. In hindsight he'd been right....

"Are you cured?" Paula said. "I checked out EMDR on the internet. It's supposed to get good results for PTSD, quickly."

"Simone is optimistic, but she won't rule out the possibility of me having another panic attack." Riley came back into the room and sat. "Maybe we should talk about this. Are you okay with me being on the team that looks for Jamie?"

She hesitated a moment then tried to make up for her qualms by speaking firmly. "Yes, definitely."

"What if Nick comes at you with a gun or a knife and I'm standing there like a gibbering idiot. You're toast." It was a worst-case scenario but he had to bring it into the open. Had to know if she had confidence in him.

"Look, I know I was reluctant before, but I need all the help I can get." She hesitated. "And you've always been there for me. You had my back when the others hazed me. You took me on as partner despite the rumors. That meant a lot to me."

Suddenly there was a whole lot more on the table than he'd expected when he'd walked into this room. He'd been looking for her confidence in him. Now she was talking about his confidence in her. And trust. But there could be no mutual trust without complete honesty.

"We're partners because I'm a mate of John's and he asked me to keep an eye on you."

Paula stilled. "What do you mean, keep an eye on me?"

"You had a reputation when you joined Summerside P.D. It's what you were talking about just now. He thought you might be bent."

"John thought that?" She spun away and turned back. "Did you think so, too?"

Riley hesitated. Then he nodded.

"But now you know differently, right? Now you know I'm as straight as they come."

He should simply say yes. She was worried about Jamie. This was no time to bring up whatever issues were between them. But the elephants had come home to roost, to mix metaphors, and they crowded the room.

"I know you're always defending Moresco. I know there's a quality in your voice when you talk to him, a flirtatious nuance that directly contradicts how you say you feel about him."

"You're jealous."

"Yes, I'm jealous, but I'm also trained in body language and to detect when a person is being honest. There's more to your relationship with Moresco than you're telling."

"I'm not lying to you," she said.

"Then you're lying to yourself. That's worse."

"You're *wrong*. Nick meant nothing to me. He was, and probably still is, a criminal of the worst kind. The kind of man I literally swore on my father's grave to take down." She paced the small area, agitated. "I'm going to keep taking those bastards down until there are no more drug lords or dealers to poison our children, corrupt our community and kill good men before their time."

She stopped moving, chest heaving, eyes wild. "I *hate* Nick Moresco. I hate that I had sex with him."

Thou dost protest too much. Riley knew she meant what she said and believed it. He also knew that on some level, it wasn't true. It broke his heart. And it made him angry. Because for a while he'd thought they really had something special, something that might last. But even the strongest connection between a man and a woman was as frail as gossamer when it came to a lie.

"I'll get started on the DMV registrations.

He walked out the door. This time she didn't call him back.

PAULA WATCHED RILEY leave, stunned at the unexpected turn their relationship had taken. What had just happened here? One minute they'd been all about propping each other up. The next he'd attacked her over Nick.

She shook her head and came back to life, sitting and moving her chair close to her desk. She didn't have time for this bullshit.

Forty-six minutes. And counting.

Systematically she shut down the emotional compartments of her brain. Mental doors slammed on her feelings for Riley, on her own self-doubt. Even on her maternal fears and imaginings about what Jamie was going through. She shut down everything but logic and reason and training.

Dry-eyed, fueled by a burning anger, she got to work. In John's absence she made decisions about deploying personnel. If she got in trouble for it, she would take her lumps. She called Jackson and Crucek in, briefed them and sent them out to interview residents on Sally's street who might have witnessed the kidnapping. Delinsky she sent to the hospital to take Sally's statement.

She called her old partner, Detective Russo, at Melbourne Metropolitan Police Department. With a combination of sweet-talk and bullying she got him to agree to email her copies of additional files on Moresco and his crime associates she'd compiled seven years ago.

While she waited for the files to arrive Paula traced the tortuous paper trail surrounding ownership of the ice-cream shop. Nick wasn't the registered owner. The owner was Palermo Holdings, an Italian furniture import store with a Carlton address in the city. A Mr. Ricardo Santorini was listed as the manager of Palermo. She had a hunch Santorini was the cousin Ricky she'd overheard Nick speak to on the phone years ago.

By the time she'd found the phone number for Ricardo Santorini, the email from Russo had arrived.

"Hey, Ricky," she said, adopting the voice she'd used in her cover's persona—western suburbs with a touch of second-generation Italian. "Is Nick there?"

"Nah, he's down the peninsula somewheres," Ricardo said. "Who is this?"

"Angela, Maria's daughter."

"Who?" Papers rustled. He sounded distracted.

"My mum is your Aunty Therese's second cousin," Paula lied fast, referring to the family tree on the screen in front of her.

"Uh, okay. Nice to hear from you. What's up?"

Paula took a deep breath and plunged in, banking on Ricky being a typical Italian male who didn't keep track of the whereabouts of his dozens of female relatives.

"Mama told me about Nonna's birthday party and said I'd better show up with a plate of cannelloni or else. But I lost the address and she's gone out of town to bloody Woop Woop for a few days, and there's no cell phone reception so I can't call her."

"So what do you want with Nick?" A trace of suspicion entered Ricky's voice. Possibly he was even wondering why she'd called him and not his mother or some other female who would know more about the festivities than him.

"I thought the party was at his house," she said innocently. "I heard he bought a flash new place when he got out of the joint. Trying to impress the rellies that he's got his mojo back."

"I don't know where you heard that pile of BS. Nick's laying low. The shindig is at Tina and Matteo's."

"Tina's house. Okay, gotcha. Ta for that." She hung up before Ricky could ask any more questions.

Tina and Matteo? Paula didn't recall anyone by those names. Nothing on the family tree. She scrolled through the list of Nick's contacts. Nope, not there, either. So much of detective work was tedious, fact-checking, eliminating possibilities, narrowing the playing field.

Paula went out to the bull pen. The night shift had arrived so she commandeered one of the uniforms and got him going through the phone book, starting with Carlton where most of Nick's relatives and friends lived, and working outward across the metropolitan area.

Dinner was a hamburger from the take-out down the road. While she munched, she called Sally to check on Chloe and heard with relief that the blood tests had come back negative for rabies. Then her mother called and Paula filled her in on developments, grateful for her mum's quiet confidence that Jamie would come home safely. It wasn't logical but it was reassuring, and Paula needed a dose of reassurance right now.

She'd just hung up when John knocked on her door. Paula automatically checked her watch. Nearly 7:00 p.m. Outside, the sun cast long shadows and glinted gold off the windows across the road.

Jamie had been missing three hours.

John dropped into a chair. "I got your message. I understand you've taken over my station." She started to explain but he held up a hand. "You did the right thing. Any progress?"

She rolled her shoulders to stretch them and shook her head. "I've got first names for the couple who are hosting Moresco's grandmother's birthday party, but that's about it. Not holding out much hope on the station wagon he was driving. The ice-cream shop registration was a dead end."

"He's covered his tracks well. Do you think he was planning something like this from the beginning?"

"I don't know."

A silence spun out.

Part of her wanted to ask if John still distrusted her but she couldn't afford the mental or emotional energy asking would demand of her. That was in a compartment of her brain that was in lockdown. Right now she didn't give a damn what anyone thought of her.

"I talked to Riley. He seems upset but he's not being very communicative. Are you two okay?"

"I don't know what you mean." Paula stared him down. Her and Riley's relationship had never been officially outed—station romances were frowned on—although Riley might have mentioned it to his friend.

Not that it mattered anymore. She and Riley were done.

"Never mind." John sighed and rose. He rapped her desk lightly with his knuckles. "We'll get your son back."

"Damn right we will."

Paula returned to the database, searching for clues, no matter how tiny.

CHAPTER FIFTEEN

RILEY RUBBED HIS eyes. They were blurred and sore from hours of going through motor vehicle registrations on the computer. This wasn't what he'd signed up for when he'd joined the police department. But it was part of the job and he had to do it. If it meant finding Jamie...

"Anything?" Paula stood three feet from his desk, arms crossed. Keeping her distance.

He didn't know how to bridge the gap. Knew she wouldn't welcome him trying right now. She was focused on one thing—finding Jamie.

"I've got a short list of a couple thousand white station wagons. I'm working on my short short list now." He put a hand up to stifle a yawn.

The day shift had long gone home. Celine was working night-shift Dispatch. The station was quiet.

"Go home," Paula said.

"I'm not tired."

"That was an order, Henning. If we get a break tomorrow, you'll need to be alert."

She didn't wait for an answer, just walked to

her office. He noticed she wasn't quitting for the night. He tried to resume the search but the letters and numbers swam in his vision. Much more of this and he'd need glasses.

All right. He'd take a break.

Riley went home, had a shower and heated leftover pizza in the microwave, washing it down with a beer. Sitting in his house alone was hard. The thought of Jamie being separated from his mum made him want to punch a hole in the wall or something.

Riley changed into jeans and a sweatshirt and headed off to the shooting range for some target practice. Maybe he could ease his frustration by imagining the bull's-eye was Nick Moresco.

He walked through the concrete bunker to one of the individual shooting lanes. Fifty meters away a red and white target was clipped to an electronic track positioned in front of a wall of thick wood.

He loaded his Smith and Wesson and donned safety glasses and earmuffs. Then he gripped the revolver in both hands, braced his legs and extended his arms straight. He lined up the sights and fired off a round of six bullets in quick succession. Acrid smoke filled his nostrils. The recoil sent jolts through his arms and up his shoulders.

He lowered his arms and lifted his safety glasses to squint at the target. Two bullets had hit the bull's-eye. All six bullets had placed inside the first three rings. Nothing wrong with his aim.

He pushed a button and the target came toward him along an overhead cable. Shots rang out elsewhere in the range, the muffled reports echoing off the concrete walls.

His fingers fumbled with the bullets, slotting two in, dropping the third. He'd thought he could get away from his thoughts, take a break from his feelings. But apparently not. He'd hurt Paula. He'd let her down.

You do it all the time.

Bullshit. Who else had he let down?

All the women in his life. Nabili, his mother, Katie…

Nabili? He'd barely known her.

His cell phone buzzed against his thigh. Shucking his earmuffs he answered without even looking at the caller ID, so sure it would be Paula with news about Jamie. "Have you found him?"

"This is Katie. I heard from Sally that Jamie's missing. I didn't want to bother Paula. What happened?"

Riley told her what he knew and tried to reassure her, but he couldn't hide the fact that they only had the flimsiest of leads.

He pulled off his safety glasses and laid his gun on the counter. "How are you doing?"

"I'm okay. Same old, same old."

It felt like too long since he'd talked to his sister. He wanted to keep her on the line, ask her about her class. But when he opened his mouth, it all poured out. "I'm sorry. Sorry I abandoned you."

"What? Riley. What are you talking about?"

"I left for Afghanistan when you had cancer. You—" He didn't want to remind her of how she'd nearly died. During the second round of chemo the doctors found cancer in her second breast. Her prognosis had been grim. Riley had left home not knowing if he'd ever see his only sibling again.

"Riley, I wasn't mad at you. I was mad at John. You couldn't help it. You'd trained and struggled to get into the SAS. You had to go when the army called you." Her voice hardened. "John had a choice."

"But you're my sister. Blood is thicker than water."

Then she laughed bitterly. "Or seawater, which is what must be flowing in John's veins."

Riley wiped a hand across his face. He'd never particularly thought of himself as emotional but he'd been on one hell of a roller-coaster ride the past few weeks. "Oh, Katie. I don't know what I would have done if I'd lost you."

"Well, you didn't."

"Anyway, I just needed to apologize."

"You've said sorry before," Katie reminded him.

"I forgave you long ago. Not that there was anything to forgive."

That left Nabili as the last person he'd wronged. Who, like Katie, had dark hair and green eyes and was a teacher. *She looks like your sister.*

"Keep me posted on Jamie," Katie added. "I'll be worried sick until he's found. And if there's anything I can do, let me know."

"I will. Take care, Katie."

He hung up. Then sifted through his received calls till he found the one from Gazza. He hit the button for reply. The call went to voice mail, so he sent a text message asking Gazza to give him Pete's email address or for Pete to get in touch with Riley. There had to be a bottom to this black hole he was in.

THE NEXT TIME Paula looked out of the blinds, darkness had fallen over Summerside. She glanced at her watch and was surprised to see it was nearly midnight.

Jamie had been missing seven hours and forty-eight minutes.

Closing her eyes, she allowed herself a moment to think about him and hope he was safe. That he wasn't hungry or cold or frightened. *I'm coming, mate. Don't worry.*

She rose and stretched her back, rotating her stiff shoulders. Staring at the computer screen had left her with a headache. She wouldn't get any more productive work done tonight.

She packed up her files and walked through the station. All was quiet except for a uniformed cop booking in a tipsy fiftysomething woman who'd reversed her car outside the pub and hit a Stop sign.

At home Paula let herself into the dark house. She made herself a cup of chamomile tea, delaying the moment when she'd have to walk past Jamie's empty room.

Fatigue was dragging her down but the thought of lying in bed alone in the dark, worrying instead of sleeping was enough to give anyone insomnia. She drifted into her sewing room thinking she could choose fabrics for the next row of patches while she drank her tea. Hopefully a few minutes with her quilt would soothe her enough to sleep.

What she wanted right now was a dark blue. She sorted through the small pile of scraps on the table. She didn't find anything to her liking so she got out the garbage bag full of old clothes and fabric oddments and dumped it in the middle of the floor. It had been a few years since she'd seen the bottom of this bag. Usually she just put her hand in and pulled out something at random. It might be a good idea to sort out the remnants by color and store them in separate bags. When her life turned to crap, when chaos threatened, she craved order.

She threw a couple of pink and red items into a small pile, a green T-shirt of Jamie's over there—Hello, what was this?

She held up a man's dress shirt, midnight blue silk. A faint whiff of expensive—and familiar—cologne wafted toward her as she shook it out.

Nick's shirt. She'd thought she'd thrown this out. It was evidence. Oh, nothing that could be used against him in a trial. It was evidence that she'd had feelings for him. That she had slept with him when she didn't have to. That she'd delayed his arrest, not telling her superior officer about the evidence she did have, so she could spend one more night with him.

She buried her face in the cool silk, crumpling it in her hands. That time discrepancy was what had gotten her busted back to uniform. Not falling asleep on the job. It was the deliberate manipulation of the investigation for her personal ends.

In the interval between the meeting with Al and the actual arrest Nick could have gotten wind of the arrest and left town, or had his goons lay in wait for the armed response unit. She'd put other cops at risk.

She'd betrayed her father's memory.

She couldn't even pretend she'd blocked this from her mind. She recalled exactly how much she'd wanted him then. She'd been young and, yes, needy—not of love so much as security. He was an experienced older lover with wealth and a big family. She could have had all that if she closed her eyes to his criminal activities.

She'd read about prisoners who became attached to their captors, or detectives who fell in love with the criminal they were investigating. She wasn't the first person to become so deeply embedded that she lost her ability to think rationally.

She was long out of his spell, if that was the right word for it. And yet, echoes of their old relationship remained, enhanced by the fact that they shared a son.

Riley had been right. That was what she couldn't bear to admit, why she'd gotten so angry at the mere suggestion. Oh, God, how must he have felt hearing her flirt with Nick?

She didn't love Nick. Not now. She *couldn't* love a man who could sell crystal meth to kids.

A man who could kidnap his own son.

Moresco as a lover had been a fantasy she'd bought into to disguise the grubbiness of undercover work, to mask what was happening to her. *Riley* was the real man, a hero in every sense of the word.

SUNLIGHT STREAMED THROUGH cracks in Riley's curtains. Yawning, he scrubbed his hands through his hair and swung his legs over the edge of the bed. Six o'clock. A couple of crows were making a racket in the tall pine across the street. He had a mind to book them for being a public nuisance.

He checked his phone messages, hoping Paula had left word that either Jamie had returned or she had a lead on his whereabouts. Nothing.

Riley padded out to the kitchen to put on the kettle for coffee. While he waited for the water to boil he studied his decor. He'd never thought he'd be using the word *decor* in a non-ironic fashion. The eggcups were lined up on the narrow shelf above the stove. Paula's black rooster fit right in. His mum would have liked the look. She would have loved the new stove.

Coffee in hand, he went to the bedroom to check his email. He scrolled through the new messages, looking them over.

Lieutenant Peter Caldwell.

Riley put down his mug and clicked open the email.

G'day, Riley. I'm in Kabul on a few days' leave. Got a message from Gazza saying you wanted to know what went down that day you ran afoul of the suicide bomber in Kabul. I was on patrol with you. Here's what I remember.

An Afghani woman named Nabili ran a school for girls, officially sanctioned by the government but a target for the Taliban. We went on regular patrols past the place to keep her and the girls safe. You gave her money to buy pencils and paper. Said she reminded you of your sister.

The day of the explosion we were walking toward the school—Gazza said you don't remember stuff. The school wasn't a big group of buildings with playing fields like Australian ones. It was just a concrete house at the end of a row of houses with a vacant lot next door.

I stopped to have a yarn with the dude who sold tea on the corner. You went on ahead. I don't know the exact sequence of events because I was talking, right? I heard a scream and looked over. Nabili had opened the door to a woman in a burka. The woman—who was really a man—grabbed her. You were still a hundred meters away. I was probably twice that. Burka man started shouting in Farsi.

The suicide bomber.

Nabili screamed at you in English, "Shoot, shoot!"

Far from the hot dusty streets of Kabul, Riley started to sweat.

The guy was holding Nabili in front of him. You couldn't get a clear shot. You ducked and dodged, but the bomber kept her between you. He was ranting something. Nabili started yelling in Farsi.

Telling the girls to run away from the school as fast as they could. Riley was starting to remember. His heart began to race. But—he noticed dispassionately—he wasn't losing control. This was "normal" anxiety, not a panic attack. Could the EMDR be working?

The little girls came pouring out of the side door into the vacant lot. Nabili screamed at you, "Shoot me. Shoot me."

If she were dead the suicide bomber would have no hostage. Riley could then shoot the bomber. He dropped his face in his hands. Killing Nabili to save her young female students would have been the correct thing to do. It was what he'd been trained to do in those circumstances.

He'd choked. But where was his backup? Why hadn't Pete come to his aid?

I was running like batshit toward the school. Once I got level with you I started firing. But it was too late. The bomber detonated. Then it was raining body parts.

Riley stared at the screen. Tears streamed down his face. It was all coming back to him. He hadn't been able to fire his gun when he'd needed to. He hadn't been able to kill an innocent woman who reminded him of Katie.

By *not* shooting her, he'd let her down. The girls she loved as if they were her own had died. Everything she'd worked for, gone. His final days in Afghanistan had been horrific. No wonder he'd blocked them out.

As corny as it sounded, all he wanted was to keep the streets of Summerside safe for his family and his friends and the ordinary people who depended on the local police.

Mate, if you're beating yourself up about what happened, don't. You're human, not a robot. Nobody should have to make the kind of choice you had to make. You're a good soldier and an honorable man.

Riley ached for the camaraderie he'd missed—plain speaking, no nonsense and good humor. The men tolerated each other's foibles, called each other on their bullshit, but underneath all the joshing was the ironclad knowledge that the guys would always be there for each other.

The mateship of soldiers was evident in cops, too. Paula was no exception. While he wouldn't call her one of the guys, she got it, she really did.

He hit reply on the email.

Pete, mate, I'm a little shell-shocked reading your account of that day. But thanks. I hope it wasn't painful for you to relive. If you can get to the ANZAC Day march in Canberra, I'll be first in line to shoot you a beer.

Riley hit Send, then logged off.

He looked at the clock. It was only 7:00 a.m but he bet Paula would be at the station early. He reached for his phone and dialed.

"Good morning," he said when Paula answered.

"Riley?" She sounded tired and anxious but determined. The woman had a spine of steel.

This wasn't the time to apologize or hash over whatever was going on—or not going on—between them. "Just letting you know I'll be at the station in half an hour, reporting for duty."

"Make it twenty minutes. We have a lot of work to do."

"Boss." Riley imbued the word with affection. There was silence on the other end as if for once Paula didn't know how to respond.

He hung up before she could reject him.

He wasn't prepared to say categorically he would never have another panic attack. But for the first time in a long time he felt in control of himself. If he were a betting man, he wouldn't mind betting on himself.

Look out Nick Moresco. Riley Henning was back.

SIXTEEN HOURS and seven minutes…

It didn't sound very long but to Paula the past night had been the longest of her life. She never wanted to experience another one like it.

Riley's phone call, while surprising and a little odd, had lifted her spirits. She absolutely did not want to bring their personal issues into the briefing room but she was dying to know what was going on with him. And if he would still care when she confirmed his suspicions that she'd had feelings for Nick Moresco. The only way they were going to have a lasting relationship would be to be completely honest with each other.

But all that was for some other time.

Paula arrived at the Incident Room just before seven-thirty. Riley and Delinsky were seated at the table. John stood against the wall. Jackson and Crucek had interviewed potential witnesses but they were off today.

It was a mammoth task to find a boy in a city of over four million people with a team that consisted of her and two uniformed cops. One of those uniforms was a solider who'd served on active duty. But still.

Riley glanced up when she entered the room. His gaze was cool, calm and confident. She breathed a quiet sigh of relief. He, too, had left the personal stuff at home.

Before she got down to business she had a word

with John. "I want more men on the ground. We need to call on Frankston."

"Not going to happen." John shook his head. "A kid in Frankston OD'd on crystal meth last night. Cardiac arrest. He's in the hospital, fighting for his life. Frankston's putting all their manpower into locating the dealer who sold him the ice."

Paula bit back a curse and squared her shoulders. "All right. We'll make do."

"Get a solid lead, something you can act on, and I'll pull another uniform for you," John conceded.

She had a lead—Tina and Matteo—but it wasn't solid enough, not without an address.

Paula nodded briefly to everyone and stood at the head of the table. "The birthday party is today. We need to locate the venue and intercept Moresco before he arrives at the party."

Delinsky put a hand up. "Do we know his current whereabouts?"

"No." Paula kept her voice level and expression calm so as to not reveal how much that bothered her. "The hosts of the party are Tina and Matteo. No last name and no first name matches among Moresco's known family, friends or business associates. We're also searching second names—lots of people go by their middle names. If Moresco is keeping a low profile, it's all the more likely he'll conceal the IDs of people in his circle."

Riley raised his hand. "I could run that for you. I did a stint in electronic intelligence in the army."

The things she didn't know about him. She wanted to hug him. Instead she simply nodded. "Excellent. How are you doing with the short short list matching the white station wagon with an address?"

"I recommend we put all our resources on Tina and Matteo," Riley said. "I suspect Moresco would have ditched the kidnapping car by now."

"You're probably right." Paula planted her knuckles on the table and leaned forward. "The clock is ticking. The party starts at one o'clock and goes till six. We need to find Jamie within that time frame. Afterward, who knows where he'll end up."

"Is it possible Moresco will simply bring back your son once he's seen his great-grandmother?" John asked.

Until now John had been leaning against the wall, taking in proceedings. Paula suspected he was evaluating her performance. If she weren't so focused on finding her son, she'd probably be offended he could do that when he must know she was in the worst emotional state of her life.

"It's a possibility, I suppose," Paula conceded. "But I don't want to take the chance that he has something more permanent in mind."

The atmosphere in the room became grim.

Paula couldn't bear it. "What are you waiting for? Get moving."

The men filed out. Riley was last to leave.

Paula looked up. "When this is all over and we have Jamie back…" She floundered and had to grip a pencil in both hands. She wanted so badly to reach out to him but didn't know how. There was so much at stake.

"I was thinking Jamie might like to march in the ANZAC Day parade with me," Riley said. "If that would be okay with you?"

She nodded, grateful he'd given her a point in the future with Jamie, a solid image of her small son marching alongside the soldier Jamie hero-worshiped. It was something she could hang on to over the next few nerve-racking hours. "That would be good."

The day passed slowly, tediously, cross-referencing phone books, government records, hospital records, every kind of record they could imagine to find a couple named Tina and Matteo.

Four o'clock came and went. Twenty-four hours and counting…

Paula's nerves were frayed. She knew in child-abduction cases that most murders occurred in the first twenty-four hours. She found it hard to believe Moresco would kill his own son, but it happened all the time.

To make matters worse, John had informed

her that because the chief kidnapping suspect was the father, the Department of Federal Police wasn't treating Jamie as a missing person. There would be no checks on airports or boat harbors. She'd done pretty well keeping an icy calm until now, but cracks were starting to form. She'd just snapped at Delinksy for taking a five-minute coffee break.

"Paula?" Riley rose from behind a computer and crossed the bull pen.

"What is it?" she barked. Then put a hand to her forehead and closed her eyes briefly. "Sorry. Start again. What is it?" she asked in a more reasonable tone.

"I've got something." He put a printout of names and addresses in her hands. "Halfway down."

"Just tell me what I'm looking at," she said through gritted teeth.

"Inmates of the prison where Moresco was incarcerated." Riley stood next to her shoulder and pointed to a name. "Matteo Tibaldi, close friend of Moresco's cousin Rocky. Matteo wasn't on your list of Moresco's contacts because he was out of action, serving fifteen years for manslaughter and drug dealing. He was released eighteen months ago. Lives in Williamstown with his wife."

Paula turned her head, searching Riley's face. "Please tell me…"

Riley grinned. "Her name is Tina."

Paula gave a whoop and threw her arms around Riley's neck, squeezing hard. He lifted her off her feet before setting her back down.

She pushed away, tugging her shirt down at the hem. "Forgot myself for a moment. Good work. Incident Room. Now."

On her way there she stopped in John's office to inform him they had an address. But looking at the assembled team, she quailed. Herself, Riley and Delinksy. They were so few in number.

Peterson hurried in and slid into a chair. "The boss told me to report to you."

Yes. John had made good on his word.

"Here's the plan," she said. "We'll surround the house. Delinksy and Peterson at the back door, Riley at the front—but stay out of sight. I'll enter."

"I don't like it," Riley said. "I'll go in with you. Delinsky at the back, Peterson covers the front."

"If you go in, too, we look like a couple of cops," Paula argued. "By myself, I might be able to pass on the mommy card. If I can take Jamie out of there without a scene, so much the better. I don't want any civilians injured. I don't want my son traumatized."

Riley scowled and looked as though he wanted to say more. Paula ignored him. He didn't have to like it. He just had to back her up.

"Henning, you ride with me," Paula said. "Let's get moving. It's an hour and a half drive."

"I bet you can make it in an hour fifteen."

"You're on." It was easier to joke around than think about what was ahead.

They were still bantering as they exited to the parking lot.

"Hey, where do you think you're going?"

Paula spun to see Jackson and Crucek approach in full uniform. "I thought you two were off."

"What, and miss all the fun?" Crucek demanded.

She'd held it together till now, but the thought of these guys coming in for her and her son almost made her burst into tears.

"You guys haven't showed so much initiative since you pulled that dumb stunt with the coffee sugar. How'd you know, anyway?"

Jackson nodded at Riley. "Wyatt Earp called us."

Riley snorted. "Don't let it go to your head."

She didn't look at him. If they still had something between them, it would be there when this was over. If they didn't... Well, she wasn't going to think about that now.

CHAPTER SIXTEEN

PARTY GUESTS WERE leaving by the time Riley and Paula cruised past the Williamstown house in the unmarked car. Riley stopped for couples and families crossing the road, giving them ample time to get a good look at the house and surrounding garden. It was a two-story, rendered brick home set on a trim lawn bordered by a low box hedge. A high wide portico over the doorway formed a second-floor balcony.

A black Ford sedan pulled out from the side of the road ahead. Riley drove into the vacated slot. Paula was on the radio to Jackson and Delinksy, finalizing the details. She sounded calm but her knuckles were white where she gripped the radio and he could feel her tension like the hum of a high-voltage wire.

"We don't make a move till the last guests are out," she said, going over the plan once more. "I will go in. If I'm not out in fifteen minutes, Riley comes in. If you don't get a signal from one of us within another ten minutes, Jackson and Crucek storm the back door, Delinsky and Peterson come through the front. Keep exits secure at all times. Do not fire unless directly ordered to. This is a family home." She took a breath. "My child is in there."

Waiting was hard. The guests lingered under the portico. Children ran around and had to be gathered. The transition to parked cars was leisurely, people stopping to chat more before departing. Some folks glanced curiously at Riley and Paula. She slunk low in her seat, a baseball cap pulled over her face. He studied a map, as if pretending to look for an address.

A rap on the glass made him glance up. A henna-haired woman in her sixties was smiling at him, motioning him to lower the window.

"I live around here," she said. "Can I help? What address are you looking for?"

"We're...trying to get back to the highway," Riley said. "Do you know the best way?"

"Go to the end of the road, turn right, left at the roundabout and you'll hit the main drag," the woman said. "Keep going straight and you'll come to the entrance to the freeway."

"Right, left, straight." Riley gave her a salute and folded his map. "Cheers."

She tottered away on her high heels then looked back to give him an encouraging smile and to motion with her hand, right at the end of the street.

Riley started the engine. "Old busybody. Now I have to go around the block."

"Make it two blocks." Paula, still slumped in her seat, radioed to the others to let them know why they were moving.

Riley drove around for ten minutes and returned to the same parking spot he'd vacated, opposite the house on the left of Matteo and Tina's.

"There are only two cars left on the street. They could belong to residents," Riley said. "The front door is shut. The yard's empty. What do you say? Is it time?"

Paula lifted her cap, assessed the situation. Even knowing how high the stakes were, her expression gave him a jolt. She wasn't only a cop going after a criminal. She was a mother protecting her child. "It's time."

Being a woman, she checked herself in the mirror. To make sure she looked good for Moresco? Riley quashed the bite of jealousy. She couldn't possibly feel that way now.

As she walked up to the door Riley had the urge to forget caution and storm the house, guns blazing, to take Jamie back. Instead he checked his watch and set the timer. This wasn't the Wild West and it wasn't Kabul. There was no place for cowboys in suburbia.

PAULA RANG THE BELL and stepped back. She glanced at her watch then took a deep calming breath.

A glamorous-looking blonde in her thirties wearing a stylish blue dress, five-inch heels and a warm smile opened the door. Her expression sobered as she registered Paula's plain gray pants and button-down with its muted maroon stripes. Clearly she wasn't a guest.

"Can I help you?" she asked.

Paula didn't want to flash her badge unless absolutely necessary. "I'm here to pick up Jamie Drummond. I'm his mother."

The blonde glanced uncertainly over her shoulder. "Wait here. I'll see what Nick says." She shut the door in Paula's face.

Paula counted to three, then stepped inside. The foyer was a marble vault accented with pink statues in recesses and an abundance of green foliage. To her left was the dining room, the table still bearing the remains of a buffet. To the right was a formal living room dotted with used glasses and plates.

From deeper in the house came the sound of voices. She was about to go looking when Nick appeared in the arched doorway to the dining room.

"So, you found me. Sadly, you're too late for the party." He sounded unconcerned.

Paula wasn't fooled. "I've been worried about Jamie," she said, matching his casual tone. "I've come to take him home."

"Why so soon, *cara?*" Nick shrugged negligently, the picture of reasonableness. "He's having a wonderful time, getting to know his cousins."

"Did you tell him you were his father?" A gritty edge crept into her voice.

"I didn't have to. He made the connection himself." Nick strolled into the foyer, circling Paula. "His aunties and grandmama and great-grandmama have been fawning over him for the past two days. I think he must be a lonely little boy."

"Not two days. Twenty-six hours and twelve minutes," Paula corrected, turning to keep Nick from getting behind her. "He doesn't belong here and you know it."

But his barb hit home. Jamie had family whom he had a right to know.

"He doesn't want to leave," Nick said, now with a hint of steel to his voice. "He calls me *Dad*."

"Bring him to me. Let him decide." She was taking a risk. Jamie might be so hyped-up on candy and attention that he'd beg her to let him stay longer. But she only had Nick's word that her son was happy.

"He's busy," Nick said. "And I'm not ready for him to go yet. You've had him for six years. I want time to get to know my son."

Paula was getting impatient. "You mean before you go back to prison for child abduction and drug dealing?"

"Tsk, tsk. I keep telling you I'm not in the drug

trade anymore. As for abduction, Jamie is my son. Taking him isn't a crime. I checked."

"It is if I have a court order granting me sole custody." She fished in her back pocket and produced a copy of the order. As she did, she noted the time. "You've got two minutes to bring Jamie out."

Nick glanced at the legal document. His expression hardened. "Or...?"

She shrugged. "Or I'll take him."

He chuckled. "No offense, I know you're tough, but you wouldn't stand a chance against the Moresco womenfolk."

"Don't make jokes where my son is concerned. My men have your house surrounded. If I'm not outside with Jamie in two minutes, they're coming in. It would be better if you cooperated. I don't want anyone to get hurt."

"My men are upstairs, with your men in the crosshairs," Nick said calmly.

"You're bluffing. My men wouldn't show themselves."

"Really?" Nick folded his arms across his chest. "When you don't come out at the appointed time, one of them will emerge. Isn't that your plan? Do you want to place a bet on whether he'll reach the house?"

Riley. She couldn't let him get in the firing line. "Jamie might be happy right now but pretty soon he's going to want his mum. What are you going to tell him if I'm not there?"

Nick considered this. "I could tell him you've gone overseas for business. That's a good story. I could tell him he's going to live with me from now on."

Paula's skin turned to ice. Was he insane? The conversation had taken on a surreal feeling. "You won't get away with this."

Nick shrugged. Clearly he felt he held all the cards.

"Jamie!" Paula yelled suddenly. "Jamie, I'm here."

She pushed past Nick, taking the route through the dining room. He grabbed her arm. She wrenched free and started to run, calling for her son.

"Mummy!" Jamie's voice came faintly from the rear of the house.

"I'm coming, mate." Paula reached the modern kitchen, left chaotic from party preparations and the half-finished clean-up. From the foyer she could hear Nick calling upstairs in Italian.

Jamie burst through the door on the far side of the kitchen as Nick ran into the room. Paula crouched and opened her arms for her son. Jamie barreled toward her. Nick slung Paula out of the way. Then he picked up Jamie, holding the boy in front of him.

Nick backed toward the rear door, picking up

a boning knife from the counter. He held it to Jamie's throat. "Don't come any closer."

Oh, dear Lord. Paula sucked in a breath. "Don't move, sweetheart. Keep very still."

But Jamie was startled. He did move. The point of the knife dug into his tender neck. "Mummy. He's hurting me."

Riley stepped out from behind the door, gun drawn and aimed at Nick. "Let the boy go." Without taking his eyes off Moresco he added to Paula, "Don't worry, I'm in control."

He meant of himself. She prayed he was right.

Where had he come from? How had he gotten through the firing line of Nick's men upstairs? It didn't matter. She'd never been so glad to see anyone in her life.

"I don't want anyone hurt," she said. "Nick, drop the knife. Think about where you are. You don't want to spoil your grandmother's party."

A flicker went over Nick's face. Appealing to his sense of family was the right tactic. Family and ego drove him.

She was aware of a shuffling noise in the dining room but couldn't take her eyes off Nick. The next words were hard but she forced herself. "Jamie's your son. Do you really want him to think of you as a thug?"

"My son will carry on the Moresco name. He's going to follow in my footsteps."

"As a drug dealer?" Paula scoffed.

"I am a businessman!" Nick tightened his grip on Jamie. The boy whimpered, his eyes huge and fearful.

"Nicky?" an elderly woman said from behind Paula. "What's going on?"

"Nothing, Grandmama. Go back upstairs." Although Nick dismissed her, he spoke with deference.

Paula shifted until the newcomer was in her line of sight. Nick's grandmother wore a black dress and had white hair piled on top of her head. She shuffled into the room with the help of a silver-topped cane.

Behind her came Loretta, his mother. Paula recognized her from her file photo. She was a big woman in a flowing blue caftan, with shoulder-length dark gray hair threaded with tiny braids.

Thank heavens the women had arrived. Paula moved her shoulders, releasing some of the tension. She spoke to the grandmother. "Please tell him to put down the knife."

Grandma's sharp black gaze darted from Nick to Paula. "Are you the cop?" she spat in a thick accent. "You keep my great-grandson a secret from his family. Is not right. Loretta, take the boy upstairs."

"Come with Nonna, Jamie," Loretta said kindly. "Nick, give him to me. You're scaring the child."

"No. He's staying with me until Paula and her goon get out of this house."

"Please let me go." Jamie had tears in his eyes. "I want my mummy."

Paula's heart squeezed. Jamie only called her mummy when he was really tired or scared.

Nick lowered the knife and turned Jamie in his arms to look into his face. "Why, *bambino?*" he said tenderly. "I can give you so much. Any toy you want, cousins to play with, all the cake and ice cream you want."

"If you let me go, I'll come another day." Jamie sniffled. "Please…Dad."

Paula held her breath.

"You see?" Nick said. "He calls me Dad. How could I give him up?"

"Can't you see he's frightened of you?" Paula said. "Let him go."

"Nicky, look out!" Loretta shouted.

When Moresco had lowered the knife Riley moved in swiftly. He wrenched Nick's hand and twisted it behind his back, pushing the barrel of his gun into the drug dealer's neck. The knife clattered to the floor.

"Jamie, get a wriggle on," Riley said. "Go, now."

Jamie squirmed his way out of Nick's grasp and slithered to the floor. He ran to Paula. She gathered him in her arms and held him tightly. Her throat was clogged with unshed tears. She had her baby back.

Over the top of Jamie's head Paula saw Riley handcuff Nick after a brief struggle. Beads of perspiration stood out on Riley's forehead but his gaze was steady, as was his grip on his gun. She gave him a nod of approval.

"I'm taking Jamie outside." The clock was ticking down to when Jackson and the others were supposed to storm the house. She wanted to get out of here without gunfire.

Loretta reached out as she and Jamie passed. "All these years, we just wanted to know what Nicky's baby looked like."

Paula paused, uncomfortable. What was she supposed to have done, send photos?

Loretta stroked Jamie's curls. "He looks like my Nicky when he was this age."

Paula hadn't expected to feel sorry for Nick's family. But she understood how Loretta felt. Her own mother would be devastated if denied access to her grandson. Paula had a fleeting image of Karen and Loretta meeting over a play date between Jamie and some of his cousins.

How could she make friends with drug dealers, the same type of scum who'd been responsible for her father's death? Almost certainly Loretta was accessory to multiple crimes even if police had never been able to gather evidence against her.

What would her father have wanted Paula to do?

No answers came to her. She was weighed down by grief and guilt. Another glance at Loretta made her think. Her father would have forgiven his daughter anything. Just as Loretta undoubtedly forgave Nick his sins. Yes, she'd betrayed her father and slept with the enemy. She could never regret that because Jamie was the result.

"Paula?" Riley recalled her to the situation at hand.

She shook her head. *Helluva time to be having a personal crisis. Get on with it, Drummond.*

"We have to go but maybe we can work something out where you can see him once in a while," she lied to Loretta. She might empathize with the woman, but no way in the world would she willingly let Jamie near any Moresco ever again.

"Don't trust her," Nick warned. "She betrayed me."

Grandma thumped her cane. "Loretta, if you let that woman into your life she'll end up arresting you."

Nick strained at his cuffs, scowling at Riley. "You have nothing on me. I'm going to sue you for false arrest."

"Abduction of a minor," Riley reminded him, jerking on the handcuffs. "You crims are never as smart as you think you are."

"We didn't mean to keep Jamie a prisoner. At

least, I didn't," Loretta said to Paula. "We only wanted him here for his great-grandma's birthday."

"I get that. I'm taking Nick in for questioning in relation to alleged drug offences in Summerside. If he cooperates, I'll drop the abduction charges."

Loretta understood what that meant. "Nicky will tell you whatever you want to know. Nicky, do you hear me?"

Then she touched Jamie on the cheek. "Come back and visit soon, *bambino*."

Riley started to lead Nick out.

Paula stopped him. "Let him say goodbye to his grandmother."

Eyebrows raised, Riley stepped back and allowed his prisoner a moment with the matriarch. While they waited he put a hand on Jamie's shoulder and squeezed. "You were brave."

Then over the boy's head he said to Paula, "You're ruining your tough-cop image, you know. What'll the guys say in the locker room?"

"I don't give a damn what anyone says. I know I did the right thing." However Paula kept her gaze fixed on their prisoner to make sure the old bat didn't slip him a .38 special. "Good work, Constable. If I were you, I'd be applying for detective."

She turned to Loretta. "Where are the owners?"

The woman in the blue dress stepped out from the living room. "I'm Tina Tibaldi. My husband is upstairs."

"Tell him and the other men to come down and bring their weapons. Again, if they cooperate they'll be dealt with lightly. My men will be coming in."

Tina ran up the staircase.

Holding Jamie's hand Paula stepped outside. Riley followed with his prisoner. To Paula's surprise Jackson and Crucek weren't taking cover but were standing on the front lawn.

"Go inside. Confiscate the guns but don't make any arrests." She squeezed Jamie's shoulder. "Come on, mate. It's time we went home."

RILEY'S LEAST FAVORITE thing about policing was the paperwork. As a two-fingered typist he had a serious disadvantage. Paula had taken Jamie home, no doubt to do some serious mollycoddling. Riley took Moresco's statement then transferred him to the Frankston lockup before going to the Summerside station to file his report. Finally around 9:00 p.m. he hit Save then Print. The printer whirred into life and began to spit out the document.

Movement to his left made him look up. Paula had returned, wearing a summery dress and sandals. "I didn't expect to see you here tonight."

She pulled up a chair and sat. "Jamie's asleep with my mother standing watch. She's got a cricket bat by the door and a can of pepper spray on the hall table. But that's just for her peace of mind. With Nick locked up, I don't anticipate any more trouble."

"We won't be able to hold him for long," Riley said. "I questioned him for two hours. There's no evidence to link him to crystal meth in Summerside."

"We have to keep digging. How is the boy who OD'd?" Paula leaned over to take a page of his report as it emerged from the printer. Her perfume—or maybe it was her shampoo—wafted over him.

"He's stabilized, doing okay." Riley leaned forward as she read, reluctant to let her out of his olfactory range. "You smell terrific."

"You're just saying that because you've been sitting in one of those stinky interview rooms for hours."

"Yeah, that's it." Why had she worn that dress if she wasn't open to a little flirtation? He blew out a sigh that expressed his frustration on more than one level. "We don't have any other leads. Maybe Moresco's clean, as he says."

"Something is bound to turn up, sooner or later." She continued to scan the report. "The other guys go home?"

"Yep." Riley collected the remaining pages. "After they catalogued and stored the small arsenal of weapons they confiscated."

"I was grateful they were there as back up. I intend to tell them so at the first opportunity."

"We could have booked Moresco's cousins on firearms offences. And maybe more if we'd searched the house."

"We didn't have a warrant for that."

"Did you mean what you said to Loretta about letting her see Jamie? I can't believe you'd still be making deals with the devil." Riley took the page from her, stacked it with the others and stapled them together.

"Is that what you think?"

"Does it matter what I think?" he asked softly, searching her eyes.

"It matters. A lot."

He let a couple of beats go by. "I think you were lying. I think you did what you had to do. As always."

She glanced away, touching the corner of her eyes with her knuckles.

Riley wanted to take her hand but he wasn't sure how she'd receive that. "That family..." He shook his head. "Mark my words, they'll be making a telemovie about them some day."

"Grandma is something else, isn't she?" Paula glanced back, laughing. "I thought for a moment she was going to raise that cane of hers and start strafing us with automatic gunfire."

"I think she came from the old country to see

how her crime dynasty was doing, not for a birth-day party."

Paula shuddered. "I can't stop thinking about Nick wanting Jamie to follow in his footsteps."

"I wouldn't put it past the old lady to have tried to smuggle him on the plane with her." Riley yawned and stretched his arms above his head. "Man, I'm tired. I could sleep for a week."

"That's too bad." Paula crossed her legs so that her dress slid above her knee. "I made a booking at that new French restaurant in the village for a late dinner. I think champagne is in order."

"Suddenly I have a second wind. As long as you don't order me to eat snails, that is. Let me drop this in John's in-tray. Then go home and shower and change." He glanced her way. "Hope you're not too hungry."

"I'm starving." A sly smile curved her lips. "I'll come with you. We can call the restaurant from your house and tell them we'll be late."

Whistling, Riley scooped up the report and deposited it.

Paula joined him at the door to the parking lot. "So tell me, how did you get past Moresco's sharp-shooters?"

"Trade secret," Riley said smugly. She punched him in the arm, surprisingly hard. "Ow. Note to self—don't piss off the boss."

She held the door open for him. "Come on, spill."

"It was simple," Riley said, using the remote to unlock the Audi. "I got Jackson and Crucek to cause a diversion. They came out of hiding and took up positions on the lawn to make it appear they were getting ready to storm the house."

He opened the passenger door for her. Paula slid inside and arranged her skirt. Riley waited until he was in the driver's seat and strapped in before continuing. "While that was going on I went to the end of the block and came toward the house through the backyards, over the neighbor's fence and into Tina and Matteo's side yard."

"How did you get into the house?"

"The laundry room door. Can you believe it? They just had a simple push-button lock."

"You could lead training sessions for the guys."

"I could." He started the car and eased onto the road. "But I might not have much time once I sit my detective exams."

Her eyebrows rose but she didn't respond to that. Instead she said, "You were pretty cool out there today. Do you think your PTSD is cured?"

Riley turned onto the main street, slowing for a young couple crossing from the supermarket to the row of shops and delis. "Today I felt the adrenaline rush you always get going into an unknown situation with potential danger. But I didn't have symptoms of acute anxiety. I'm going to keep up the sessions with the shrink for a while, if that's what you mean."

"Could you have fired your gun if you had to?"

Riley met her gaze. "I believe I could."

He drove a couple more blocks before he turned right. Then he pulled over. To hell with this pussy-footing around. Riley leaned over and cupping her cheek, kissed her soundly, tenderly, taking his time. He wanted her. He wanted her forever.

He murmured against her lips, "I'll be asking you for a recommendation."

"For your application to make detective? You're not allowed to get promoted till I am. But I think I could sign off on a recommendation." Paula reached her arms around his neck and drew him close. "Just give me one more example of how you operate so I can be sure."

"I HAVE A CONFESSION to make," Paula said, very early the next morning. After dinner the night before they'd gone to her house and let her exhausted mother go home for some well-deserved rest.

"Should I book the interview room, get out my tape recorder?" Riley idly sifted his fingers through her hair. He would never get enough of the silky texture, the living gold.

Ignoring his lame joke, she propped herself up

on her elbow to look at him. Her expression was serious.

"What is it?" He found himself holding his breath.

"I *wanted* to sleep with Nick."

The breath released—he'd known that—but his chest was still tight. He kept silent. What did she expect him to say?

"Don't you want to know why?"

"Not really." Why would he want to hear how sophisticated and charming she found a criminal who preyed on human weakness and destroyed lives? Riley could look past her weakness. Wasn't that enough? She thought he was jealous—and he was, a little. But she had so much strength and goodness in her that he hated anything that reflected badly on her.

"After my father was killed, Mum and I struggled, not just financially but emotionally. Dad was the rock on whom we both depended," Paula continued anyway. It almost seemed as though she was speaking to herself, not Riley. "I floundered for the next few years, questioning the meaning of it all, railing against fate. It was teenage angst magnified by grief."

"I'm sorry." Riley pulled her closer. He knew how that felt.

"When I met Nick, at first I saw him in black and white, as pure evil. But as I got to know him, the shades of gray crept in. He took care of his family, he would do anything for them at the drop of a hat. His brothers, cousins, mother…they only had to ask."

"It helped that he had buckets of money at his disposal," Riley pointed out dryly.

"When he started taking care of me, in an odd way and despite my being an undercover cop, I felt…safe."

"Safe?" Riley snorted. "Far from it."

"I know," she said patiently. "Didn't I qualify that remark? I know now it was all an illusion. As well as being kind to those close to him, Nick can be terrifyingly ruthless. But as long as he believed I was a massage therapist and loyal to him, I was golden." She paused to think. "Maybe I was looking for a father figure, someone to take care of me."

I'll take care of you. The thought leaped to Riley's mind. He knew better than to voice it. Her explanation hadn't changed anything as far as he was concerned. But he could see that something in her had changed. She could accept herself. That was enough for now.

"Anyway, you were right—I was attracted to him. I just didn't want to admit it." She sighed. "But I'm cured, completely and utterly over him. I'm a cop and an adult. I can take care of myself."

"Even cops have partners." Riley kissed her

lightly. "Even grown-ups look out for each other. Needing someone in your life isn't a weakness. It's what makes us human."

"I—I need you," she said in a husky whisper. "Jamie does, too."

Was this, then, what she was really confessing? It didn't look easy for his tough detective to say. Riley was finding it hard to speak himself. He touched his lips to hers, feeling her warmth, the softness of her skin. "If you want me, if you…trust me, I'll have your back—and Jamie's—always."

Her tears spilled over. She buried her face in his neck. "Yes. Oh, Riley, I love you so much."

The words were muffled but he heard, and rejoiced. "I love you, too." The lump in his throat garbled his words but he got them out.

She drew back, wiping her eyes, smiling brilliantly. "I think I hear Jamie up. Shall we go tell him?"

"Definitely. You and Jamie are coming to Canberra with me next week for the ANZAC Day ceremony, aren't you?"

"Canberra?" Paula sat up in bed. "What's wrong with Melbourne?"

"My army mates meet every year for the ceremony at the National War Museum. I bought airplane tickets for us all. I wanted it to be a surprise. My dad and stepmother are coming, too. It's the first time I've taken part in the ceremony since I was discharged. It's special."

"I wouldn't miss it." She hugged him. "Jamie will be over the moon."

IN THE DARK OF A CRISP Canberra predawn, a lone trumpet sounded reveille. Riley stood at attention with his fellow SAS mates, Gazza, Pete, Simpkins, Dunlop and Blue. Riley's father was standing a few rows away with members of his regiment who'd fought together in Vietnam.

The year of being incommunicado hadn't mattered to Riley's mates. They'd warmly welcomed him back into their ranks as if there'd been no estrangement. He and Pete held each other for a long hard hug that left both of them brushing their eyes afterward.

Thousands of veterans and civilians were gathered for the ceremony commemorating Australian soldiers' contribution to all wars. It was a sad occasion, Riley thought. There was no glory in war but it was important to bear witness to those who had fallen.

Nabili and her students were at the forefront of his mind. Not as they appeared in his nightmares, but as he remembered them in life, quietly engaged in teaching and learning. The young girls' shy giggles and their thirst for knowledge, the way they flung their hands in the air in their eagerness to answer questions. Nabili's leadership and courage had been an inspiration. He felt privileged to have known her.

The ceremony continued with speeches and prayers and the laying of the wreath at the tomb of the Unknown Soldier. Then the ceremony was over and the trumpeter stepped up to play *The Last Post*.

Riley lowered his head in a silent prayer to Nabili and her students. *Forgive me.* If he had to do it over again, he wasn't sure he could do anything different.

When the final lonely note sounded, Riley raised his head. He sought out Paula and Jamie in the crowd of civilians. She was standing with Sandra, their two blonde heads bright spots in the pale morning light.

Paula met his gaze and smiled. One chapter of his life had ended. A new one was beginning. He saw Jamie waving at him and grinned.

With the official ceremony over, the soldiers disbanded, to regroup in a few hours for the march.

Riley arranged to meet his mates then he went to find Paula and Jamie. He kissed Paula and squeezed Jamie's shoulder.

"Am I really going to march with you and all the soldiers in the parade?" Jamie asked.

"You bet." Riley unpinned the Victoria Cross for Australia from the row on his left breast and attached it to the boy's thick pullover sweater. "There you go, soldier."

Jamie touched the brass and ribbon in awe. "What's it for?"

"Bravery in combat. You deserve it after what you went through." Riley gave Paula a twisted smile. "He deserves it more than me."

She shook her head. "Didn't you ever watch the *Wizard of Oz?*"

"Yes, but—" He wrinkled his brow trying to get the connection. "Refresh my memory."

"The lion that thought he was a coward? You don't need medals to be brave."

"Oh, yeah, I remember now. Weren't there some evil monkeys? I liked the Scarecrow best. We should watch that together. I bet Jamie would love it."

"Whatever you say." She leaned up to kiss him, her eyes full of love. "Partner."

* * * * *

LARGER-PRINT BOOKS!
GET 2 FREE LARGER-PRINT NOVELS PLUS
2 FREE GIFTS!

◆ Harlequin®

Super Romance

Exciting, emotional, unexpected!

YES! Please send me 2 FREE LARGER-PRINT Harlequin® Superromance® novels and my 2 FREE gifts (gifts are worth about $10). After receiving them, if I don't wish to receive any more books, I can return the shipping statement marked "cancel." If I don't cancel, I will receive 6 brand-new novels every month and be billed just $5.44 per book in the U.S. or $5.99 per book in Canada. That's a saving of at least 16% off the cover price! It's quite a bargain! Shipping and handling is just 50¢ per book in the U.S. or 75¢ per book in Canada.* I understand that accepting the 2 free books and gifts places me under no obligation to buy anything. I can always return a shipment and cancel at any time. Even if I never buy another book, the two free books and gifts are mine to keep forever.

139/339 HDN FEFF

Name _____ (PLEASE PRINT) _____

Address _____ Apt. #

City _____ State/Prov. _____ Zip/Postal Code

Signature (if under 18, a parent or guardian must sign) _____

Mail to the **Reader Service:**
IN U.S.A.: P.O. Box 1867, Buffalo, NY 14240-1867
IN CANADA: P.O. Box 609, Fort Erie, Ontario L2A 5X3

Not valid for current subscribers to Harlequin Superromance Larger-Print books.

**Are you a current subscriber to Harlequin Superromance books
and want to receive the larger-print edition?
Call 1-800-873-8635 today or visit www.ReaderService.com.**

* Terms and prices subject to change without notice. Prices do not include applicable taxes. Sales tax applicable in N.Y. Canadian residents will be charged applicable taxes. Offer not valid in Quebec. This offer is limited to one order per household. All orders subject to credit approval. Credit or debit balances in a customer's account(s) may be offset by any other outstanding balance owed by or to the customer. Please allow 4 to 6 weeks for delivery. Offer available while quantities last.

Your Privacy—The Reader Service is committed to protecting your privacy. Our Privacy Policy is available online at www.ReaderService.com or upon request from the Reader Service.

We make a portion of our mailing list available to reputable third parties that offer products we believe may interest you. If you prefer that we not exchange your name with third parties, or if you wish to clarify or modify your communication preferences, please visit us at www.ReaderService.com/consumerschoice or write to us at Reader Service Preference Service, P.O. Box 9062, Buffalo, NY 14269. Include your complete name and address.

HSRLP11B